Say It With Murder

SAY IT WITH MURDER

Emma Page

Constable · London

First published in Great Britain 2000
by Constable, an imprint of Constable & Robinson Limited
3 The Lanchesters, 162 Fulham Palace Road
London W6 9ER

Copyright © 2000 Emma Page

The right of Emma Page to be identified as the author of
this work has been asserted by her in accordance with
the Copyright, Designs and Patents Act 1988

ISBN 0 094 80430 3

Printed and bound in Great Britain

A CIP catalogue record for this book is available from the
British Library

For G.
for all the years

1

On a calm, bright Tuesday morning in mid-October, Lorraine Clifford lay dreaming in the bedroom of her flat in Wychford. In her dream she was a child again, playing ball with her beloved mother in the garden at Beechcroft, running and laughing in the sunshine, under a cloudless sky, her father sitting on a nearby bench, glancing up from his Sunday newspaper to look across at them with a loving smile.

She came slowly awake, surfacing through the dream layers to the realities of the present day, where she was no longer a carefree child but a hardworking young woman a few weeks from her twenty-fourth birthday, lying in her bed, ten miles from Beechcroft, both her parents dead. Her father had been twenty-two years older than her mother. It was seventeen years now since a totally unlooked-for heart attack had carried him off with appalling suddenness; twelve long years since her mother had drifted away down that bleak and lonely road, into the dark tunnel from which she had never returned.

Lorraine lay for a few moments longer, engulfed in memories, then she forced these thoughts aside and threw back the bed-clothes. Time to ready herself for the day. She was a social worker, employed in the area for the best part of three years now. She was highly regarded by her superiors and by the disadvantaged folk among whom she worked.

She thrust her feet into slippers, pulled on her dressing-gown and went swiftly along to the bathroom. She was of average height, carrying not a spare ounce of flesh. She had her share of looks but made nothing of them. The habitual expression of her dark-blue eyes was intent and serious; twin frown lines were already deeply indented between her brows. She had no truck with make-up, kept her pale blonde hair in a short, no-nonsense cut. Her clothes were spartan-plain and trouble-free.

A hasty shower, a quick breakfast; everything cleared rapidly away, leaving the flat immaculate, as always. Then off to face the rigours and chances of the day.

In the best bedroom, overlooking the front garden at Beechcroft, a substantial Edwardian villa, half-way along Wedderburn Road, in a residential suburb of Cannonbridge, Lorraine's stepfather, Philip Harvey, was also rising from his bed. He was a tall, athletically built man of forty-seven, good-looking still, with a purposeful cast of countenance; his thick, dark hair showed a light sprinkling of grey. He had married Veronica Clifford, Lorraine's mother, two years after she had been widowed. Veronica, a delicately pretty, highly strung woman, was thirty-five at the time, Philip thirty-two.

As Veronica was greatly attached to Beechcroft, her home throughout her first marriage, and had no wish to leave it, Philip had moved in there from his bachelor flat. Veronica had been very happy in her first marriage; it had given her stability and security. She had been very dependent on her first husband, John Clifford, and his sudden death had come as a shattering blow.

John Clifford had been the founder and sole owner of Clifford Workwear, a prosperous concern occupying a prime position on the Cannonbridge industrial estate; the firm manufactured an extensive, up-to-date range of protective clothing used in industry. The business, together with everything else her husband owned, had passed to Veronica on his death. She had been overwhelmed by shock and grief, horrified at the weight of her new responsibilities, for which she was totally unprepared. She had found herself barely able to cope, staggering along from day to day, crisis to crisis.

At the time of Clifford's death, Philip Harvey had been employed by the firm for some years, working his way through various departments, to the point where he became Clifford's right-hand man. Philip was quiet and hardworking, with a shrewd head for business; he lived alone, had no close relatives. Veronica very soon found in him a tower of strength and before long was entrusting him with all major decisions. He never let her down, never put a foot wrong, never presumed, never stepped out of line. He arrived early for work, he stayed late.

8

Within a few months of Clifford's death, the entire running of the firm had passed into Philip's more than capable hands.

During the whole of her marriage to Philip, Veronica never managed to regain such fragile stability as she had ever possessed. She suffered more than one breakdown and was admitted, on occasion, as a voluntary patient to Chelmwood Hospital, a large Victorian mental institution in a rural situation some three miles from Cannonbridge. The hospital was now no longer in existence; the land had been sold off and the buildings put to other uses.

Veronica's final admittance to Chelmwood – during a prolonged spell of severe wintry weather – came three years after her second marriage. Two weeks into her treatment, she disappeared from her ward, at some time during the night.

The hospital stood in extensive grounds, on the edge of open country; the search took the best part of two days. Her body was found at last, frozen stiff, curled up at the foot of a tree in dense woodland; she was barefoot, clad only in a nightdress.

The post-mortem revealed that she had taken a massive overdose, a lethal mix of various medicaments she had been prescribed over the last year. She had seemed to be making progress and had spent part of the day before her disappearance at home, at Beechcroft – such home visits being a standard feature of the hospital treatment. Philip had collected her after lunch and driven her back after tea; he had thought her much improved.

She would appear to have taken the opportunity to pick up a hoard of capsules and tablets she must have earlier amassed and hidden away. She had died from the effect of the drugs before the sub-zero temperature had time to kill her. She had left no note but her intention appeared plain and the inquest duly recorded a verdict of suicide.

At the time of their marriage Philip and Veronica had both made straightforward wills, each bequeathing everything to the other. Veronica's death had thus left Philip sole owner of the firm, the house and all Veronica's other assets. He had never remarried, had never entertained any thought of it.

For the first year or two he had attempted to manage the domestic side of his life with the help only of daily women but this had proved far from satisfactory and he decided to employ a resident housekeeper.

It had turned out to be a good deal more difficult than he had imagined to find someone both competent and pleasant to have living in the house. He had been able to tolerate the presence of his first choice for only six weeks and that of her successor for barely a month. But he had pressed doggedly on, determined to make a happy home for his stepdaughter, Lorraine. He had counted himself extremely fortunate in lighting on Rhoda Jarrett for his third choice. He had been reluctant at first to take her on: she was only twenty-seven years old, a good deal younger than he had had in mind; she was a single mother with a daughter of three. But in all other respects Philip considered her admirably suitable for the post and after a good deal of thought he took her on for a trial period.

Rhoda hadn't disclosed to Philip any more of her personal circumstances than she deemed absolutely necessary and Philip had felt no compulsion to press her in the matter. In fact, she had been abandoned by her boyfriend as soon as he learned of her pregnancy; he had swiftly taken himself elsewhere. They hadn't been living openly together; the relationship had developed while both were living at home with their families, in a small town at some considerable distance from Cannonbridge. Highly respectable, strait-laced families, of the type that bred church-wardens, shopkeepers, clerks. When her boyfriend took to his heels, Rhoda was turned out of her home without ceremony. She had immediately left the area and had never been back since.

By the end of her trial period, she had established a highly satisfactory order at Beechcroft. She was an excellent cook, a meticulous housekeeper; quiet, well-mannered, tactful, in no way presumptuous or pushy. The atmosphere in the house was harmonious. She got on well with Lorraine; her little girl, Vicky, was no trouble.

In addition to all these virtues, it was no hardship to look at Rhoda, though there was nothing at all flamboyant or showy in her appearance. She was tall, with a graceful figure. Green eyes, large and wide-set; abundant, dark-gold hair, taken up into a casual knot on top of her head.

At the end of the trial period Philip had no hesitation in

10

deciding to keep her on. Within another few weeks he had taken her into his bed. It wasn't a matter of romantic love or irresistible passion on either side, but a discreet and convenient arrangement that suited them both.

Rhoda had been ten years now at Beechcroft and Philip had never regretted taking her on. One aspect of the situation that particularly commended itself to him was the skill and delicacy Rhoda had always displayed in never allowing the slightest suggestion of familiarity to creep into their daily dealings; she was scrupulous at all times to maintain a professional attitude towards him, courteous and impersonal.

Rhoda had at first permitted herself to entertain the hope that they might one day marry, and, though time had slipped by and the matter had on no occasion been mentioned between them, she had never entirely abandoned that hope. It remained stubbornly rooted in her mind, an unfailing source of confidence, of comfort and security, even though Philip now no longer came to her bed and dealings between them these days never at any time departed from the entirely businesslike.

Today, on this mid-October morning, Philip switched on his bedside radio and took in the news headlines. His bathroom was next door to his bedroom. Rhoda and Vicky – now thirteen years old – shared a bathroom on the floor above, where their bedrooms were located. Rhoda was always an early riser. She had been up and about for some time, though no sound of her movements drifted about the passages; Philip had made it clear from the start that he liked a quiet house, particularly at the start of the day.

Vicky had been out of bed for only a few minutes and was giving her whole attention to the absorbing business of checking her weight on the bathroom scales, running a tape measure over her waist, her hips and thighs, to determine if she had lost or gained an ounce or an inch while she was asleep. She was short for her age, inclined to plumpness; a plain girl with bright, alert eyes, a naturally forceful personality she had early learned to subdue when strategy demanded it.

She had no idea who her father was. Her mother had never touched upon the subject and Vicky had long ago realized that it would be a waste of breath to ask questions. She had by now lost all curiosity in that regard.

In spite of the circumspection rigorously exercised by her mother and Philip Harvey, Vicky had, in time, become aware of the true state of affairs between them, though she never, by word or look, made it plain that she knew. She had persuaded herself that her mother would one day succeed in marrying Philip and she looked forward to that day with happy certainty. Philip would be certain to adopt her legally; her surname would be changed to Harvey; she would be in every way his daughter. The three of them would be in all respects a complete and genuine family. When she left school she would undoubtedly be found a job – well paid and with first-class prospects – at Clifford Work-wear. In the fullness of time she would be bound to come into a substantial inheritance from her adoptive father. Her entire future appeared secure and rosy.

She frowned now as she assessed the results of her personal scrutiny: she had achieved only the most infinitesimal reduction since yesterday – and she had half-starved herself over the twenty-four hours. Something a good deal more drastic was definitely called for; it must be thought up and put into operation without delay.

When she was dressed, ready for school, she went downstairs to the big kitchen where her mother was putting her breakfast on the table. The two of them always ate in the kitchen; Philip's meals were served in the dining-room. Rhoda had finished her own breakfast some time ago but she sat down, as usual, to drink a cup of coffee with her daughter. Neither was in a talkative mood, each occupied with her own thoughts, barely aware of the other's presence.

Rhoda was roused from her musing by the ringing of the telephone in the hall, though the sound didn't pierce Vicky's absorption. It had always been Rhoda's duty to answer the phone but that had changed in recent weeks; the rule now was that when Philip was in the house he would answer the phone himself.

At the first ring, Rhoda left the table silently and crossed to the kitchen door. She opened it a fraction and stood with her head inclined at an angle. She heard Philip come swiftly out of the dining-room to snatch up the receiver. She didn't return to her seat but remained in the doorway, intently listening. Vicky didn't glance up, didn't even register that her mother had left the table; she went on drinking her coffee, immersed in thought.

At the other end of the phone, in the village of Rivenoak, half a mile from Cannonbridge, Martine Faulkner was conducting her side of the conversation in a rapid undertone, subdued almost to a whisper, in case Owen, her husband, should suddenly appear in the bedroom doorway.

She daren't close the bedroom door as that would reduce her chances of catching the whisper of Owen's footfall in time to replace the receiver and adopt the posture of some innocent activity. The domestic quarters, spacious and comfortable enough, adjoined the sizable commercial premises of the Faulkner enterprise. Owen had taken, in recent weeks, to moving from one area to the other, with a speed and silence far greater than she would ever have credited, for a man of his build; it lent her days a spice of danger and excitement that she found highly diverting. What she was, by temperament, always least able to endure was the daily tedium of domesticity and she had had to stomach her share of that in the three years of her marriage.

Her husband, Owen Faulkner, had begun his working life by serving his time as an electrician. He was an only child, born late in his parents' marriage. They had owned and run the large general store in Rivenoak, a prosperous concern started by Owen's grandfather.

Owen wasn't lacking in ambition and he had lost no time in setting up as a master electrician, employing others. His parents were happy for him to take over part of the commercial premises of the property, to provide him with an office and workshop. His scope widened over the years; he took on men from other trades, enabling him to offer an increasing range of services; it became necessary to build on to his original portion of the premises.

Both his parents were now dead and Owen was sole owner of the entire concern. The territory he served had grown steadily; in addition to surrounding villages and hamlets, it now included several Cannonbridge suburbs.

This morning, as Martine continued to exchange intimate

endearments with Philip Harvey, she was, as ever, careful to keep an ear cocked. She had just arranged to meet Philip in the evening, at one of the quiet country hotels they favoured, when she caught a murmur of sound at the head of the stairs. She broke off on the instant and was sitting serenely at her dressing-table, calmly arranging her hair, when her husband materialized on the threshold.

Owen was thirty-eight years old, tall and solidly built, a muscular, broad-shouldered man with a driven look, heavy features that scarcely ever relaxed into a smile, hair already plentifully streaked with white. He darted a piercing glance at his wife's mirrored face as she smiled back at him from the glass with cheerful composure. She rose gracefully from her seat and turned to face him.

She was twenty-one years old, an eye-catching redhead with a supple, sensuous figure. She had come from a far from privileged background in the neighbouring village of Northwick; she had begun to work at the Rivenoak stores on leaving school, five years ago. She had applied for the job after due deliberation. More than anything at that time she had yearned for a secure, settled position in life, with no necessity ever to worry her head about money. She had a shrewd idea of her own worth and Owen Faulkner struck her as by far the best catch in the area.

Owen's mother, an astute matriarch, was still alive at that time, although in failing health; she kept a keenly watchful eye on all that went on. She died eighteen months after Martine began work at the stores and before many more weeks had passed Martine had said yes to Owen, who was under the impression all along that it was he who had done the pursuing.

It was through her husband's business that Martine had met Philip Harvey. Philip had from time to time made use of the various Faulkner services; he had encountered Martine one day last summer when he had called in at the stores to speak to Owen. Owen had been out and Philip had spoken instead to Martine.

Although Martine now had an infant son, Jamie, she had reached a stage in her marriage where she was ripe for mischief. She had never been remotely in love with her husband and had all along had to school herself to receive his embraces with a convincing show of affection. She set her cap deliberately at Philip and was very soon engaged in an affair that proved to be exactly what she needed, gratifying her vanity and egotism, providing ongoing excitement and romance, a focus for her daydreams, a deeply satisfying awareness of her own desirability, her provocative sexuality.

In a matter of weeks, however, things had begun to change. What had started out on both sides as no more than a passionate interlude had now assumed the character of something conceivably more meaningful and more lasting.

The notion of marriage at some point in the future was beginning to invade their thoughts. Martine could visualize now the possibility of leaving Owen, taking Jamie with her, naturally. She was supremely confident that in such a situation she would automatically be entitled to custody of her son; the thought of any other outcome never so much as crossed her mind.

And Philip was permitting himself to contemplate the idea of Martine occupying an open, conventional place in his life. She had by now contrived an encounter between himself and Jamie, and Philip had found himself charmed by the little boy, delighted to take him on as a son, if that day should come. And the thought that there could, perhaps, in time, be a brother or sister for Jamie was distinctly appealing.

From being at first highly circumspect in all their dealings, anxious that not even the slightest hint of what was going on should emerge, they were now both beginning to relax, to the point of allowing, on occasion, a degree of outright carelessness to creep in. A growing feeling of recklessness had entered the air of late, an exhilarating sense of inviting events to rush towards them, be the consequences what they may.

Now Martine sat at her dressing-table, chatting easily to her husband, with an engaging, artless air; she saw the intensity of his gaze begin to slacken. From the adjoining bedroom came a gleeful little crowing sound. Owen's expression lightened on the instant. Martine stood up, smiling. 'Jamie's awake.' She moved to the connecting door with a glance at her husband, inviting him to follow.

Jamie, a sturdy, handsome infant of ten months, greeted them with a gurgle of laughter, chubby fists waving in the air. Owen

15

crossed swiftly to the cot and lifted him tenderly out, his face glowing with love and pride.

A few minutes later Martine asked casually if Owen would be at home that evening, to babysit; she thought of going over to see a girlfriend in her home village of Northwick; she wouldn't be late getting back.

Owen was absorbed in playing with his son and didn't glance up. Yes, he told her, with no more than a flick of thought, he would definitely be at home.

Footsteps sounded outside, on the gravel. Martine crossed to the window and looked down. Harriet Russell, ahead of time, as usual, was walking past, to her office at the end of the property. A woman of thirty-four, neat and businesslike in appearance, comely enough in an everyday fashion, her expression invariably easy and composed, Harriet had worked for the Faulkners since leaving secretarial college.

She had originally been taken on by Owen Faulkner's father, to assist in the running of the post office side of the stores; she had proved an invaluable asset, markedly efficient and reliable, level-headed and trustworthy. Later, when Owen started his own venture, it was Harriet who set up his office for him. For a number of years now she had acted as deputy to Owen, in most aspects of the business.

Still stationed at the bedroom window, Martine watched Harriet turn into her office. 'If it's not convenient for you to be at home this evening,' she remarked airily to her husband, 'I can always ask Harriet.' Harriet was devoted to Jamie.

She had also been devoted since childhood to Jamie's father. Before Martine came to work at the stores there had been a long understanding between Owen and Harriet. They had been regarded locally as indisputably a couple, though there had never been anything as formal as an engagement – and certainly never anything approaching passionate or romantic love. Both families, Faulkners and Russells, were long established in Rivenoak, pillars of the local community, on friendly terms with each other for generations. A match between Owen and Harriet would have been warmly welcomed on both sides.

When Martine appeared on the scene, sixteen years old, in the glow of her blossoming beauty, things underwent a rapid change: Owen was very soon paying open attention to the newcomer. His mother, far from pleased at this turn of events, made it her business to look into Martine's background and found what she discovered anything but reassuring.

Martine, it seemed, was a by-blow; no name had ever been put to her father. Her mother, a single woman, an illiterate, itinerant field-hand from some far-off part of the country, had left her new-born daughter in Northwick, in the care of a middle-aged, childless couple, a farmworker and his wife, who were only too happy to take the infant on an informal basis: no questions asked, no disclosures to any branch of authority, no legal adoption ever to be sought, no maintenance ever to be looked for, the mother to depart the scene forthwith, never to return, never to attempt any form of contact.

When the farmworker died, ten years later, his widow continued to bring up the child with care and devotion.

It appeared blindingly clear to Owen Faulkner's mother that the redheaded Martine was no more than a fortune-hunter but her trenchant observations on that score produced not the slightest alteration in her son's conduct.

Harriet Russell never at any time made any comment on all this to anyone. She gave no sign of distress or resentment when the marriage took place; she accepted an invitation to the wedding and sent a handsome present. She remained in her job, as self-possessed, as loyal and efficient as ever, invariably courteous and helpful to Martine, never making the slightest difficulty for her; always friendly in manner – but not a whit more than that – towards Owen.

Harriet was an only child, both parents now dead, having passed away within weeks of each other, in the last twelve months. Harriet had invested her considerable inheritance with her customary acumen. She continued to live, on her own now, in the same house, a large, solidly built dwelling, standing alone on rising ground, overlooking the residential quarters of the Faulkner property.

2

Over at Beechcroft, Philip Harvey had finished his breakfast. He was later than usual this morning, as he wanted to speak to Tom Guthrie, the gardener, before leaving for Workwear.

Rhoda Jarrett came into the dining-room, to clear the table, and they spoke of household concerns in the impersonal, practical fashion customary between them in such matters; the exchange didn't take long.

Philip left the room and went out into the hall, where Vicky Jarrett stood, buttoning her blazer, about to leave for school. Philip gave her a kindly word in passing, before going out through a side door, in search of Guthrie, whom he found pruning the roses.

Tom Guthrie was in his late fifties, a quiet, reflective man, slow-spoken and methodical; he had always worked at gardening. He came of farming stock; he had been born in Rivenoak and still had relatives in the village. He had left Rivenoak twenty-five years ago, being by then married, with a young family. He had decided on the move to Cannonbridge to enable his children to attend better schools.

He had been taken on, shortly afterwards, by John Clifford and had worked at Beechcroft ever since. He remembered John Clifford with respect and affection and Veronica, his wife, with heartfelt compassion. Lorraine Clifford he had known since her birth. He regarded her with almost fatherly fondness, touched with admiration for the way she had fashioned for herself a life of useful service, after the shocks and sorrows of her early years.

Lorraine had been such an appealing child, merry and high-spirited, trusting and vulnerable. Guthrie had felt the profoundest sympathy for her in the desolating time after the sudden death of her beloved father, the long period of emotional instability afflicting her grieving mother, culminating in her mother's death, deeply harrowing in its tragic circumstances,

18

leaving Lorraine, at the tender age of twelve, utterly bereft – except for such care and affection as she might look for from her stepfather. And Philip Harvey had been good to Lorraine; there could be no denying that.

Lorraine had continued to live at Beechcroft until she went away to university, and she had always returned for some part of every vacation. She still paid regular visits, still kept her old bedroom in the house, with some of her belongings left there still. She always had a word for Guthrie, always made a point of seeking him out, chatting to him with lively interest, friendly understanding.

Guthrie was a widower now, living alone, his children grown up and married, parents themselves, scattered to distant parts of the country.

The garden layout at Beechcroft had been greatly simplified in recent years and Guthrie's hours had correspondingly dwindled. He had worked full-time for John Clifford but now came only three days a week: Tuesdays, Thursdays and Fridays. But he managed very well, being able to supplement his income sufficiently with part-time and occasional work in other gardens.

Philip spoke to him now about various tasks to be carried out in the immediate future, then he went along to the garage. By the time he edged the car out, all thought of the garden, the house, of Guthrie, Rhoda and Vicky had dropped away from his mind. He drove off to Clifford Workwear, to set about the serious business of the day.

Vicky Jarrett came out of Beechcroft a minute or two later. She would have walked past Guthrie without a word or look, wrapped in her own thoughts, had he not spoken a few words of greeting, when she jerked herself momentarily from her musings and gave him a smiling reply. Guthrie had never found Vicky at all troublesome but he had never been able to develop any real fondness for her, not even when she was a small child. She had always struck him, right from her early days, as remarkably calculating, for one so young.

Five minutes' brisk walk took Vicky to a terrace house where her best friend – indeed, her only friend – Avril Byrne, lived with her mother who had been widowed for some eighteen months. Mrs Byrne was employed as a senior assistant at Ashdene, a privately run care home for the frail elderly, conveniently situated for Mrs Byrne, only ten minutes' walk from her front door; she had worked there for several years.

Avril Byrne was thirteen, the same age as Vicky, in the same class at the local comprehensive school. They had known each other nearly all their lives, having first met at a community playgroup, ten years ago.

Avril was even shorter than Vicky, equally given to plumpness. Compliant by nature, she was long accustomed to being dominated by her friend and would indeed have found it distinctly alarming to be compelled to take everyday decisions on her own.

Avril was, as always, stationed at the window, watching out for Vicky; she ran to open the front door as soon as she spied her. Vicky went inside the house for a moment, as she wanted a word with Avril's mother.

Mrs Byrne was busy in the kitchen. She didn't have to scurry round this morning, she wasn't due at Ashdene till after lunch; her hours today were two o'clock till ten. She was a sturdily built woman in her late forties, on the plump side, with an amiable expression and a ready smile. Eternally optimistic, she was invariably in some mild degree of muddle but never much bothered by the fact, always confident that she would, for sure, catch up with herself tomorrow.

'Will it be all right if we come along to Ashdene this evening?' Vicky asked her, with the ingratiating air she always employed towards Mrs Byrne. The two girls went to each other's houses after school, turn and turn about. When they had eaten and done their homework, they had the rest of the time to themselves; as often as not, they liked to go along to Ashdene, where there was always pocket money to be picked up, in return for carrying out various undemanding chores. They always caught the same bus home, boarding it outside Ashdene, at 9.10 p.m.; it stopped close to both Beechcroft and Mrs Byrne's house. At weekends and during school holidays they frequently put in extra time at the home.

Rhoda Jarrett had no objection to her daughter visiting

Ashdene in this fashion. Rhoda sometimes gave a hand at the home herself, at Mrs Byrne's request, when the staff were particularly hard pressed and Rhoda was able to spare a few hours. She felt the time Vicky spent at Ashdene provided useful training: helping the elderly residents, running errands for them, reading them the newspapers, as well as performing light domestic tasks – and the pocket money earned in this way was by no means to be despised.

Mrs Byrne and Rhoda Jarrett had, like their daughters, first met at the community playgroup. It had never been in Rhoda's nature to make close female friends, a tendency greatly heightened during the difficult years after she had found herself pregnant and alone. Mrs Byrne, far more outgoing and gregarious, would have been happy to be on terms of free and easy friendliness with Rhoda but after ten years she had accepted, in her good-natured, uncritical fashion, that this was never likely to be the case and that Rhoda's customary courteous and co-operative attitude was as much as could be looked for.

Before Mrs Byrne was widowed, she had been able to work her due share of night shifts at Ashdene, leaving Avril in the care of her husband; but after his death this was no longer possible as she couldn't make satisfactory arrangements for her daughter. It meant a noticeable drop in income – night work being markedly better paid – at a time when every penny counted.

A few months ago, shortly after Vicky and Avril had started earning pocket money at Ashdene, Avril had suggested to her mother that if she wanted to take her share of night duties again, Avril would be happy to go along with that decision, provided Vicky could stay overnight with her. She added that Vicky had mentioned the idea to her mother, who thought something might be worked out.

Mrs Byrne mulled it over and then spoke to Rhoda Jarrett, who proved willing to give the scheme a try. What particularly appealed to Rhoda was the freedom it would give her to stay out as long as she liked on those evenings when Vicky would be sleeping at Mrs Byrne's. In all her time at Beechcroft, Rhoda had never been free to go out in the evenings. She had joined some women's organizations but could only ever attend their afternoon meetings. If she went to a theatre or cinema, it must always be to a matinée performance. She had no wish to visit pubs or clubs, had never had any such wish – her teetotal upbringing had seen to that.

After due discussion, satisfactory arrangements had been established. Mrs Byrne would regularly work the night shift on Thursdays, Fridays and Saturdays, with the possibility of an occasional extra night shift, if required. She was able to assure Rhoda that the two girls would be as safe overnight in her house as in any dwelling in the land; her late husband had been a DIY enthusiast, priding himself on having rendered the house impossible to break into, but easy to escape from, in case of fire. And the situation of the house was in itself reassuring: a middle terrace house, adequate street lighting, good neighbours on both sides.

Mrs Byrne would see Vicky and Avril into bed before setting off for the 10 p.m. shift and would leave Ashdene next morning at 6 a.m., in good time to send the girls off to school on Friday mornings – there being, of course, no school on the two following mornings, Saturday and Sunday.

Now, in reply to Vicky's inquiry, Mrs Byrne answered with an amiable smile: 'Yes, sure, come along this evening. There'll be plenty for the pair of you to do.' She was fond of Vicky, always so well mannered and deferential.

On the way to school, Vicky bombarded Avril with questions about the results of her morning's weighing and measuring. As instructed by Vicky, Avril kept a conscientious daily check on these vital matters. Her tally today was even more disheartening than Vicky's, all figures showing a marginal increase. As they walked along, Vicky outlined her new plan of attack against the excess poundage. Avril listened, with dismay at first and then with resigned acceptance. If, as Vicky assured her, that was the only way forward, then, disagreeable as it sounded, that was what they would have to do.

Shortly after eleven, after Jamie Faulkner had had his mid-morning snack, Martine took him out on to what had been the rear verandah, transformed by Owen, after Jamie's birth, into an enclosed, sheltered area, out of direct sunshine, with glass panels that could be slid open or shut, according to the weather; here the child could play or take a nap, in safety and comfort.

A minute or two later, Harriet Russell came soundlessly by, making a detour on her way to her car. She was bound for Cannonbridge, on a routine round of the various jobs currently being undertaken by Faulkners.

She stood watching, unobserved, as Martine settled Jamie and then went back into the house. When the sound of her going had died away, Harriet went silently up the verandah steps. Behind the glass, Jamie smiled a rapturous greeting. He pulled himself to his feet, took a few staggering steps and flopped down again, chattering away to her in his own brand of language, delighted with his performance. She gave him a loving smile before going back down the steps, turning at the foot to wave goodbye.

It was not far off 6.30 when Vicky and Avril let themselves in through the back door of Ashdene. The home was owned and run by Miss Newman and the girls at once sought her out, as they always made a point of doing.

Doris Newman was still a few years away from fifty. For much of her time as a hospital nurse she had chosen to work on geriatric wards and had always entertained the notion of one day setting up her own establishment.

She was a strongly built woman, ebullient and outgoing. She was always smartly dressed and plainly devoted much thought and effort to her appearance. Her abundant, coarse hair was skilfully and expensively cut, curled and tinted. The shade, between gold and chestnut, did as much for her as any shade could do. She might have been thought handsome, were it not for the set of her jaw, the flinty look in her eyes, persisting even when she smiled – something she had trained herself to do with marked frequency, especially in the presence of visitors to the home – rare though visitors were – and particularly if those visitors should be official callers – official callers being very rare indeed – and, most particularly of all, if the official callers should be male.

She had, as ever, a number of little jobs awaiting Vicky and

Avril. When she took over the home and set her own stamp on it, she had before her one paramount aim: to make as much money in as short a time as possible, to enable her to retire while her personal charms were still in bloom, take off for a warmer climate and bluer skies, the kind of well-heeled, free and easy way of life she dreamed of, with no shortage of available males, personable and accommodating.

To this end she kept her wage bill as low as possible, resulting, inevitably, in a cutting of corners all round, a regular turnover of staff and the speedy departure for a better post of any employee with above average standards or skills. She had grown, from long practice, adept at sailing close to the wind without giving rise to searching official scrutiny.

Although Ashdene had no declared policy of excluding males, there were never, at any one time, more than two or three males in the home. Doris greatly preferred female residents, finding them, in general, a good deal more amenable. They were, without exception, women in advanced old age, with no close or caring relatives, no friends; a fair proportion had struggled all their lives with learning difficulties; a number had slipped into a state of confusion or suffered from mild dementia.

Now Doris told Vicky and Avril what needed doing and they took themselves off to set about their tasks. They worked well and with dispatch; they never failed to give excellent value for what they were paid. They had, in addition, devised methods of rewarding themselves with such little bonuses as they were able to come by, here and there: biscuits filched from the kitchen; sweets and chocolates spirited away from residents' private supplies; a coin or two purloined from small sums of money left carelessly about.

To all these extras must now be added the discreet procurement of laxatives – their new weapon, according to Vicky's latest decree, in the fight against unwanted flesh. It should prove easy enough to come by adequate amounts. Every resident, apparently, was in permanent need of laxatives and supplies were always at hand. Bottles and boxes were never locked away but stood in full view, in bedrooms and bathrooms.

24

3

Lorraine Clifford's twenty-fourth birthday fell on Friday, 14th November. She rose at her usual hour, showered and dressed as swiftly as always. As she ran a comb through her hair she paused suddenly and leaned forward, to stare intently into the dressing-table mirror, studying her reflection, the set of the eyes, shape of the face, curve of the cheekbones, angle of the jaw. She turned her head and looked over to where a number of framed photographs were ranged on top of a chest of drawers: family photographs, dating back to her childhood.

One large studio portrait, taken at the time of her mother's engagement to her father, showed Veronica at the age of twenty-four – the same age as Lorraine was now. She went across to peer down at the likeness, study the eyes, the features. She picked up the photograph and carried it over to the mirror, glancing back and forth, from her mother's face to her own reflection, comparing every detail of both, trying yet again to determine the question that rose in her mind these days with increasing frequency: was she growing more or less like her mother, with every passing year?

In the hall, a few minutes later, she picked up her mail, heavier this morning because of birthday greetings. Over coffee and toast in the kitchen she began to slit open the envelopes. Cards from colleagues, from girls she had known at school and university, and kept in touch with now only by means of an exchange of Christmas and birthday cards.

An expensive, formal-looking card from her stepfather, enclosing his usual substantial cheque. Philip had all along treated her with considerable generosity. He never forgot her birthday, was equally open-handed towards her at Christmas. During her student days he had provided her with a liberal allowance and a car, replacing the car, after her student days were over, with the handsome blue Peugeot she still drove; it was the car she had chosen herself – he would have bought her any car she wanted.

In like manner, when she started work in Wychford, he would have bought her any property she decided on, but she had looked for nothing better than a flat of no great size, coveniently located, easy to run, easy to maintain.

And Philip's manner towards her had always made it plain that he never expected – or would welcome – any fulsome display of thanks. He never patronized her, never questioned her or plied her with unsolicited advice, never made the slightest attempt to influence the way in which she chose to live her life.

There were cards from Rhoda Jarrett and Vicky; they always remembered her birthday. She had never harboured any degree of ill feeling or resentment against either of them. Rhoda had been unvaryingly kind to her and it had at no time seemed to Lorraine that Rhoda was in any way trying to take her mother's place. Even after Lorraine came to realize the true state of affairs between her stepfather and his housekeeper, she felt no animosity towards Rhoda. She could never, by any stretch of imagination, see Philip marrying a domestic employee and she looked on the relationship as a safeguard against his marrying anyone else, someone who might try to step into her mother's shoes.

She picked up next a pretty card, depicting an old-fashioned cottage garden in exuberant bloom. The card was from Jessie Dugdale, an elderly woman Lorraine had known all her life. Jessie had been at school with Lorraine's maternal grandmother – Veronica's mother. Jessie had never married; she had kept up with her old schoolfriend till the schoolfriend's death, kept up with the schoolfriend's daughter, Veronica, till Veronica's death; she kept up now with the schoolfriend's granddaughter, Lorraine.

Enclosed with Jessie's card was a handkerchief of finest lawn, exquisitely embroidered by Jessie. She was no longer in the best of health, frail now and alone, her parents dead years ago; no living relatives. She still occupied the dwelling in which she had been born, in which she had lived all her life: a little rented cottage, in the village of Bowbrook, a mile or two from Wychford. Until her retirement, almost twenty years ago, Jessie had managed a wool and needlework shop in Wychford; the shop was no longer in existence. Since her retirement she had lived in modest comfort on her savings and pensions.

Lorraine went over to Bowbrook regularly, to see Jessie, looking on her as one of the last remaining links with her dead mother. She would go again within the next few days, to thank Jessie for remembering her birthday – and to keep an eye on the state of her health. Jessie was never one to complain and would always soldier on for as long as she could, sometimes beyond the point where prudence should have sent her to bed or to visit her doctor. She would take Jessie, as she often did, some little gift: fruit, maybe, or a box of her favourite dark-chocolate mints.

Lorraine picked up the final envelope, studying it for some moments with a puzzled look. She didn't recognize the handwriting; the envelope bore a Cannonbridge postmark. She slit open the flap and drew out a card. It showed a young girl in a summer garden, sitting reading on the grass, in the shade of a tree. The card carried a friendly message, wishing her a happy birthday. It was with some astonishment that she read the signature: Greg Mottram. Underneath the signature was a Cannonbridge phone number; there was no address.

'Well! Well!' she said aloud. 'Greg Mottram! After all this time!' She made a swift mental calculation. It must be twelve and a half years since Greg had left Cannonbridge; he had gone six months before her mother's death.

She sat lost in thought, staring back into the past. She remembered Greg well. After such a lengthy absence, such an unbroken silence, she had thought never to see or hear from him again.

Greg was a relative of Lorraine's mother. Greg's father and Veronica's father had been cousins; Veronica's maiden name was Mottram. Greg was two years older than Veronica, making him now, Lorraine reckoned, fifty-two. He and Veronica had known each other as children but there had been a gap of a good many years, after both Greg's parents were dead, during which Greg and Veronica had never met.

And then Greg had turned up in Cannonbridge one day, as a grown man. Veronica had been Veronica Clifford for some years by then; Lorraine was a small child. Greg, it appeared, was looking for a job and Veronica's husband was in a position to offer him one, in the general office at Clifford Workwear. Greg remained there for seven and a half years, before abruptly taking himself off again, in circumstances of which Lorraine – a child then, not twelve years old – had known nothing at the time and still knew nothing.

Now, gazing down again at Greg's card, she drew a deep sigh. Did she want to get in touch with Greg, after all this time? Did she want to set eyes on him again? Reawaken the past?

She became suddenly aware of the time. She dispatched the last of her toast, finished her coffee, cleared the table. If she did decide to respond to Greg's card, she could try ringing the number on his card, during her lunch hour, see if she could catch him in, find out what he had to say.

And she did catch him in. He answered the phone at its first ring, as if he had been sitting beside it, waiting for its shrill summons.

His voice was exactly as she remembered it: level in tone, quiet and unassertive. She thanked him for his card and asked how long he had been back in Cannonbridge. A matter of ten days, he told her. He had found himself a flat to rent.

How had he discovered her address?

It seemed he had called at Beechcroft a few days ago, hoping to find Tom Guthrie, whom he knew of old, hoping Tom might be able to give him Lorraine's address.

He had found Guthrie, who told him Lorraine was living and working in Wychford but couldn't supply the exact address. Guthrie had, however, introduced him to Rhoda Jarrett and her daughter, and Rhoda had given him Lorraine's address.

Lorraine's mind made itself up on the instant. 'I can't stop now,' she told Greg. 'I've got to get back to work. Can we meet? Tomorrow afternoon, perhaps? I'll be over in Cannonbridge for some shopping, I could meet you afterwards for tea.'

He agreed at once, in a tone of pleasure. She suggested a quiet café in a side street, near the centre of town. Yes, that would suit him fine. They arranged to meet there at five o'clock.

'I hope we manage to recognize each other after all these years,' she added on a lighter note. 'But I can remember very well what you looked like.'

28

'I haven't got any younger,' he responded on the same easy note. 'I'm losing my hair. And you're all grown up now. Do you still look like your mother?'

There was a moment's silence before she replied: 'I'll leave that for you to decide.'

St John's church was an imposing Victorian edifice in the vicinity of Beechcroft. On Saturday afternoon the sexton, a hardworking man in his late sixties, was busy in the church grounds. He glanced round at the sound of approaching footsteps. A man was coming up the incline, a few yards away, a man he had seen a number of times over the last ten days: lean and narrow-shouldered, not the most prepossessing physical specimen, well into his middle years; thin hair, wispy and mousy, liberally touched with grey; bony features, a preoccupied look. Clothes that had never cost a great deal and had plainly seen long service, though neat enough, brushed and pressed. He carried a handsome bunch of white chrysanthemums.

The sexton didn't bid him good afternoon, having learned by now that the only reply he could expect was an abstracted grunt, not even a turn of the head.

The bony-faced man continued at his usual steady pace towards the corner of the churchyard he always visited: the corner where the Clifford family graves were grouped in the shade of ancient trees. The most recent occupant of one of these graves was Veronica Harvey, formerly Clifford, who had joined her first husband and his forebears twelve years ago. It was before Veronica's grave that the bony-faced man invariably halted, on her grave that he reverently placed his offering of flowers, never other than white.

Some time later, the bony-faced man turned from the grave and left the churchyard, at the same unhurried pace. He set off in the direction of the town centre, the quiet café in the side street, where he had arranged to meet Lorraine Clifford.

The graves of Greg Mottram's parents lay in another church-yard, over the border of the next county, in the town where his childhood and early youth had been spent. He hadn't visited those graves, hadn't so much as set foot in that town for a good many years and doubted that he would ever do so again. He no longer had any relatives living there. In fact, the only remaining relative he was aware of was Lorraine Clifford. He had been deeply attached to Lorraine's mother, when they had known each other as children; it had been a long-abiding grief to him when an abrupt end was put to their friendship, after the death of his father.

His mother had died when Greg was five; he could barely remember her. His father, a quiet man, diffident and undemonstrative, had married again, a year or two later. He had met the lady not long before the marriage and had found himself, somewhat to his surprise, swept swiftly and surely towards the altar. His new bride was a widow, a good deal younger than himself, on the look-out – though he wasn't aware of it – for a secure, comfortable berth for herself and her eleven-year-old son. She was possessed of great charm when she cared to exert it and she had no difficulty in persuading him, when it came to making a new will, that he could safely leave everything to her, confident that she could be relied on to look after Greg.

After the wedding ring was safely on her finger, her temperament turned out to be a good deal more steely than she had previously allowed to be apparent. In particular, her attitude towards her new stepson underwent a change, though she was careful never to reveal her true feelings in the presence of his father, who was often away from home in the course of his business. In private, she treated Greg with icy formality, making no secret of her preference for her own son, who in turn took his attitude from his mother; the lad was in any case distanced from Greg by the gap in age.

Greg perceived, young as he was, that he could do nothing to remedy his situation. He bore it as best he could, withdrawing into himself, watchful never to provoke his stepmother in the smallest degree.

Then, when Greg was ten, his father died. His stepmother's manner towards him became even more icy. He was consumed with unhappiness, he felt utterly alone in the world. He withdrew even further into himself, he was unable to make friends, to do himself justice in his studies.

He left school at the earliest possible moment, intent only on escaping from home, from an intolerable situation. His step-mother made not the slightest effort to prevent his going, indeed she did all she could to speed him on his way, though she offered not a penny by way of assistance.

He found work on the lowest rung of the ladder in an office in a neighbouring town. The work was grindingly dull; he could afford only the cheapest accommodation. He lived with the utmost economy, saving every penny he could, fearful always of sliding further still, into the very lowest depths of poverty. The days passed in a grey blur.

The years that followed took on a pattern of their own. When the bleak tedium grew too much to bear, he moved on to another town, another job – invariably some minor clerical or book-keeping post. He assuaged the wretchedness of his days in the only way he knew: with alcohol. He kept his intake to the absolute minimum, careful, even in his worst moments, never to put his job at risk. He bought always the very cheapest brand on offer; he had no concern for such niceties as flavour or bouquet. He was never without a packet of mints or breath fresheners.

When he had lived in this fashion for some fifteen years, the firm currently employing him collapsed. He moved on to the next town, which chanced to be Cannonbridge, and immediately set about his usual search for work.

A few years previously, he had read in the county newspaper a report of the wedding of Miss Veronica Mottram. The accompanying photograph showed a slender, elegant young woman, in whose face he could recognize the child he had known. Veronica, it seemed, was now Mrs John Clifford, her new husband the owner of a thriving Cannonbridge enterprise: Clifford Workwear.

When Greg arrived in Cannonbridge, the telephone directory supplied him with the Cliffords' address. In the course of the next few days, in between his job-hunting efforts, he walked round several times to Beechcroft and was lucky enough at last to catch a glimpse of Veronica at the wheel of a car, driving out through the gates.

After a full week of fruitless job-seeking he nerved himself to call at Beechcroft. He found Veronica and her four-year-old daughter at home. Veronica was delighted to see him and listened with interest to the greatly softened and muted version he gave her of the twenty years and more that had gone by since they had last met. She offered at once, without any prompting, to ask her husband if there might be a vacancy for Greg at Workwear. Clifford was happy to oblige his wife and Greg was very soon installed in the general office, with better pay and conditions than he had ever previously enjoyed.

4

At a minute or two before five o'clock, Lorraine approached the side-street café, laden with the fruits of her shopping. She glanced about the pavements but could see no one resembling the image of Greg Mottram she had in her mind. No one stood waiting outside the café.

She positioned herself discreetly to one side of the front window and peered in at the tables.

There he was! She had no doubt of it. He was still recognizably the man she had last seen twelve and a half years ago, though undeniably older and a good deal more careworn. He was sitting at a corner table, stiffly upright, his back against the wall, his eyes fixed on the door.

She moved to the entrance and stepped inside, looking across at him. He knew her at once. She saw that he recognized her from her likeness to her mother; she saw, too, from his instant change of expression, the pang of anguish this recognition had plainly caused him.

He stood up, waiting for her to reach his table. There was some initial awkwardness in their meeting but it quickly disappeared under the little rituals of dealing with Lorraine's shopping, settling themselves down, consulting the menu, giving their orders to the waitress.

As Lorraine poured the tea she asked him about his flat. It was comfortable enough, convenient enough, he told her; it would do him for the present. He didn't add what was equally true: he could have found accommodation a good deal cheaper, of a type he had grown well used to over the years: some cramped, tatty bedsitter in a seedy neighbourhood. But he was determined, now that he was back once more in Cannonbridge, where he was to some extent known, in however limited a fashion, and however long ago, that he would not start out in a despondent, down-at-heel fashion but on as respectable a footing as he could contrive, in the hope that it would, before too long, begin to pay worthwhile dividends.

He was equally determined not to exhaust his precious savings; he must find a job of some kind, any kind, without delay, to safeguard that vital lifeline.

He went on to ask about her work, her life, and she answered readily. He listened with keen interest as she spoke about her relationship with her stepfather, the current state of affairs at Beechcroft, what she believed to be the true standing of Rhoda Jarrett in the household. When she had finished, he made no comment but embarked on an account of his job-seeking since returning to Cannonbridge. No success so far, he told her, but it was still early days. If he found nothing acceptable soon – and he certainly wouldn't be over-fussy – he would fall back on his old standby: agency work. There were two agencies in Cannonbridge; he had seen their windows, plastered with stickers, offering steady employment, flexible hours.

Lorraine asked him – in words that seemed to Greg to echo in part what her mother had said to him twenty years ago – if he would like her to put in a word for him with her stepfather, see if there might be a vacancy for him at Workwear.

'It's very kind of you,' Greg responded after a pause. He had no idea how much, if anything, she might know of the past. 'But I don't know that it's a good idea. I can't see anything coming of it.'

She shook her head slightly. 'I think you're being much too gloomy. Whatever difficulties there may have been between you and Philip, it was all a long time ago. I can't really see Philip nursing hard feelings against anyone for years, he's far too busy for that. And I've always found him a very reasonable man.' Her voice took on a persuasive tone. 'Do let me speak to him, see what I can do. You might be in for a pleasant surprise.'

'Maybe you're right,' he conceded after another pause. 'If you can do anything, I'd be very grateful.'

She asked no questions now about what it was that had led to his abrupt departure from Workwear, twelve and a half years ago, and he didn't volunteer the facts, though they were as sharply clear in his brain at this moment as they had been then.

He had settled down well at Workwear, deeply grateful for the opening, anxious to prove himself worthy of Veronica's confidence in him, determined to do his utmost. He had enrolled for evening classes to improve his skills, had studied assiduously. He kept his head down at work, carried out his duties conscientiously. His work rarely brought him into direct contact with Philip Harvey, who appeared scarcely aware of his existence.

Greg rented a modest flat; he attempted no social life. His leisure was spent in solitary walking, reading, watching TV, listening to the radio – and drinking. Solitary drinking in his flat and nowhere else. He was at all times vigilant to keep it within bounds, mindful that he must never cause the slightest embarrassment to the Cliffords.

He never expected – or, indeed, wanted – any social acknowledgement from the Cliffords and had made it plain to Veronica from the start that he had no wish to intrude on her personal life. Nevertherless, once in a while, Veronica would invite him to Beechcroft for a simple meal.

When John Clifford died, three years after Greg came to Cannonbridge, Greg immediately offered to do anything in his power to help Veronica, but his services were never called on. Not long after Clifford's death, Greg began to feel that Philip Harvey had developed a dislike for him. Far from being unaware of his existence, Philip now appeared to go out of his way to criticize Greg's performance at every opportunity. Greg bore it as best he could; he redoubled his efforts at work, was scrupulously respectful in all encounters with Philip. But it made no difference; Philip continued to harry him. He began to fear that Philip's purpose was to drive him from the firm altogether. He was increasingly plagued by nervous tension. He made mistakes in his work, he began to drink more. Once or twice, in consequence, he failed to arrive at work on time in the morning. He was given a formal warning. His nervous tension grew almost unbearable. He couldn't appeal to Veronica; her state of health was too precarious to allow her to be troubled on his account.

And then Veronica married Philip Harvey.

The wedding was a very quiet affair. Greg received no invitation. Philip's needling of Greg didn't abate but rather increased; it played more and more on Greg's nerves, he relied even more on the bottle. He was given a second warning.

The day inevitably came when he turned up for work not only late but very obviously in the grip of a hangover. He was instantly dismissed. He made no effort to fight his dismissal but accepted his fate, almost relieved, in fact, that it had come at last. He packed his few possessions and moved to a neighbouring town. He didn't attempt to say goodbye to Veronica.

Six months later he read in the county newspaper of Veronica's death, the inquest, the findings. He was devastated but not totally surprised.

Now, sitting across the café table from Lorraine, in the belief that she might perhaps know something of the circumstances of his leaving Workwear, he felt impelled to offer her some reassurance. 'I did have a little trouble with alcohol at one time.' He gave her a direct look. 'But that's all in the past.' It was very far from being the whole truth but he was able to feel it wasn't exactly a lie. He had had his ups and downs in the last twelve and a half years, there had been spells of drinking and spells of abstinence. It was two whole months now since he had touched a drop and this time he intended it to stay that way.

Lorraine gave him an encouraging smile. 'I've never had any problem of that kind myself,' she said easily. 'I suffer from migraine. For me, alcohol is the very worst trigger for an attack, I found that out a long time ago, so I never touch alcohol in any shape or form, I wouldn't dare.' She made a wry face. 'Not even a single liqueur chocolate at Christmas or a spoonful of sherry trifle.' She smiled again. 'I'll certainly do what I can for you with Philip. Leave it to me.'

She waved aside his thanks and made a swift change of subject. 'Do you by any chance remember Jessie Dugdale? She was at school with my grandmother. My mother always kept up with her.' It was the first time either of them had mentioned Veronica today; her frail ghost hovered now in the air between them. 'Jessie's an old lady now, of course,' Lorraine went on. 'She'll be eighty in another couple of months. She still lives in the same cottage, in Bowbrook. I'm going to see her tomorrow afternoon, I've invited myself to tea. I try to keep an eye on her, she has no relatives.'

'I certainly do remember her,' Greg acknowledged. 'I remember her very well. After she retired, she used to come over to Beechcroft sometimes, when your father was away on business. She would come over in the afternoon and stay the night. Your mother would sometimes invite me for supper while Jessie was there. I must have met her six or seven times. I always found her very friendly and unassuming, very easy to talk to. I liked her a lot.'

Lorraine looked at her watch. 'I wish I could stay longer but I must be going.'

'I'm afraid I can't offer you a lift,' Greg said as he picked up her shopping. 'I don't run a car.'

She waved that aside too. 'I have my own car, I couldn't do my work without it. So it's me that can offer you a lift.'

He thanked her but didn't accept, indicating that he still had things to do in town. The truth was he had no wish to be returned so early to the solitude of his flat. He could easily pass another hour or two walking about the lighted streets; it would all help to shorten the evening.

As he carried her shopping to the car-park she said: 'I'll let you know how I get on with Philip, what happens about the job. I'll give him a ring and see if I can invite myself to supper, one evening next week. Of course, he might be away on business, he goes away a fair amount and he goes abroad more often these days. So it's possible I might not get to see him at all this week. Anyway, I'll be sure to ring you as soon as I have any news, let you know what the situation is.'

Again he thanked her. But his first action on leaving the car-park was to call at a newsagent's to buy an evening paper. He found a seat in the brightly lit pedestrian precinct, opened the paper and began to scan the job-vacancy columns.

*   *   *

36

Jessie Dugdale was a slightly built woman, somewhat stooped these days, with a calm, gentle face, softly curling hair, almost all white, still showing traces of its original auburn, her large hazel eyes a little faded, a little sunken. Lorraine found her a shade frailer each time she called.

'You will be sure to take proper care of yourself,' she urged as she was leaving the cottage at the end of her tea-time visit on Sunday. 'They're predicting a bad outbreak of flu later on. I hope you'll be having your injection?'

'Of course I will,' Jessie smilingly assured her. 'I have it every year.'

'But the injection won't protect you against the common cold,' Lorraine reminded her. 'If you neglect a cold it can be pretty serious, it can lead to bronchitis or pleurisy. You will take care, won't you?'

'You mustn't worry so much about me,' Jessie protested mildly. 'I never behave in a foolhardy fashion, you should know that by now. Of course I'll take care, I always do. I've got my winter routine going now: I stay indoors if the weather's bad, I make sure I keep warm and eat well. I do my shopping and other errands in the fine spells.'

'I'm glad to hear it.' Lorraine put an arm about her slender shoulders, kissed her soft cheek. 'I'll be over again before too long. You know how it is. I'm always so busy at work, but I'll do my best.'

'I do understand.' Jessie pressed her hand. 'It's good of you to come over as often as you do. You know how much I look forward to seeing you.'

Lorraine got into her car and pulled out. As she turned to wave, a thought rose in her mind: she had said not a word to Jessie about Greg Mottram's return.

During her lunch hour on Monday, Lorraine snatched a moment to phone Greg, to say she had now rung Philip and would be going to supper at Beechcroft on Tuesday. She could call in at Greg's flat on Wednesday evening, if that would be convenient, to let him know how she had got on.

Yes, Greg assured her, Wednesday evening would suit him

very well; he looked forward to seeing her. The moment she had rung off, Greg embarked on a tour of the flat, assessing the rooms through the eyes of a visitor – and a young, sharp, female visitor, at that.

He occupied flat number one, a one-bedroom flat on the ground floor of a four-storey block of eight flats of varying sizes, purpose-built forty years ago by private developers and modernized since then. The property had changed hands shortly before Greg moved in and the new owner had indicated his intention of carrying out minor improvements, in consultation with the tenants.

But that lay some little way off in the future; what was concerning Greg now was what he might do right away to brighten the general impression.

By the end of his survey he had decided on a number of immediate steps he could take. He set about the first of these at once, in a burst of energy that felt almost light-hearted.

Over supper at Beechcroft on Tuesday, Lorraine chose her moment with care, to broach the subject of Greg Mottram. She began by saying how surprised – and pleased – she had been to receive a birthday card from him.

At the mention of Greg's name she saw Philip's jaw tighten but he said nothing. She pressed easily on, describing her meeting with Greg, raising, as it were in passing, the possibility of an opening for Greg at Workwear.

Before she had finished, Philip was already shaking his head, with an air of unbending decision. 'I wouldn't want him working for me again. I remember only too well what he was like years ago. People don't change to that extent. If he's looking for work in Cannonbridge, he can go to one of the agencies, they'll fix him up. If he's any good, one of the employers he comes across will offer him a job.'

She said nothing but he saw by her face that she thought his attitude harsh.

'I don't know if he's told you how he came to leave Workwear, years ago,' he queried. 'Maybe he's given you some prettied-up version of what happened.'

'He's told me nothing,' she replied flatly. 'And speaking to you about a job was entirely my idea.'

'I was forced to get rid of him.' There was no softening in Philip's tone. 'He was going steadily downhill, he was worse than useless, he was a bad example to everyone else. You can't keep up a good standard of performance if you're seen to tolerate some deadbeat for family reasons. I thought it was a mistake, taking him on in the first place. He struck me as a sponger, from the word go. He'd got round your mother, got her to talk your father into giving him a start. I couldn't interfere with that, of course, not at that time. But later on, when I took over the running of the firm, I made it pretty plain to him he'd better smarten up in his work if he wanted to be kept on.' He shook his head again, with vigour. 'There's no place in any firm for hangers-on, you can't keep dead wood. He was drinking heavily, turning up late in the mornings, making serious mistakes. He was given warnings but he chose to ignore them.' Once again he shook his head. 'No way I'd ever take him on again.'

When Lorraine rang Greg's doorbell on Wednesday evening, he eyed her face as he admitted her, searching for signs of hope. She didn't keep him in suspense but broke the news as gently as she could, omitting all reference to Philip's scorching comments. He dropped his gaze, he made no reply but sat with all expression wiped from his countenance. She went on in a kindly fashion to encourage him to keep applying for jobs in as wide a range as possible.

He replied, as cheerfully as he could: 'I'll certainly do that. And I'll call in at both agencies in the morning. I'm sure one or other of them will find me temporary work, till I land something better. A part-time job would be ideal, it would let me go for interviews.'

Lorraine had intended staying an hour or so but couldn't bring herself to remain for even half that time; Greg's company was anything but enlivening. He looked relieved when she rose to go. As he walked out with her to her car, she promised she would be in touch again shortly. He gave her no more than a brief nod in response.

After she had driven off, he went slowly back into his flat. He was badly in need of a drink but he thrust the thought from him. He'd managed without a drop, all these weeks, he mustn't slip back now.

He wandered in and out of the rooms, flung himself down into an easy chair, switched on the TV, picked up the newspaper, but couldn't keep his mind focused for two minutes together.

He got to his feet again. After another ten minutes of pacing to and fro, he suddenly exclaimed aloud: 'What the hell!' and plunged out of the flat.

He made at speed for a nearby corner shop that held an off-licence. He came tearing back to his flat a few minutes later, clutching his bottle. And a packet of mints; he hadn't forgotten those.

In due course he slumped asleep in his chair before the TV, kept switched on, to give him the illusion of company. Time drifted by. The TV voices droned, laughed, sang; the faces smiled and frowned. But he heard nothing, saw nothing; he remained sunk in slumber.

It was almost three in the morning when he stirred and came awake, the lights still on, the TV still churning out its offerings.

He glanced at the clock. Hardly worth bothering now to undress and go to bed. He settled back into his chair and closed his eyes again, more at ease in this familiar situation than he had felt for weeks. Another few hours, then a wash and shave, a strong cup of black coffee, and he could begin the day in earnest, as he had begun countless others, in the long stretch of years behind him.

5

At 4 a.m., in his bed at Rivenoak, Owen Faulkner came suddenly and sharply awake. He hadn't been sleeping at all well lately; he had deliberately stayed up till well past his usual hour, striving to occupy his brain by going over accounts and estimates, in the hope that when he did put his head on the pillow he would fall at once into an annihilating sleep.

Moonlight stole in around the edges of the curtains; by its rays he was able to make out the time on the bedside clock: still two hours before his alarm was due to ring.

He glanced across at the other bed, to where Martine lay curled in slumber. She had gone to bed early, standing up abruptly in the middle of a TV programme, simply saying she was tired, brushing his cheek with a fleeting kiss, vanishing from the room in a trice.

It wasn't the first time in the last week or two that she had behaved in this way. They seemed to spend almost no time together now in the evenings. Either she would announce without warning that she was going out to one of the women's groups that had recently caught her attention, or she was off to bed, pleading tiredness, the moment supper was cleared.

He eased himself silently out from under the covers, into his dressing-gown and slippers, and made his way noiselessly from the room, down the stairs and into the kitchen. He set the kettle on to boil, made himself a hot drink, paced restlessly about, sat at the table, cradling his drink, staring at the wall, his brows drawn together in a fierce frown, striving to rid his brain of the torturing suspicions plaguing him now night and day. The phone calls that ended in a flash on his approach, the elegant new designer outfits, the frequent – expensive – hairdos. Above and beyond all else, the turning away from him in bed.

He dropped his head into his hands. It couldn't be, mustn't be, what he feared in his guts it must be. It was surely all capable of innocent explanation. She was still very young, still growing up, adjusting to marriage and motherhood. She was really just starting to spread her wings, it was no more than that. It would be asking for trouble, surely, to attempt to rein her in.

He expelled a long, wavering breath, finished his drink and got to his feet, feeling fractionally more cheerful. Yes, that was it. Patience and understanding, open-mindedness and love, above all, love; that was the answer.

He left the kitchen and went soft-footed back up the stairs. He

41

halted by a landing window, standing for some moments sunk in thought. He fingered the curtain aside and stood looking out at the house opposite, planted on top of rising ground, standing four-square and solitary in the moonlight, the dwelling where doubtless at this moment Harriet Russell lay sound asleep.

He let the curtain fall back into place and went slowly along to the bedroom.

Shortly before eight o'clock on the evening of Saturday, 22nd November, a service engineer, by the name of Yoxall, came out of the back door of an upmarket country hotel, ten miles from Cannonbridge, and crossed the car-park to where he had left his van. He worked for a firm that supplied and serviced catering equipment and had been called out to deal with a malfunctioning appliance.

As he sat in his van, filling out his work sheet, a car drove into the space beside him and a couple got out. Yoxall didn't raise his head but went on writing. The woman spoke, an instant later, and the man said something in reply. The moment Yoxall heard the man's voice he knew who it was: Philip Harvey. He glanced out and saw that it was indeed Harvey.

And he recognized the woman, too: Mrs Faulkner, wife of Owen Faulkner. Yoxall was in his late fifties; he lived in Rivenoak, had lived there all his life. He knew Owen Faulkner and had some passing acquaintance with Mrs Faulkner. He had spent several years as a maintenance engineer at Clifford Workwear, jogging along comfortably enough, but had left for his present job a month or two after Clifford's death. He had never been able to hit it off with Philip Harvey and hadn't been happy at the thought of working under him after Harvey took over the running of the firm.

He watched now with intrigued attention as Harvey and Mrs Faulkner, arms about each other's waists, went off, laughing and chatting, towards the hotel entrance. He sat for several moments after they had disappeared inside, digesting what he had seen. Well, well, well, he said to himself with keen relish, if that isn't an interesting turn-up for the book. I know someone who could be mighty surprised to hear this bit of news: Tom Guthrie,

Harvey's gardener. Yoxall had known Guthrie all his life. And he knew the pub where Guthrie drank his nightly pint. It was always possible, of course, it occurred to Yoxall as he returned to his work sheet, that none of this might be news to Guthrie; he might already be well aware of what was going on.

But Guthrie had known nothing of it, as at once became evident when Yoxall dropped into the pub for his chat on Monday evening. Guthrie listened impassively, expressing neither surprise nor disapproval, offering no comment of any kind but making it plain, all the same, by his manner, that he considered any such goings-on on the part of his employer no business of either himself or Yoxall. He turned the conversation abruptly to other topics, resisting all attempts on Yoxall's part to bring out his juicy titbit again for a more thorough chewing over.

Guthrie stood up to leave the pub earlier than usual. He wanted to mull over in solitude what Yoxall had told him, without having to endure any more of Yoxall's ill-natured tittle-tattle. They parted outside the pub, going their separate ways.

Guthrie made his way slowly homeward, deep in reflection. Mrs Faulkner he knew well by sight, from his regular visits to Rivenoak; he had often seen her in the stores and had spoken to her on several occasions. A very good-looking young woman; there could be no denying that. And pleasant enough in manner.

Could it have been merely a once-only light-hearted jaunt that Yoxall had seen, an evening's frolic, born of some purely chance encounter, meaning nothing, leading nowhere? Or could it be something more?

He didn't know Mrs Faulkner well enough to be able to make any kind of sensible guess. Philip Harvey would, of course, know Mrs Faulkner through her husband – could it even be that Owen Faulkner knew all about the evening's junketing and had given permission for it? After a little further thought Guthrie was forced to the conclusion that this last notion didn't seem at all likely.

Suppose, just suppose, that Yoxall had hit the nail on the head, there was something going on between Philip Harvey and Mrs Faulkner. Why should it concern him? He was only the

43

Beechcroft gardener, not a judge set up in some court of morals. True, he had known Owen Faulkner a long time; he liked and respected him. And he took a dim view, in general, of married women – particularly married women with young children – playing around. But in what way could it conceivably be considered any of his business?

His thoughts moved inescapably on to Rhoda Jarrett. He had always got on well with Rhoda, though always careful to maintain a certain distance, never to veer towards the over-friendly. And Rhoda had always responded in the same fashion.

He had never known for certain – and had never had the slightest wish to know for certain – on what precise personal footing things stood between Philip and Rhoda but he had formed a shrewd notion, years ago, that matters between them were not confined to the purely businesslike.

If, indeed, something was going on between Philip Harvey and Mrs Faulkner, was Rhoda aware of it? And if aware of it, how was she taking it? What would Rhoda's position be now at Beechcroft? What would her future be? And Vicky's future?

His footsteps had by now brought him to his own front door. He thrust away all these troublesome thoughts, took out his key and let himself in.

Wednesday morning saw Greg Mottram once again making his way along the churchyard paths to the Clifford burial ground; he carried yet another tribute of white flowers.

He had a job now – of sorts. One of the agencies had found him temporary work in the office of a Cannonbridge supermarket, where influenza was beginning to cut a swathe through the regular staff. The post was part-time and the hours flexible – all the flexibility being on the side of the management. Three full days a week for certain, the days variable, as staffing requirements dictated. Additional days and half-days to be worked, as needed, particularly during the approach to Christmas.

Routine work, monotonous and undemanding, the pay by no means generous, but any job was a marked improvement on dispiriting idleness, and the chances of finding a decent position, full-time and permanent, were always outstandingly better for an applicant in work of any description.

Today Greg spent longer than usual before Veronica's grave. When at last he turned away, he walked slowly back towards the gates, lost in thought. He stepped out on to the pavement and stood for several moments, pondering, then, with an air of sudden resolution, he set off in the direction of Wedderburn Road and Beechcroft.

That same evening Owen Faulkner found himself once again in a state of restless agitation, barely able to sit through the evening meal opposite Martine, sustain an appearance of interest in her breezy chatter.

The moment the meal ended he murmured an excuse about some imaginary business appointment and left the house; he got into his car and headed for Cannonbridge. His sights were set on the pub Tom Guthrie frequented.

He reached the pub ahead of Guthrie and stationed himself in a corner where he could watch the door. When Guthrie arrived he showed no surprise at seeing Owen.

Owen wasted no time in casual chit-chat but came straight to the point, speaking in low tones, his voice urgent and compelling, his eyes burning. Guthrie listened in attentive silence and then, as one old and trusted friend to another, appreciating that old friend's deep disquiet, answered as fully and candidly as he could the questions Owen fired at him.

When they parted company, half an hour later, Owen stood for some minutes outside the pub, sunk in reflection, before going off to his car.

Next morning Owen sought out a retired police inspector he had some acquaintance with and got from him the name of a small private inquiry agency in Cannonbridge that the inspector could unreservedly recommend.

Owen went along at once to the agency and discussed with one of the partners the kind of work he might require the agency to undertake. He went as far as discussing fees but at the last moment he drew back from actually giving definite instructions. He couldn't bring himself to do it. It was too shocking, too final a step. 'I'll be in touch if I decide to go ahead,' he said and took his departure. The partner watched him go with a shrug. He'll be back, he told himself with certainty. And before much longer.

There could be some perfectly innocent explanation, there must be a perfectly innocent explanation, Owen kept assuring himself on the drive home, I have absolutely nothing to worry about. It was only too easy to give free rein to wild surmises. It was unthinkable that Martine, his beloved Martine, could ever behave in a deceitful, treacherous fashion. She would be horrified if she knew what he'd been letting himself imagine.

He stopped on the way home and in a flood of remorse called at a high-class chemist's and bought his wife a bottle of hideously expensive French perfume.

6

Eight days later, shortly after 9.15 on the evening of Friday, 5th December, Lorraine Clifford came out of a Cannonbridge school that had lent its premises for a public meeting which had aroused considerable interest among the general public, as well as among pressure-group lobbyists, campaigners and crusaders of every description, and had brought along reporters, not only from the local papers but also from Wychford and from the county press.

Lorraine stood talking for several minutes in a small knot of folk, all chatting with animation, fired by the flood of ideas surging about in the course of the evening. The meeting had been called to discuss the terms of a trust set up under the recently published will of a Cannonbridge citizen, a maiden lady of ninety-two, without relatives, active and in full possession of her faculties to the last, who had died early in November.

She had lived alone, quietly and frugally. No one except her solicitor and her bank manager, whom she appointed joint trustees, had ever credited the old lady with possessing more than a couple of brass farthings and even these two gentlemen had been taken aback by the size of her estate, when it came to be fully valued, after her death.

The trust was designed to benefit the residents of the region the old lady had known and loved: the town of Wychford, where she had been born, Cannonbridge, where she had lived all her adult life, and the rural area in between, with its villages and hamlets. The trust would seek to provide a wide range of opportunities for the less privileged in society – individuals and groups – with the proviso that all applicants must raise by their own efforts some portion, however small, of the necessary funds.

The meeting had ended in a unanimous and enthusiastic decision to support the trust in all possible ways. After some minutes of spirited conversation, Lorraine said goodnight to the others in her group and went off to her car. She felt altogether too stimulated, too wide awake, merely to drive back to her flat, go to bed and try to sleep.

She looked at her watch as she opened her car door: 9.45. She could be at Beechcroft before ten; Philip was hardly likely to be in bed. She was sure she could persuade him to back the trust, join with her, maybe, in various projects, lend his undeniable weight as a leading local employer to any suitable proposal she might put forward.

Philip might be out, of course, in which case she would find no one at home. Friday was one of Rhoda Jarrett's regular evenings out; Rhoda was never home this early and Vicky would be sleeping at Avril's.

She made up her mind as she switched on the engine. She would give it a try, see if she could catch Philip, commandeer half an hour of his time.

She reached Wedderburn Road, pulled up near the gate of Beechcroft, got out of her car and started off along the drive. She had covered no more than a few yards when the outside light on the corner of the house suddenly came on. The front door opened, light streamed out from the hallway. Philip, with a woman at his side, stepped out on to the gravel. They left the front door open and strolled across to where a car was drawn up at the side of the house.

Lorraine had come to an instant halt. She stepped aside into the shadows of the shrubs lining the drive. She had at once clearly recognized the woman at Philip's side: Martine Faulkner, Owen Faulkner's wife.

It was immediately plain that the two were on highly affectionate terms. Philip had his arm about Martine's shoulders, he was smiling down at her; she was laughing and chatting, gazing lovingly up at him.

The pair halted when they reached the car; Philip folded Martine in a passionate embrace. Lorraine came to with a start. She turned and darted silently back along the drive. She was inside her car again, in a flash, equally silently. Then she was off and away, headed for the Wychford road and the haven of her flat.

Friday morning, one week later, was crisp and invigorating. Rhoda Jarrett set briskly about her usual quick tidy-up before starting out on her shopping trip, always the longest of the week. She whisked through the downstairs rooms and then darted upstairs.

In Philip Harvey's bedroom she was adjusting his bedcover when her eye was caught by a glint of metal by the skirting boards. She stooped to retrieve the object, half hidden in the folds of the cover. She straightened up and stood for several seconds, staring down at it.

A lipstick. An expensive-looking lipstick.

The notion had crossed her mind with increasing frequency of late – though she had done her best to resist the notion – that Philip was involved with some other woman. There was the matter of the phone calls. And the trace of perfume lingering sometimes in the air of his bedroom.

She had almost succeeded in persuading herself that she had simply allowed her imagination to run away with her.

But she very definitely hadn't imagined this lipstick, lying now in the palm of her hand.

The question at this moment was no longer: is it so? but: who is the woman? And: is it serious?

Doris Newman, sole owner and manageress of Ashdene, had

48

never married, never had any wish to marry, never had any serious or long-term attachment. But she was far from indifferent to the charms of the opposite sex, her appetite in that regard being decidedly keen and certainly not starved of satisfaction.

Just before six o'clock on Friday evening, one of her current men friends turned his car into the Ashdene drive and halted by the front door; he and Doris were off to London for the weekend; they would be returning on Sunday evening.

Doris came promptly out, carrying her overnight bag; she stepped into the car and they were away.

She had made her customary arrangements for her absence: Mrs Byrne would be in charge of the home and would sleep there on Friday and Saturday nights. Mrs Byrne had worked at Ashdene for only a year or two before Doris promoted her to senior care assistant. She was exactly what Doris wanted in that post: easy to get along with, efficient enough to do what had to be done but not so super-efficient as to be critical of the standards Doris deemed good enough for the establishment.

Over breakfast on Saturday morning, Rhoda Jarrett listened with close attention for the ring of the phone in the hall. It came at the expected time. Philip left the dining-room, to snatch up the receiver with his accustomed speed.

Some minutes later, when Philip had left the house and driven off, Rhoda was now alone in the premises – Vicky was sleeping over at Avril's, in accordance with the arrangement. Rhoda went to the phone, picked up the receiver and dialled the code number that would tell her where the last call had come from.

She made a note of the calling number and stood frowning down at it; it definitely rang a bell in her brain. Within a moment or two, she was pretty sure she had the answer: surely it was Owen Faulkner's home number?

She hurried along to the kitchen and found the card Owen had recently given her. His men had carried out an emergency repair to the central heating system one Friday afternoon; Owen had written his home telephone number on his card, in case there should be further trouble and she needed to get in touch with him over the weekend.

49

She looked at the card now. No question about it: it was from the Faulkner number that someone had just phoned Philip and, unless she was greatly mistaken, was regularly phoning Philip.

She returned to the hall, to the phone, her face set. She tapped out the Faulkner number. At the other end the receiver was picked up almost at once. A young female voice spoke the number. Rhoda said not a word. The voice spoke the number a second time. Still Rhoda said nothing. The voice said: 'Hello?' on a slightly sharper note. And again, sharper still: 'Hello?'

Martine Faulkner. Not a shadow of doubt: Martine Faulkner. Still in silence, Rhoda replaced the receiver.

That same evening was one of Rhoda's regular evenings out. She often went to the theatre on Saturday evening and that was where she was going tonight. She made a point of mentioning the fact to Philip in a casual way. She never used her car in the evenings, finding the local bus service very convenient. In the ordinary way, she would return to Beechcroft between 11.15 and 11.30 p.m., never earlier than 11 p.m.

The evening was fine but chilly, with a keen breeze, and she took especial care to wrap up well.

The play was one she would normally have greatly enjoyed, well acted and well produced, but she couldn't keep her mind on it. She left the theatre early and caught a bus home. It dropped her off, close to Beechcroft, at a minute or two before ten.

She made her way slowly and silently along the drive, halting the moment she had a good view of the front of the house. Light showed from only one room: Philip's bedroom. She saw a car standing at the side of the house.

It was now that her care to wrap up well paid off. She retreated to the shrubbery on the left of the drive, prepared to stand in the chilly shadows for as long as it took. In the event, she had been waiting a bare five minutes when she saw the bedroom light go off, the landing light come on. The outside light at the corner of the house sprang to life. The front door opened. Light streamed out. She didn't budge as two people emerged.

There could be no mistaking the woman at Philip Harvey's side: Martine Faulkner; her glorious, red-gold hair shone in the glow from the hallway. Rhoda stood motionless, watching as the pair made their light-hearted, lover-like way across the front of the house, to the car. She began to inch her way towards them.

As they closed in a farewell embrace, Rhoda stepped out of the shadows, her footsteps clear on the drive. At the sound, they broke apart, heads turned sharply to look her way. She made no alteration to her pace but went smoothly on.

'Good evening,' she said to Philip in a tone of bland courtesy, adding, a moment later, an equally pleasant 'Good evening, Mrs Faulkner.'

Neither attempted any reply. They stood like stone images, gawping at her. She experienced a moment of the keenest pleasure.

In the ordinary way, Rhoda used the back door to come and go but now, without slackening her steady pace, she moved serenely on towards the front door, still standing wide open. As she put a foot over the threshold, Martine's unnerved, high-pitched giggling, swiftly suppressed, reached her ears but she didn't turn her head.

7

Lorraine Clifford's duties took her over to Cannonbridge on the following Monday afternoon, ten days before Christmas. Before driving back to Wychford, she called at Greg Mottram's flat, as she often did now, when circumstances permitted. She never stayed long, never imposed on his hospitality.

Greg had got in from work a few minutes before she rang his bell. He looked, as always, pleased to see her. She waved aside his offer of tea. She wouldn't even step inside but remained standing at the door. 'I can't stay,' she told him. 'I've just stopped by for a moment, to see what you think about an idea I've had.' She broke off, to ask if he'd had any luck with his job applications.

Not yet, he told her, striving to keep his voice cheerful. But he was still hopeful, applying for anything that looked at all promising.

'It occurred to me,' she said, 'that it might be an idea if I were to put in a word for you with Owen Faulkner. He might have an opening for you himself, or he might know of someone who has. He has business contacts all over this area. What do you think?'

He was immediately taken with the notion. 'It sounds a first-class idea.' He had never met Faulkner but he knew who he was. 'I'd be very grateful for anything you can do.'

'Don't get your hopes up too high,' she warned, as she turned to go. 'It might come to nothing.'

One of Doris Newman's part-time care assistants was currently off work with a sprained wrist and Rhoda Jarrett had agreed to help out by doing the 10 a.m. to 2 p.m. shift in her place, for four days: Tuesday to Friday. Rhoda didn't have to prepare a midday meal for Vicky during term-time and Philip Harvey never came home to lunch on weekdays. He had no objection to Rhoda giving a hand at Ashdene in this way, provided it didn't interfere with her duties at Beechcroft – and she was always scrupulously careful in this regard.

Rhoda always found Doris Newman an easy employer, not given to breathing down the necks of her staff; she never pressed Rhoda to give her more hours than she could comfortably manage. Rhoda liked the work well enough, finding it a change from the daily round at Beechcroft – and the extra money was always useful, particularly in the run-up to Christmas.

Promptly at 9.45 on Thursday morning, Rhoda set off at a smart pace for Ashdene, taking with her today some women's magazines she had finished with; there was always someone among the residents who would enjoy looking at them.

Rhoda got on well with the old ladies, who found her quiet manner, kindly and sympathetic, her unhurried attentiveness, her readiness to listen, a welcome contrast to the speedy ministrations of the regular staff.

She reached Ashdene and went round to the rear entrance, to report for duty. As she passed the windows of the ground-floor rooms, more than one old face lit up at the sight of her, more than one feeble hand was raised in a friendly wave.

On Saturday morning, Lorraine was up even earlier than usual. She drove over to Cannonbridge, intent on catching Greg before he left for work. She wanted to give him his Christmas card and present – and to ask if he had heard anything from Owen Faulkner.

He was delighted to be able to tell her that he had received a visit from Harriet Russell, who had asked him about the kind of work he was looking for, what he could offer. She must, he felt sure, have reported favourably on him as Owen Faulkner had stopped by next day to say he would certainly keep his ears open and would be sure to contact Greg as soon as he knew of anything.

Lorraine's next stop on her festive delivery round was at Beechcroft, where she managed a word with Philip and then had a minute or two with Rhoda and Vicky who received her offerings with smiles of pleasure. Nor had Lorraine forgotten Avril Byrne, whom she had often encountered at Beechcroft; she gave Vicky a small gift to pass on to Avril.

Lorraine drove next to Bowbrook, to Jessie Dugdale's cottage; she had taken particular care in choosing Jessie's card and present. She found Jessie in the throes of a heavy cold, sitting coughing and sniffling in an armchair by the fire in the living-room, sipping a steaming beaker of honey and lemon. The cottage looked nowhere near as clean and tidy as it usually did, a sure sign that Jessie was far from well.

She questioned Jessie closely about her condition and insisted on taking her temperature but she could find none of the specific signs of influenza.

'You should be in bed,' she finally pronounced. 'I'm not too happy about that cough. I think the doctor ought to see you.'

Jessie uttered a groan of protest. 'I'm sure that isn't necessary.'

She strove to suppress her cough. 'It's only a cold. It'll be gone inside a week. I've got a bottle of cough mixture from the chemist, it's very good. You can't go bothering the doctor, the poor man's rushed off his feet with all this influenza about, he won't thank you for calling him out for a common cold.' The doctor was past sixty, sole practitioner in a scattered rural practice.

Jessie's cough wouldn't be suppressed any longer but suddenly erupted in a loud explosion. Lorraine gave her an eloquent look. 'I'll call in at the surgery on the way home,' she declared with finality. 'I'll have a word with the receptionist, I'll leave a message, asking the doctor to look in on you. You can probably expect him on Monday.' Lorraine knew the doctor, as she knew other doctors in the area, encountering them in the course of her work. And she had met Jessie's doctor here at the cottage, more than once, when he had called to see Jessie. 'It won't take him five minutes to sound your chest and write you out a prescription,' she maintained. 'He won't be too busy for that.'

She added, as she was leaving: 'I'll make time to pop over for a moment on Monday afternoon, to see how you are, and if the doctor's been. If he's left you a prescription I can nip along to the chemist and get it made up.' She wouldn't be able to look in on Jessie as often as she would have liked, for the next week or two. This was always a very busy time at work and she had already volunteered for extra duty, as she did every Christmas and New Year; she couldn't go back on her word now. With no close family ties of her own and little taste for the seasonal festivities, she never minded the extra work over the holiday. Her colleagues with families, particularly those with young children, always wanted, naturally enough, to be at home as much as possible at this time of year.

Greg Mottram spent Christmas Day, as he had spent every Christmas Day for many years, on his own. It didn't at all sadden him; he would, in fact, have been disconcerted, at this stage in his life, to be invited to share someone else's Christmas.

He had selected an especially handsome, and expensive, bouquet of white flowers – lilies, carnations, roses – to take to Veronica's grave, keeping the bouquet carefully overnight, to be at its best today. He waited until the last of the church services had ended and the congregation had finished their seasonal chatting, before he approached the churchyard. It was almost deserted now and he spent a long time by the grave, deep in thought.

He felt refreshed, buoyed up, not in the least lonely, when he let himself into his flat again. He settled down to enjoy the rest of his Christmas. No work for four whole days; there was his tasty dinner to look forward to, courtesy of the supermarket frozen food cabinets; there was his particular treat in the shape of more expensive bottles; he had the wide range of festive programmes on TV and radio.

He had his memories of the past.

And his designs for the future.

As soon as Avril Byrne had eaten her breakfast and helped her mother clear up, on Boxing Day morning, she ran round to Beechcroft, where she knew Vicky would be waiting for her, impatient to begin wielding her new camera – a topnotch camera, a Christmas present from Philip Harvey – out of doors, on this sparkling morning.

Vicky had been delighted with her present. She had taken indoor snapshots of them all yesterday and couldn't wait to try her skills further afield, lining up anyone she could persuade to pose for her.

She was down by the gate, looking along the road, when Avril rounded the corner and raced into view.

But first things first. As soon as Avril came panting up to the gate, Vicky cross-questioned her about every morsel that had passed her lips in the last twenty-four hours, how far she had ignored their current diet restrictions, what the tape measure and scales had revealed this morning.

Avril had to confess to a certain amount of slippage but promised faithfully to be even more careful over the next few days, in atonement.

With that important matter dealt with, a start could now be made on the photography.

At half-past ten, Martine Faulkner announced that she intended to take advantage of the fine weather to pop over to Northwick, to see Bertha Pearce, the woman who had brought her up.

She couldn't ring Bertha, to say she was on her way, as Bertha wasn't on the phone and never had been; she was a keenly thrifty woman who had managed well enough without such a frivolous inessential all her life and certainly didn't feel the need of such an expensive luxury now, in her late sixties. She could be reached via the phone of a neighbour, in dire emergencies only; she wouldn't countenance her neighbour being disturbed for everyday trifles.

Not that there was any necessity for Martine to let Bertha know, when she took it into her head to pay a visit; she was always sure of the warmest of welcomes, at whatever hour of the day or night she might choose to turn up; Bertha was, and always had been, utterly devoted to her.

'You'll be all right with Jamie?' Martine inquired casually of Owen. Yes, perfectly all right, Owen assured her.

She gave him a perfunctory kiss. 'I won't be late back.' She waved a hand blithely as she went towards the door.

Her mood over the last couple of weeks, since the evening when Rhoda Jarrett had suddenly materialized out of the shadowy recesses of the Beechcroft drive, had been one of unvarying exhilaration, so confident was she now of the explosion that must surely at any time erupt, changing all their lives, fundamentally and for ever. The humdrum Rivenoak days were almost at an end, the glorious new life was about to begin.

After the sound of her car had died away, Owen strove for the next hour or two to keep himself occupied, to push to the back of his mind the searing suspicions that kept surging up in his brain.

He played with Jamie, did his best to watch TV, tried to read the Christmas newspapers and magazines. He had to fight down the strong temptation to snatch Jamie up, drop him off at Harriet Russell's, jump into his car and drive over to Bertha Pearce's cottage, to check up on Martine, see if she was where she said she would be.

He well knew that such a course would be madness. If his suspicions should prove ill-founded, if he should come upon Martine cheerfully chatting to Bertha in all innocence, he would then find himself in the highly unpleasant position of having falsely and foolishly mistrusted his wife. Martine wouldn't lightly forgive him for that; nor would Bertha.

He returned to playing with Jamie. What he had to struggle against now was an urge to go rooting through Martine's belongings, something he had never done before, something he would normally consider indefensible.

But the urge grew stronger by the moment. It was impossible to continue like this, the uncertainty was poisoning his life. He had to find out, one way or another. He saw Jamie's eyelids beginning to droop. In another minute or two the child had fallen asleep. Owen settled him down and then darted off to make a rapid search of his wife's things, upstairs and down. It yielded nothing until he tried the drawers of Martine's bureau, an old piece that had belonged to Owen's grandmother. He found the lowest drawer locked. He went at once to a box of keys that had been in the house for as long as anyone could remember. He carried it back to the bureau, knelt down and set about trying to find a key that would operate the lock. It took him some time but he found one in the end. He slid open the drawer and began removing its contents, piece by piece, careful to preserve the order in which they lay, so that all could be exactly replaced.

The very last item was a large white envelope, unsealed. Inside was a glossy menu folder with the name, stamped on the cover, in gilt, of a high-class restaurant in a town several miles from Rivenoak. Inside the folder lay a spray of orchids, carefully pressed.

All the thoughts he had refused to allow himself to harbour came flooding back now into his brain. Decision hardened all at once into granite. The time had come to face the truth.

He sprang to his feet, went at speed to the phone and rang the home number the inquiry agent had given him. When his ring was answered he apologized profusely to the agent for disturbing him at a holiday time, but the agent, submerged in the torpor of a family Christmas, was in a mood to welcome the interruption. Owen asked if he might call in at the agency next morning. By all means, he was told; it would be business as usual in the morning. An appointment was fixed for nine o'clock.

It was turned ten when Martine returned home in a relaxed and cheerful mood; Jamie was long ago in bed. Owen was sitting in front of the TV, striving to focus his thoughts on the festive film offering. Martine greeted him with an easy show of affection. She didn't appear in the least tired; she didn't sit down but moved about the room, chatting brightly, picking up Christmas cards, giving them a glance before replacing them.

Bertha Pearce was very well, she told Owen. They had spent an enjoyable day together. In the afternoon they had gone out to tea, at the home of friends she had known since childhood. Other friends had also been there and had invited herself and Bertha to a party tomorrow evening. Two families of Bertha's relatives, known to Martine from way back, would be driving up from Devon, for the party; others would be coming from the next county. It would be a large and lively reunion.

'You won't mind if I go?' Martine employed the wheedling tone that had always worked so well with Owen.

'No, I don't mind.' He kept his eyes on the TV.

'I'll go over in the afternoon.' Her voice was light and carefree now. 'It should be a good get-together. It'll give me a chance to see some of the girls I was at school with, catch up on all the gossip.'

Martine slept late on Saturday morning; Owen had slept hardly at all. It was he who rose at the first sound from Jamie, attended to him and then prepared to open up the business premises, ready for the day's trading. He was on the look-out for Harriet Russell who arrived early, self-possessed and dependable as always, all set to handle the rush of phone calls requesting skilled assistance following the spate of domestic mishaps and

58

emergencies that seemed an inescapable feature of all public holidays.

Owen remained deep in conversation with Harriet for some time before going off to his car, to drive to Cannonbridge for his appointment with the inquiry agent. Harriet stood looking after him as he went, knowing herself unobserved, not bothering to mask her feelings but allowing them to surface briefly. Then she dropped the shutter again. Her features took on their customary look of control and competence. She turned and went briskly along to her office.

It was almost noon when Martine finally rose from her bed. She spent a long, leisurely, enjoyable stretch of time making herself ready for what lay ahead. She was set to leave at last by the middle of the afternoon. Jamie had been cared for, during all this time, by the daily woman, back at work, after the break, and, intermittently, by Owen, in between other calls on his time.

Owen mustn't wait up for her, Martine announced breezily as she bade him goodbye. She couldn't say exactly when she would be back. She would try not to make it too late but she wouldn't want to spoil the party by being the first to leave.

The next few hours passed more slowly than any Owen could ever remember. It was shortly after eight when the phone call he was so restlessly awaiting, so deeply dreading, finally materialized.

He snatched up the receiver, drawing a long, trembling breath as the inquiry agent identified himself. Owen listened with avid attention to what the agent had to tell him; he fired off a string of questions. When a name was given, he closed his eyes and uttered a groan, despairing and disbelieving. He made the agent repeat the details, unable to accept immediately that they could possibly be true, there hadn't been some monstrous error. When at length it was all over and he had replaced the receiver with a shaking hand, he stood gasping and shuddering, scarcely knowing where he was.

At last he drew a succession of convulsive breaths, endeavouring to regain control of himself. He went at a lurching rush up the stairs, stumbling his way to the boxroom, snatching down a couple of cases.

Some time later, he went along the corridor to look in on Jamie, sleeping soundly. He went downstairs again but couldn't settle. He went out through the front door and walked about. He looked up the slope at Harriet Russell's house, seeing a light on downstairs. He went back inside, went to the phone, picked up the receiver and rang Harriet's number.

8

Martine returned home shortly before midnight. The house was in darkness; just one outside light left on for her, by the garage. Nor did any light show from the dwelling on the slope opposite, where the sound of Martine's car brought Harriet Russell, still fully dressed, to an unobtrusive stance at the side of a window overlooking the Faulkner property.

Martine put her car away and went across to the front door, letting herself noiselessly in. As she closed the door the hall light snapped suddenly on, as Owen stepped from the sitting-room. In an instant he was before her, silent and hatchet-faced. In a single fierce pounce he tore her bag from her shoulder. She stood in frozen shock as he zipped open the bag, thrust in a hand and whipped out a long, slim jeweller's case. He jerked the case open and stood for a moment staring down at its contents: an exquisitely wrought necklace and ear-rings. He slapped the case shut, threw it back into the bag and flung the bag across at her. It struck her on the arm and she staggered sideways, clutching at the bag.

Still neither of them had uttered a word. Owen turned back into the sitting-room and seized hold of the two cases standing to one side of the door. He banged them down in front of her.

'Take these and get out!' His voice crackled with fury.

She regarded him levelly. 'Jamie –' she began but he broke in on her.

'You can forget Jamie. You've forfeited any right to Jamie. He's staying here, with me. For good.'

She set her jaw. 'We'll see about that.'

'I've no intention of divorcing you,' he informed her brusquely. 'You'll have to wait the full five years if you want to marry your precious lover.' He shot her a glance of acute loathing. 'You've no grounds for divorcing me.'

'I'll get Jamie,' she responded with icy calm. 'I can promise you that.'

He gave a short bark of a laugh. 'Try it,' he invited. 'Try it and see how far you get.'

She turned without another word and opened the door. She slung her bag on her shoulder, picked up the cases and stepped across the threshold.

On the front step she halted, setting one case down to lay a hand on the door knob. 'I'll let you know, in a week or so,' she announced coolly, 'where you can send the rest of my things.' She closed the door and a moment later he heard the rhythmic click of her departing footsteps.

He remained motionless until she had got into her car and driven off. When the sound of her engine had finally died away, he locked and bolted the door. He made his way upstairs with dragging steps, went silently into Jamie's room and stood looking down at his sleeping son, in the shaft of light shining in from the passage.

In the dwelling opposite, Harriet Russell didn't go to bed until all lights had been extinguished in the Faulkner property. She didn't at once drift off to sleep but lay awake for a long time, in the dark, thinking.

The moon slipped out from behind a cloud, illuminating the face of Bertha Pearce's cottage. No light showed from within; Bertha was long ago sound asleep.

Martine couldn't risk alarming Bertha by ringing and knocking at her door at such an hour. She would stay in the car until the first light showed in the dwelling. Bertha was an early riser, always out of bed by five.

Martine slid her car to a halt, as quietly as possible, on a patch of waste ground from which she could observe the property.

She settled herself as comfortably as she could on the rear seat, wrapped in the rug she always kept in the car.

She wasn't in the least fazed by the events of the last hour. She was in buoyant good spirits as she contemplated the future. She felt a sense of joyful relief, now that the explosion had at last taken place.

There was no way Owen would be able to keep Jamie, however hard he tried. Philip would get her a first-class solicitor who'd take care of that.

She must ring Philip first thing in the morning, arrange to meet him at one of their country hotels, put him in the picture, discuss matters, make decisions. Philip was off to Europe on Monday morning, on a business trip, he wouldn't be back till the following Sunday afternoon.

The situation with Rhoda Jarrett must be settled before he left. Martine had been fully aware all along of the nature of Philip's relationship with Rhoda; he had been frank with her from the start.

She snuggled happily down under her rug and slipped into a carefree doze.

Philip Harvey rose particularly early on Monday morning. He had a number of details to finalize at Workwear and he had to sandwich in an appointment with his solicitor – he had rung his solicitor at home yesterday, after his talk with Martine, and had been promised a few minutes of his time if he presented himself at the office promptly at 8.30 a.m.

Before going out to his car, Philip asked Rhoda Jarrett on no account to leave the house before he returned – most probably in an hour or so; it was essential that he speak to her before departing for Europe. It seemed an ordinary enough request to Rhoda; he would merely be intending to issue some last-minute instructions about the management of the household while he was away.

During the time – more than two weeks now – that had elapsed since Rhoda had stepped out of the shadows to bid Philip and Martine goodnight, Philip's manner towards Rhoda had altered not one jot. The encounter had by now assumed a dreamlike quality in Rhoda's mind, as if it had happened only in her imaginings. But upstairs in her bedroom, tucked safely away inside a plastic bag at the back of a dressing-table drawer, she had the lipstick in its elegant case, to remind her of the indisputable face of reality.

Philip's personal assistant and his secretary were both at Workwear when he arrived. He checked through with them that all arrangements would be properly in place for the arrival, in a week's time, of the foreign trade delegation on whose visit he was pinning such hopes.

As always in the last few years, he was happy to leave the daily running of Workwear, during his absence, in the more than capable hands of his personal assistant, a thirty-eight-year-old man by the name of Shannon, who had been with Workwear since leaving school. Shannon would, as ever, be ably supported by Philip's secretary, a middle-aged spinster with first-class qualifications and training, devoted to her work; Philip had taken her on very soon after assuming control of the firm.

When everything had been checked, Philip left for his session with his solicitor, calling in briefly again, afterwards, at Workwear, to ask his secretary to go along with him to Beechcroft. He offered no explanation and she was far too well trained to dream of asking for one; she rose at once to her feet, to accompany him. During the short journey he drove in silence, which she made no attempt to break. When he pulled up by the front door, he indicated that she should remain in the car but hold herself ready to go indoors, if he were to summon her.

He found Rhoda Jarrett busy in the kitchen. He was relieved to discover that Vicky was not in the house – Avril had called for her and they had gone off together.

He asked Rhoda to sit down at the table and took his own seat, facing her. His look and manner alerted her to the fact that this was going to be something more than a run-of-the-mill briefing before his departure.

He plunged straight in. 'I imagine you're aware, to some extent, of my personal situation, but you're probably not aware of recent developments.'

She made no response but sat very still, looking down at her hands clasped before her on the table.

He plunged on again. 'Mrs Faulkner wishes to move into Beechcroft, as soon as possible.' Her head jerked up at that but the movement was swiftly controlled. 'You realize,' he went on, 'that it won't be possible for you and Vicky to remain here, in the circumstances.'

Now she did respond. She gave him a direct look. 'Do you intend to marry Mrs Faulkner?'

He gave her back a look equally direct. 'Yes, in due course, when her divorce comes through.'

She sank back into silence, looking down again at her hands.

'I'll be back here from Europe on Sunday afternoon,' he told her. 'Mrs Faulkner wishes to move in on Saturday morning, so I can give you until Friday.'

Her head shot up again. 'Friday?' she echoed in disbelief. 'This coming Friday?'

'Yes,' he replied, in a tone that brooked no argument. 'This coming Friday. I'd like you and Vicky out of here, at the very latest, by Friday afternoon. I trust you will be able to make your arrangements by then.' He paused for a moment before continuing: 'I'm sure you will agree that it will be best all round if you leave the area altogether.' When she made no reply, he continued: 'Guthrie will be here, as usual, on Friday.' He asked if she knew where Guthrie was working today and she was able to tell him. 'I'll call in there,' Philip decided, 'and have a word with him. He'll give you any help you need. You can hand over your keys to him, he'll lock up when you leave.' He would also arrange for Guthrie to be on hand on Saturday morning, when Martine would be moving in – though he didn't articulate that thought now, to Rhoda.

'Naturally,' he went smoothly on, 'in view of all the circumstances, there'll be a suitable financial adjustment, to take account of the lack of proper notice, the disturbance to yourself and Vicky, the fact that you're being required to leave the area – and the fact that you will not be figuring in any way in the new will I intend making as soon as I get back from Europe.' As he well knew, Rhoda was fully aware of the extent to which she stood to benefit under his existing will. She had never been shown a copy but he had discussed the matter with her at the time the will was drawn up. 'What I propose paying you now, in full settlement,' he added, 'is an absolutely final sum. I must make this clear: there will be no further payments of any kind. If you agree to the terms I have just outlined, I'll hand you over a cheque now, for the full amount.' He named the sum; he was well aware that it was more than generous. It had been arrived at in consultation with his solicitor, who was firmly of the opinion that a display of open-handedness at this moment would put Rhoda into a far more amenable frame of mind. 'And you'll be keeping the car,' Philip went on. He had provided her all along with a car for her own use as well as for shopping and other duties but its ownership had always remained with him.

'Well, what do you say?' he asked after a minute or two in which she had sat in silence, still gazing down.

She raised her head again. 'Vicky won't want to leave her school, her friends.'

'Vicky's a bright girl.' His voice was persuasive, reassuring. 'She'll soon adapt. It's the school holidays now. You've got time to make arrangements before next term begins. You might think of going back to your home town. You must have family there, old friends.'

Her tone was unbending. 'There's nothing for us there. I've no intention of ever setting foot in the place again.'

He stole a glance at his watch. 'I must press you for an answer, I have very little time.' At that moment he couldn't predict what that answer would be.

She suddenly sat up straight and gave him a full, open look. 'I accept your offer, your terms,' she told him with a briskly businesslike air.

He felt a sharp thrust of surprise but managed not to betray it. 'I'm sure you're being very wise.' He pushed back his chair. 'I'll get you to sign an agreement.' This had been drawn up in readiness by his solicitor. 'My secretary's outside in the car. I'll get her to come in, to witness the signatures.'

Ten minutes later found Philip and his secretary on their way back to Workwear, where Philip at once rang his solicitor to let

65

him know that everything had gone as smoothly as could have been hoped for.

Philip also intended to permit himself the liberty of phoning Martine, via Bertha Pearce's neighbour, to assure her nothing had gone awry in his final dealings with Rhoda Jarrett; Rhoda and Vicky would definitely be gone from Beechcroft and from the area, by Friday afternoon.

Alone in the house again, Rhoda made a strong cup of coffee before planting herself down at the kitchen table, to think things out.

Some little time later, she went upstairs with an unhurried step, to make herself ready to go out, then she took from the dressing-table drawer the plastic bag containing the lipstick she had found in Philip's bedroom.

She went downstairs without haste, down to the ground floor and on down into the cellars, one of which had been used as a workshop, years ago. It still held a workbench and a cupboard containing an assortment of ancient tools. She looked these over with an appraising eye before selecting a lump hammer, stubby and heavy.

She folded over the edges of the plastic bag and set it down on the workbench, before standing back and swinging aloft the lump hammer, smashing it down with all her force on to the lipstick, with pounding blows: once, twice, three times. She halted to contemplate the result of her efforts: the lipstick case was now squashed flat. Satisfied, she replaced the lump hammer, closed the cupboard door, took the plastic bag and made her way, still unruffled, back upstairs to her bedroom.

She picked up her shoulder bag and left the house. She didn't take her car but walked serenely off in the direction of the High Street. Within a few minutes she found herself approaching a builder's skip, standing outside a property undergoing alteration. She paused just long enough to toss the plastic bag into the skip and then continued on her tranquil way to the bank, to pay in Philip Harvey's cheque.

9

Yoxall's taste for gossip and innuendo had by no means been satisfied by his merely passing on to Tom Guthrie what he had seen in the hotel car-park that November evening. He was very soon dropping a knowing word here and there; by Christmas there were few people in Rivenoak who hadn't heard that Martine Faulkner was carrying on with another man. It occasioned little surprise. Martine's eye-catching looks and carefree manner had caused her from the start to be regarded with a certain amount of suspicion in the village, in no way lessened by the cavalier fashion in which she had set about nudging aside Harriet Russell and marrying Owen Faulkner.

Yoxall's tale certainly chimed in with the strained air Owen Faulkner had been wearing of late.

Business resumed on the Tuesday morning, after Christmas; the day was damp and blustery, with gales forecast by evening. Martine Faulkner was nowhere to be seen and it soon became plain that young Jamie was being cared for by his father, with the ready assistance – it was noted with many a significant exchange of glances – of Harriet Russell, who maintained a public face of cool reserve, a calm refusal to respond to all approaches driven by idle curiosity. Bona fide inquiries about Martine evoked the bald explanation from Owen – pure guesswork on his part, as at this stage he didn't know his wife's whereabouts – that she had gone to Northwick, to stay with Bertha Pearce; he couldn't say when she would be back.

The tide of tittle-tattle reached the ears of Lorraine Clifford as she made her regular Tuesday morning calls in Rivenoak. She listened with sharp attention. So it was out in the open now and Martine had, it would seem, left home.

Throughout the day, the weather grew progressively more stormy, the wind increased in force. It roared and rampaged throughout the first part of the night, slackening towards dawn,

67

dropping by breakfast-time to little more than a stiff breeze. By the time Lorraine was ready to leave her flat on Wednesday morning, she had reached a decision. She had a duty call to make in Cannonbridge in the course of the morning, with no specific time arranged. She would drive over, first thing, to Beechcroft, to catch Rhoda Jarrett before she could leave the house for shopping, or some other errand. Lorraine's aim was to find out, from Rhoda, as precisely as she could, how the land now lay with regard to Philip and Martine. She had a number of ready-made excuses for calling: to wish Rhoda and Vicky a happy New Year, to inquire how Beechcroft had weathered last night's storm and to ask if Rhoda was able to cope, in Philip's absence, with any problems arising from the storm.

On her way to Cannonbridge she had to drive with caution along roads strewn with broken branches. Tattered sheets of newspaper, ragged streamers of plastic, clung to hedges, littered the pavements. It was a good thing, she reflected, that she had previously decided to look in on Jessie Dugdale this evening, to wish her a happy New Year, take her a little gift; now she could at the same time make sure Jessie was all right, that she – and the cottage – had come through the storm in good order.

At Beechcroft she found Rhoda outside, making a tour of inspection; she looked pleased to see Lorraine. 'Things aren't as bad as I feared,' she said with relief as Lorraine joined her on her tour. 'I've been wondering what I ought to do about the damage. Philip always sees to anything of this sort, but he's not due back till Sunday. In the ordinary way I'd get on to Owen Faulkner but I can't very well do that now, things being the way they are.' She gave Lorraine an inquiring glance. 'I imagine you know what's happened? About Philip and Martine Faulkner?'

'More or less,' Lorraine said. 'I've heard gossip.'

'Didn't Philip explain things to you?' Rhoda asked with a frown. 'I think he might have done.'

'He's explained nothing,' Lorraine replied. 'But I haven't spoken to him all that recently. If things happened in a rush, and he had to get off to Europe, I don't suppose he ever gave me a thought, I couldn't really expect him to.'

In a restrained and unemotional fashion Rhoda related frankly what had passed between herself and Philip on Monday morning – she had long ago realized that Lorraine was aware of the nature of her own relationship with Philip and, far from resenting it, appeared to approve of it. She ended her recital by saying: 'You can see now why I can't very well ring Owen Faulkner about the storm damage.'

'I think the best thing now,' Lorraine responded, 'would be for me to go along to Workwear, see if I can get in touch with Philip, ask him what he wants done about the damage, and then come back here and let you know what he says.'

At Workwear she spoke to Shannon, without giving her reason for wishing to speak to Philip. Shannon told her Philip's movements were always difficult to predict on his trips abroad; he travelled a good deal, visiting firms in various countries. The arrangement had long been the same: Philip rang the office once daily, around noon. If Lorraine cared to return at that time, she would be able to speak to Philip then. Alternatively, she could leave a message now with Shannon, for him to pass on to Philip, asking, maybe, for Philip to ring her at her flat in the evening.

Lorraine didn't take up either of his suggestions. She told Shannon it wasn't necessary for him to tell Philip of her attempt to contact him. She then returned to Beechcroft, with her mind made up.

She assured Rhoda she would take full responsibility and then she phoned the insurers, getting from them the name of a reputable firm specializing in emergency building repairs. She rang the firm and was promised men would be along shortly.

Greatly relieved, Rhoda made them both a cup of tea.

'I had intended wishing you and Vicky a happy New Year,' Lorraine said wryly as she drank her tea, 'but it doesn't seem very appropriate now.'

Rhoda grimaced. 'No, indeed. I won't be making much of the New Year this time, I've too much on my mind.'

'You won't be completely on your own?' Lorraine inquired. 'Vicky will be here?'

Rhoda moved her shoulders. 'As a matter of fact, she won't. She'll be sleeping over at Avril's. Doris Newman went to London yesterday afternoon, she won't be back till Sunday evening, so Mrs Byrne's in charge at Ashdene.' She attempted a smile. 'But

I'll be too busy to feel lonely, I've so much to see to, ahead of Friday.'

'Have you decided yet what you're going to do, when you leave here?'

'One thing I have decided,' Rhoda replied with energy. 'I'm definitely not leaving the area immediately. It wouldn't be fair to Vicky and I can't see why she should be made to suffer over this. I feel now I was manoeuvred into signing the agreement. I was given no more than a minute or two to consider it. Later on, perhaps, when Vicky's had time to get used to the idea, and I've been able to look at the various possibilities, we may decide then to leave the area. Or we may decide to stay, at least till Vicky leaves school – that won't be all that long now.'

Lorraine asked if they had found somewhere to go when they left Beechcroft on Friday.

'I did think about renting a little furnished flat.' Rhoda drew a sigh. 'But I phoned a few yesterday and they all seem to insist on a minimum let of six months, and I don't want to be tied down for as long as that, not at this stage. So I've settled on a bedsit, for the time being, while I decide what I'm going to do. We can move in there on Friday afternoon. It's a good large room, with two single beds, it'll do for the present well enough. It's not as if I've got any furniture or kitchen things to fit in, it'll just be our clothes and personal belongings. And it's near Vicky's school, that's one big advantage.'

She directed a look of appeal at Lorraine. 'I know it won't be long before Philip discovers I haven't left Cannonbridge, but I'd like to have time to draw breath before he does find out.'

Lorraine reached across and touched her hand. 'He won't hear of it from me. You can be sure of that.'

When Lorraine left Beechcroft she rang the supermarket, asking to speak to Greg. When he came to the phone, she explained her presence in Cannonbridge, adding that she was snatching a moment now to wish him a happy New Year, and to pass on the news she had just learned from Rhoda Jarrett about the upheaval at Beechcroft, the new direction in Philip's life. Greg listened with absorbed interest.

When she was about to ring off, mindful of the duty call she had to make, Greg said: 'If you're not doing anything tomorrow evening, perhaps you'd like to come and have a bite of supper with me here, then we can have a proper chat.'

'I'd love to come,' she responded warmly. 'I shall look forward to another of your tasty supermarket specials. I'll see you about 6.30.'

Towards the end of the afternoon, with the light beginning to fail, Owen Faulkner got wearily back into his car, at the end of his final call of the day, at a house on the outskirts of Cannonbridge. He drove slowly along to the nearest lay-by, switched off his engine, closed his eyes and leaned back in his seat, allowing all conscious thought to drain from his mind.

He had scarcely had time all day to give even a passing thought to his personal situation. He had spent a night of badly broken sleep, aware from the fury of the storm what the morning was likely to bring, by way of urgent appeals for help from distressed householders.

From the moment he set foot in his office, the phone never ceased to ring. He had had to deploy his men like a general, doing what he could, when and where he could. He had spent much of the day driving from job to job, assessing, advising, inspecting, reassuring.

After some blessed minutes of peace and quiet, he opened his eyes and shifted in his seat. Thought came flooding back, personal, disquieting.

It had taken him the best part of three days to come to terms of any sort with the events of last Saturday. He had progressed through a succession of emotional states, none of them at all pleasant, arriving finally at a point early yesterday evening when he felt he could now trust himself to speak to Martine. He had almost succeeded in persuading himself that Martine could be starting to have second thoughts, might even be regretting what she had done, could be soberly contemplating the harsh fact that she might actually lose Jamie.

Spurred on by these notions, he had decided to attempt to speak to her. He was pretty sure she would have gone to Bertha

71

Pearce's cottage and so rang Bertha's neighbour, who certainly appeared to be under the impression that Martine was staying next door and went obligingly off to relay his request.

A few minutes later, the receiver was picked up, not by Martine, but by Bertha, her tone markedly cool. No, Martine had no wish to speak to him, over the phone or in person, no wish whatever to see him. There was no point in his trying again; the response would be exactly the same. He would be hearing, before long, from Martine's solicitors. Bertha herself expressed no view on what had happened but her tone was eloquent. Having delivered her message, she didn't wait to hear his reply but at once replaced the receiver.

Owen was acutely anxious now to know precisely how matters stood between Martine and Philip Harvey. After his fruitless phone call yesterday evening, it had taken all his self-control to resist the impulse to jump into his car there and then and make for the pub where he would find Tom Guthrie, pump Guthrie for anything he might know of the current situation. But he hadn't been able to leave Jamie, peacefully asleep upstairs – he couldn't call on Harriet Russell to come over and keep an eye on him; Harriet, in her capacity as secretary of a village organization, had had a meeting yesterday evening that she couldn't turn her back on.

Unaware that Philip Harvey was now in Europe, Owen yearned to confront him in a vehement showdown, but common sense warned him that such a course would only make matters worse, would rouse Martine to fury when she learned of it, would provoke her into digging in her heels even more firmly.

On a sudden decision he switched on his engine, pulled out of the lay-by and turned his car in the direction of Beechcroft. He had always been on good terms with Rhoda Jarrett and he might do worse than speak to her frankly now. She could be in a position to tell him what he wanted to know – and, reticent and discreet as she normally was, she might very well now be in a mood to talk. He had long ago reached his own conclusions about the likely relationship between Philip Harvey, a widower, ambitious and highly driven, almost totally absorbed in his business, with little time or inclination for social life, and Rhoda Jarrett, a good-looking young woman, amiable and sensible, conveniently installed in his own household. If he was correct in his conclusions, then the turmoil of the last few days must surely have repercussions for Rhoda and her daughter.

As he came within sight of Beechcroft he saw a builder's van turning out of the driveway. Until a few days ago, he reflected bleakly, that would have been one of his own vehicles. He waited till it had gone and then drove in.

He left his car in the parking bay at the side of the house and walked round to the back door. A light showed in the kitchen and he set his finger firmly on the bell.

New Year's Eve proved to be even more miserably depressing for Rhoda Jarrett than she had feared. She felt a sense of total aloneness so acute as to afflict her almost like a physical pain. She strove to occupy herself with the countless tasks arising from her imminent departure. When, at last, fatigue drove her to an easy chair, she tried the TV, the radio, a book, newspaper, magazine; none did anything to raise her spirits. At ten o'clock she gave in and took herself off to bed.

But she couldn't sleep. Her brain wouldn't rest but kept churning things over. She switched on her bedside radio, keeping the sound low; she lay in the dark, listening to the thin thread of orchestrated jollity, the whole world linked in companionable rejoicing; it served only to underline her solitude, plunge her into deeper gloom.

It was well past one o'clock when she sank at last into an uneasy slumber, punctuated by dreams filled with images of dread. Each time she surfaced to consciousness she was aware of the relentless merriment continuing unabated from the radio, until at last the alarm clock released her into the new day, the new year, the seas of change ahead.

Greg Mottram didn't waste time lying in bed on the first morning of the New Year but set about an energetic sprucing-up of his flat, invigorated at the prospect of Lorraine's visit.

In the middle of the morning, with the flat to his satisfaction, he set off for St John's churchyard, to lay his New Year flowers

73

on Veronica's grave. He would go along afterwards to Beechcroft. He had been turning over in his mind what he might do to assist Rhoda in her move and had decided he would offer to store for her such items as Rhoda and Vicky wouldn't be needing for the immediate future or wouldn't have room for in the bedsit.

At a few minutes before six o'clock, as arranged with Greg on his morning visit, Rhoda drove into the parking space allotted to Greg's flat. Vicky and Avril rode with her, to give a hand with the boxes for storage. Rhoda would be taking the two girls along afterwards to Ashdene, for their evening stint; she would then return to Beechcroft, to spend her last evening and night there, alone.

Vicky jumped out of the car and ran across to press the bell; a moment later, Greg threw open the door, smiling a welcome. All four of them set smartly about unloading the cargo of boxes, carrying them indoors, stacking them neatly in the allotted area. The boxes had all been marked in a businesslike fashion with the nature of their contents, Vicky's belongings being packed separately and now being stacked separately, to facilitate later access. 'If either of you wants anything from the boxes at any time,' Greg told them, 'don't hesitate to come along. It'll be no trouble to me. No need to phone first, I'm here pretty well every lunchtime and evening.' The bedsit Rhoda had taken was within easy walking distance of Greg's flat.

They had almost finished their task when Lorraine Clifford's blue Peugeot turned in at the entrance, coming to a halt as Lorraine caught sight of Rhoda's car and the energetic activity surrounding it. Rhoda at once broke off to go across to speak to Lorraine, assuring her they would all be off shortly and Lorraine could then drive into Greg's space.

A few minutes later, as Rhoda was running the two girls to Ashdene, she told them she intended going inside the home for a moment. She wanted to wish one of her old ladies a happy New Year. This was a gentle, simple soul who had taken a particular fancy to Rhoda.

She halted the car by the gate and took a small gift-wrapped parcel from the glove compartment. 'I've brought her a little present,' she added. 'It's nothing much, but it can mean a lot to someone old and frail, with no relatives left.'

The hands of the clock in the bedsit that was now the temporary home of Rhoda Jarrett and her daughter were advancing towards 6.30 on Friday evening, as Rhoda cast a critical eye over her reflection in the long mirror of the wardrobe. Vicky had left the bedsit a little earlier, to call round for Avril; the pair were going along to Ashdene for their usual stint.

The move from Beechcroft had gone smoothly enough; no disasters or oversights, no unpleasant surprises. But Rhoda would have found it only too easy at this moment to give in to feelings of weariness and despondency, to spend the evening alone in this one room, lolling in front of the TV. She was determined to do nothing of the sort; she would not embark on this new phase of her life in a spirit of moping and brooding. She would continue to go out on her regular evenings; she would maintain the existing arrangement with Mrs Byrne, who was equally anxious to preserve it.

Now that she was able to please herself how she arranged her time, Rhoda intended, for the present, to work part of most days at Ashdene, where any help she could offer would be more than welcome, with the influenza season well under way. It would suit her well enough until she was able to make her plans for the future with greater precision.

And now she had the whole evening before her. She turned from the mirror and left the room, stepping out with a purposeful air into the chilly, light-splashed darkness.

10

Martine Faulkner sprang out of bed early on Saturday morning, in a mood of joyous optimism. Today she would be moving into Beechcroft; tomorrow afternoon Philip would return from Europe.

Shortly before nine, she bade farewell to Bertha Pearce and got into her car, bound for Cannonbridge. She would drop her things at Beechcroft and have a word with Tom Guthrie, before driving into town to keep her ten o'clock appointment with the solicitor Philip had found for her.

She had heard nothing from Philip since he left, nor had she expected to; he had told her he would ring her via Bertha's neighbour only in the event of some mishap or if he was likely to be much delayed in returning. But he had promised to phone her without fail this evening at Beechcroft, to see if she had settled in, and to give her, more precisely, the time he could be expected tomorrow.

She intended spending much of the rest of the day in a pleasant stroll about the Cannonbridge shops. She would take particular care in choosing food to prepare for tomorrow evening. Philip would no doubt expect that they would go out to eat but she had it in mind to surprise him: she would have a meal ready for his return, the first meal she had ever cooked for him.

Yes, she would cook him a truly delicious dinner. She had been assiduously grounded in the housewifely arts by Bertha and cooking had proved to be one of the very few that held any appeal for her. A really good beef casserole, she decided; welcoming and warming at this time of year; a dish that wouldn't spoil because of uncertain timing, one that would improve by standing overnight, to be put back in the oven tomorrow afternoon. She would set the table beautifully, in the dining-room. She would buy candles for the table: beautiful, elegant candles, enough to be able to dispense altogether with other lights.

It was turned five when Martine drove in through the Beechcroft gates after her final trip out. Tom Guthrie had long gone home. She had spent a highly enjoyable day; she didn't in the least mind being on her own for the next twenty-four hours – and Philip would shortly be ringing her.

The alluring odour of the beef casserole greeted her as she let herself into the house. She would give it another half-hour before removing it from the oven.

She stowed away her shopping and made herself a cup of tea. She was clearing up in the kitchen, humming along, in great good spirits, to lively music from the radio, when she heard the sound of the front door opening and closing. She froze instantly. Surmise flashed through her brain. Rhoda Jarrett? Returned for something left behind? Tom Guthrie? Come back for some reason? But surely neither would now have a key. Ah! Lorraine Clifford! She would have a key. She was probably unaware of developments at Beechcroft. She went swiftly into the hall.

But it wasn't Lorraine Clifford. Striding towards her, his arms outstretched, smiling broadly, was Philip.

On Sunday morning, Vicky and Avril let themselves out through the front door of Mrs Byrne's house as a nearby church clock was striking nine. They were due at Ashdene at 9.30 but they didn't immediately turn in that direction. They set off instead for Wedderburn Road, running lightly through the overcast morning with an air of high-spirited, giggling mischief.

When they reached the Beechcroft gates they slackened their pace and fell silent. They went cat-footed along the drive to the front of the house. They stood surveying the windows, all closed, all the heavy, lined curtains drawn together, not a peep of light showing anywhere. Vicky moved on tiptoe to the sitting-room windows and put her ear to the glass but could detect not a whisper of sound.

They made their noiseless way around the house, then Vicky darted over to the garage, with Avril at her heels. Vicky was almost there, intent on peering in through the windows, when she came to an abrupt halt. A car had slowed by the gates, as if about to turn in. Avril tugged at her sleeve and they raced into the shelter of the shrubbery. The car moved on again. Vicky turned a second time towards the garage but Avril pulled at her arm. 'Let's go,' she whispered urgently. 'Someone might come.' Vicky gave a nod and they ran off, along the drive and out through the gates, bound for Ashdene, laughing now without restraint, loudly and freely.

Philip Harvey's secretary and his personal assistant, Shannon, were at their posts particularly early on Monday morning, to make sure every last detail had been attended to, in readiness for the visit of the foreign delegation, scheduled to begin at ten o'clock. On a day such as this, the pair would expect to find Philip already at his desk and were more than a little surprised to discover this wasn't so.

When Philip hadn't shown up by a quarter to nine, they began to feel a degree of alarm. Perhaps he had failed to return home yesterday evening from Europe. Could something have happened to him? An accident? Illness? Shannon picked up the phone and rang Beechcroft, with the secretary standing beside him. But the phone rang without reply.

'I'm going round there,' Shannon said with decision as he replaced the receiver. 'You stay here, in case he rings.'

At Beechcroft, Shannon halted his car in the parking bay. He got out and glanced over at the house. It looked closed up; he could hear no sound, detect no sign of activity. He went across to the garage and peered in through a window. He could see two vehicles: Philip's car and another, smaller and older, that he didn't recognize.

He turned and crossed rapidly to the front door. He knocked and rang, without response. He made a circuit of the house, knocking and ringing at the side door, the back door. He put his ear to windows, he sent raking glances over the upper floor. Still he could detect no sound, no movement. He stood for a moment in thought and then ran along to the neighbouring house, a detached villa in a sizable garden.

The door was answered by a middle-aged woman with a harassed air. Shannon apologised for disturbing her and offered a brief explanation of his presence at her door. Did she by any chance know anything of the whereabouts of Mr Harvey or his housekeeper, Miss Jarrett?

She was sorry, she knew nothing. Her husband had already left for work and she was busy, as always, looking after her invalid father, in addition to all her other chores and responsibilities. She had never been on close terms with anyone at Beechcroft. She showed no disposition to linger further and made to close the door.

Shannon raised a hand to halt her. Could she suggest anyone who might have a key to the house?

She began to shake her head and then stopped. 'I don't know if Faulkner's men would be any help – Faulkner's, from Rivenoak. They were working at Beechcroft only two or three weeks back, they often work there. They're at a house along there . . .' She gestured in the direction. 'They should be there by now, it's gone nine.'

Shannon thanked her and asked if he might use her phone to ring Faulkner at Rivenoak. She agreed without enthusiasm and admitted him to the hall.

His ring was answered by Harriet Russell who listened intently to what he had to say. She told him Owen Faulkner had left a little earlier on a routine inspection round. He would probably be looking in about now at the job in the next road to Beechcroft. If Shannon were to go along there right away he might catch him or could be told where to find him.

When Shannon reached the property he found that Faulkner had just arrived. When he heard what Shannon had to say he at once saw the seriousness and urgency of the situation. He said little but acted instantly. He directed one of his men to bring along an aluminium ladder and a putty knife and the three of them left at speed for Beechcroft.

The downstairs windows, it appeared, were fitted with security locks, but not so those on the upper floor. The workman put his ladder up at the side of the house and with the blade of his knife released the catch on a corridor window. He climbed inside, ran down the stairs and opened the front door to them.

Owen burst into the house ahead of Shannon. He raced in and out of the ground-floor rooms, coming to an abrupt halt on the threshold of the dining-room. He uttered a terrible piercing cry. Shannon ran over and looked in, over his shoulder.

The room was in darkness, only the daylight from the doorway casting a feeble illumination over the scene: the man and woman seated opposite each other at the table, slumped forward in their chairs, heads cradled on arms, among the plates and dishes, the glasses and coffee cups, the candlesticks with the candles burned right down.

11

In the brief interval before the police arrived at Beechcroft, Owen Faulkner found a quiet corner to make a speedy call, unheard and unobserved, on his mobile phone. Over in Rivenoak, Harriet Russell was alone in her office. She listened with razor-sharp attention to what he had to say. She made no comment and was asked for none; she put no questions to him. When she had replaced the receiver she sat for some moments with her hands over her face, until recalled to everyday business life by another phone call, this time from someone requiring urgent assistance in the matter of a non-functioning boiler.

Shannon occupied the minutes of waiting for the police by pacing up and down outside the Beechcroft gates, glancing at his watch every few seconds. The moment the first police car drew up he was alongside, explaining what he could with great rapidity, stressing the urgency of his need to get back at once to Workwear, if he was to arrive there ahead of the delegation. He would give the police as much time as they wanted tomorrow. On this firm assurance he was allowed to leave.

By the time the forensic team got to work, news of the deaths had leaked out into the local community.

Mrs Byrne was busying herself in her kitchen with domestic chores; she wasn't due at Ashdene till after lunch. It was approaching 10.15 when her next-door neighbour, an elderly widow, came hurrying round, with what speed she could muster, to press Mrs Byrne's bell with urgent force. She had just heard a news-flash on the local radio of the discovery of the bodies at Beechcroft. The instant the front door opened, she poured out her tale.

Mrs Byrne couldn't take it in, couldn't believe it when she did take it in, had to be steered along to the kitchen, made to sit down while her neighbour switched on the radio, tuned it into the local station, to wait for the next report. It wasn't long in coming.

Mrs Byrne heard it in appalled horror; she buried her head in her arms. The neighbour bustled about, making tea, firing questions, proffering conjecture, all of which flowed over Mrs Byrne's head. One agonizing thought alone reared up out of the shock and disbelief: how was she to break the dreadful news to Vicky? The two girls were upstairs in Avril's bedroom, readying themselves for a descent on the Cannonbridge stores, now in the ferment of the January sales. At any moment the pair would come charging down the stairs, laughing and chattering, sticking their heads into the kitchen, to bid her goodbye. Impossible to let them go off, in happy ignorance, into town, to learn what had happened as they roved about the shopping aisles.

She stood up from her chair, switched off the radio – now delivering traffic reports – and propelled her voluble neighbour, as civilly as she could, out of the kitchen, along the hall and out through the front door. She had barely closed the door behind her when the two girls came swooping out of the bedroom, plunging down the stairs in high spirits, calling gaily out to her. She turned from the door and stood staring up at them, frowning in distress, unable to speak, clasping her hands before her, her face pale.

The girls came to an abrupt halt at the foot of the stairs, arrested by the strangeness of her manner. Her gaze rested on Vicky. 'Something I've got to tell you,' she managed to say. They didn't ask questions. Her tone froze them into apprehensive silence.

Without another word she shepherded them before her into the kitchen, sat them down at the table and took a seat herself, opposite them. She drew a trembling breath and made a ragged start on what must be said, keeping her eyes all the while on Vicky's face.

Vicky sat rigid, her face at first wiped clear of expression. At her side, Avril flashed her a nervous glance. Mrs Byrne went on speaking in a stumbling monotone.

Before she had finished, Vicky's face contorted suddenly. She gave a piercing shriek and sprang to her feet. Her chair fell back with a clatter. 'Not Philip! Not Philip as well!' She gave vent to an appalling high-pitched screaming of terrifying intensity, as if she would never stop. She flung herself forward on to the table, still screaming, arms and legs wildly flailing.

Rhoda Jarrett had left her bedsit shortly after ten, to go out to a couple of local shops. Her second call was at a small, family-run bakery.

There were several customers in the shop when she arrived. She had just been served and had paid for her loaf, she was turning from the counter, when she was halted by the sound of footsteps racing along the passage from the kitchen. A young apprentice lad in a flour-dusted apron burst into the shop with the news he had just heard over the radio.

A stunned silence fell before a buzz of talk erupted. Rhoda stood transfixed and speechless before edging her way outside, on to the pavement. She remained for another minute or two, sunk in thought, and then set off at a rapid pace in the direction of Wedderburn Road.

When she rounded a corner and came within sight of Beechcroft, she saw the line of vehicles drawn up, the police barrier tapes, the uniformed constable standing guard.

She crossed over to the other side of the road and went by. She must go along to the main Cannonbridge police station, they would want to talk to her. But first she had another call to make. She continued on till her steps brought her to Mrs Byrne's house. As she unlatched the gate she became aware of a horrifying sound from inside the house, a terrible, high-pitched screaming. She stood frozen for a moment and then let herself in through the gate, closed it behind her and went up the path. She drew a deep breath, squared her shoulders and set her finger on the bell.

In the Beechcroft sitting-room Detective Chief Inspector Kelsey had spent several minutes talking to Owen Faulkner. A big, solidly built man, the Chief, with a head of thickly springing carroty hair, shrewd green eyes, craggy features, a freckled face dominated by a large squashy nose.

Owen Faulkner was plainly hanging on with grim tenacity to

his self-control. He answered all the Chief's questions in a straightforward manner, though from time to time dropping his head and drawing long, shuddering breaths before continuing. He had already made the formal identification of his wife's body, a proceeding which had manifestly brought him to the verge of collapse; he had recovered sufficient composure, by a visibly immense effort, to be able to go along with the Chief to the sitting-room to make a statement.

He no longer had to be prompted by questions from the Chief; it all poured out of him in a ceaseless flow: the state of his marriage, the inquiry agent's report, the expulsion of Martine from the house. He broke down from time to time but recovered himself with determination, as if compelled to get every last bit of it off his chest with all possible speed.

When he had at last finished, he asked the Chief, in a tone of urgent appeal, to see that Bertha Pearce was informed without delay of what had happened. 'Martine was the centre of her life,' he told the Chief in broken tones. 'All she had.' It was plain he both liked and respected Bertha and shrank from the idea of her suffering being compounded by hearing the dreadful tidings from some other source.

On Monday mornings Tom Guthrie tended the garden of a married couple, both out at work all day. Guthrie usually took a mid-morning break in the shed he looked on as his own territory, where the machines and tools he used in his work were housed. It was almost eleven as he sat down on the old chair that stood in a corner and addressed himself to the snack he had brought from home.

He leaned across to switch on the portable radio he kept on a shelf; he liked to keep up with the local news. He had barely settled back in his chair when the name Philip Harvey leapt out at him. He jerked himself upright as he listened, scarcely able to credit what he heard.

When the report ended he sat frowning down at the floor. The police were sure to want to talk to him. Better scrub his afternoon job for today, get along to the police station instead. Even as he formulated the thought, another part of his mind kept

83

saying: It's not possible, it can't be true, it's some weird kind of mistake.

It was not far off 11.30 when DC Slade pulled up by the gate of Bertha Pearce's cottage. He spotted her at the side of the house: a stoutish, rosy-cheeked woman, wrapped up against the January chill in a baggy old coat, a woollen cap on her greying hair. She was stooping over a wheelbarrow piled with garden refuse; she raised her head at the sound of the gate. She straightened up as he followed the path round to where she stood, surveying him. Calm grey eyes; a look that seemed to indicate considerable reserves of strength and fortitude.

He introduced himself and her features at once grew taut, in the certainty of bad news. 'If we could go inside,' he suggested. She said nothing but walked before him to the back door and into the house. Still without speaking she led the way along a passage into a sitting-room. She motioned him into a seat and sat down opposite him. She clasped her hands, fixed her eyes on his face.

He said what he had to say.

She closed her eyes and drew a shaking breath she sank down into her chair. Silence lengthened in the room, broken by the ticking of a clock. Outside, a band of children went by, laughing and shouting.

'I'm afraid there are questions I shall have to ask you,' Slade said gently, 'but it needn't be today. I can come back tomorrow.'

Still in the same posture, without opening her eyes, she said: 'That's kind of you, but I'd rather get it over with today.'

'Is there some relative or friend in the village you'd like to be present while we talk?' he inquired. 'Or a neighbour, perhaps?'

She shook her head. 'There'll be enough gossip and speculation. I prefer to talk to you in private.' She drew a long, deep breath, opened her eyes and sat up, giving her head a quick little shake.

'I can make you a cup of tea,' he offered.

'What I'll do,' she said suddenly, 'I'll take a walk round the garden. I won't be long, I'll be up to it better afterwards.' She managed a smile of sorts. 'You can make the tea. I'll be back in time to drink it.' She went ahead of him along the passage, indicating the kitchen. 'Don't worry about me,' she said as she went towards the back door. 'I'll be perfectly all right.'

As he set the kettle on to boil and laid out a tray, he kept shafting a glance of concern out through the kitchen window. She was striding along the garden paths, looking neither to right nor left, never slackening, never pausing, round and round, gazing straight ahead.

The kettle came to the boil and he made the tea. He sent another glance out through the window. She was still striding about, she never looked his way.

He carried the tray along to the sitting-room and set it down. His eye was taken by the array of framed photographs on the walls, the mantelpiece, the top of a china cabinet. He moved about the room, studying them. Bertha Pearce, and a man who was clearly her late husband, made a succession of appearances, from their wedding day onwards. But pride of place was given to Martine: as a tiny baby, lovingly cradled by Bertha, with her husband beside her, gazing fondly down at the infant; Martine as a toddler, as a schoolgirl at various ages, as a blossoming teenager, a beautiful bride, with Owen Faulkner standing proudly at her side; Martine as a young mother, holding her new-born son.

He turned from his perusal when he heard the back door open. Bertha came into the room a few moments later. She had removed her coat and woollen cap; she looked younger now, a more conventional figure; the fresh air had put colour in her cheeks.

She held herself tensely upright. She spoke a word to Slade, sat down and poured the tea with a steady hand. She kept her eyes resolutely averted from the display of photographs as if only too well aware that a single glance at any one of Martine's smiling images could shatter her composure.

She handed Slade his tea. 'Go ahead,' she invited. 'Ask me anything you want to know.'

In response to his gentle questioning, she outlined for him – still with the same air of steely self-control – Martine's history, her own relationship with her and what she knew of the break-up of the marriage; she described Martine's mood in the days

85

following the break-up, particularly on the Saturday morning when she had left for Beechcroft.

Bertha had, it appeared, met Philip Harvey once, briefly – on the Sunday morning after Martine had turned up on her doorstep. She had liked what she saw of him, had felt he was a man to be trusted. And she had seen Martine look at him in a way she had never once seen her look at Owen Faulkner.

As Slade was leaving, Bertha asked to be informed of the date of the inquest.

'There's no need for you to attend,' Slade pointed out. 'It will just be the formal opening and adjournment. It won't take more than a few minutes.'

She set her jaw. 'I intend to be there. I wouldn't dream of staying away.'

It had been an unusually busy morning for Lorraine Clifford. Two meetings to attend; calls to be fitted in, before, between and after. It was close to noon when she pulled into a lay-by on the outskirts of Wychford, to snatch ten minutes for herself before going on to her next call. She switched on the radio and leaned back in her seat, closed her eyes and drew a long, luxurious breath.

Almost at once she found herself listening to the noon bulletin on the local radio; the name Beechcroft flashed out at her. She jerked up in her seat, her eyes shot open. As the bulletin progressed she put her hands up to her face and crouched forward, shaking and gasping. When at last the bulletin was over and she had regained control she looked at her watch. She must ring the Cannonbridge police station, she must get over there right away. But she would have to call in first at the department and let them know – she had no idea how long the police might require her presence.

It was almost a quarter to one by the time she drove into Cannonbridge and turned her car in the direction of Wedderburn Road. As she neared it she saw the house-to-house teams already at work. When she was within sight of Beechcroft she slowed her car, glancing across at the vehicles drawn up, the

86

constable by the gate. She picked up speed again, heading for the police station.

DCI Kelsey had not long returned to the station from Beechcroft, where he had left the forensic team at work. The two bodies had now gone to the mortuary; the post-mortems were due to start at five o'clock. House-to-house inquiries were also getting under way out at Rivenoak. There had been no difficulty over photographs; Owen Faulkner and Bertha Pearce had supplied excellent recent prints of Martine, and Rhoda Jarrett had produced some good clear snapshots of Philip Harvey, taken by her daughter as lately as Christmas Day.

Lorraine was kept waiting only a few minutes before she was taken along to an interview room where the Chief and Detective Sergeant Lambert joined her. She was plainly shocked and grieving and the Chief kept his routine questioning as brief as possible; she had little to tell him of any significance.

He asked if she knew of any relatives of Philip Harvey. She told him that the only one she had ever heard of was an elderly man, a childless widower, a cousin of Philip's father; he was a crofter, living on an island off the north-west coast of Scotland; neither Philip nor his father had ever met him.

The Chief allowed a short pause to elapse before he went on to ask her in a gentle tone to prepare herself for a difficult task: to go with him to the mortuary to make the formal identification of Philip's body.

She gave a little gasp. Tears sprang into her eyes.

'It will take only a few moments,' the Chief assured her.

She nodded briefly, without speaking, and they left without further delay.

The early days of the New Year had brought a seasonal rush of work to the supermarket office and Greg Mottram had spent an unremittingly busy morning, with scarcely a moment for a break. He left his desk at one o'clock to set off for his flat where he dispatched his customary snack lunch, cleared up, had a quick spruce-up, and then it was back to work, to face an equally wearing afternoon.

The moment he set foot inside the office again, he knew

something was amiss. Folk stood about in little groups, talking in low, earnest tones. He latched on to the nearest group; as usual, no one noticed him. He asked no questions, made no comment, but listened with close attention. Inside a very short time he learned what it was that had generated so much discussion: the discoveries at Beechcroft.

He stood silent and motionless for some little time; no one noticed.

The sudden entry of the supervisor, perceiving with an eye of keen displeasure this rampant idleness at a time when they should all be working flat out, produced an instant hush and sent everyone swiftly back to work.

After being interviewed and making his statement, Tom Guthrie was on his way out of the police station, at a quarter to three, when a new thought brought him to a halt: tomorrow, Tuesday, was one of his regular Beechcroft days. What was he to do? Go along there as usual in the morning, get on with the next job confronting him? Would there still be police about the property? From whom would he now take orders? Who now owned Beechcroft? Would the house be sold? Pass into the hands of strangers? What would happen to the garden in the meantime?

He resumed his progress towards the exit, slowly now, revolving his thoughts. At the junction of two corridors he caught sight of a familiar figure coming towards him: Lorraine Clifford, looking pale and lacklustre.

He hadn't spoken to her, hadn't seen her so far today, and he hesitated now. What could he possibly find to say to her? He had known her in the two great losses of her childhood, he felt he had some faint understanding of what she must be going through now.

She had seen him, she was approaching, he couldn't escape. He must find some words, however feeble.

She couldn't manage a smile but her expression lightened a little as she came to a halt before him. He got out some awkward words of sympathy. She said nothing in reply but gave a little nod, reaching out to touch his hand for a moment.

Emboldened, he found himself explaining his dilemma: was he to go to work at Beechcroft tomorrow or not? He saw at once that in asking her advice he had done her a favour. The necessity to weigh up the situation, come to a decision, advise him on his best course, jerked her up, out of her low spirits. Her eyes brightened somewhat, she spoke with a degree of animation. 'I'll be having a word with the solicitor – Philip's solicitor – later this afternoon. I've just been on the phone to him, he's fitting me in for a few minutes. I'll know better after I've seen him what the position is about Beechcroft but whatever it is, I can't see that it would serve any purpose to let the garden run wild.'

She touched his hand again, looking earnestly up at him. 'I'm pretty sure you'll have your job at Beechcroft for the time being, at any rate.' She remembered something. 'But I don't think you can go there tomorrow, I gather the forensic team may not finish today, we'll all have to keep out of their way for the next day or two. I'll give you a ring tomorrow, let you know how things stand. My guess is you'll be able to go along to Beechcroft as usual, on Thursday and Friday.'

When they had parted company, Lorraine went along to the reception hall to ring her department, to arrange some leave for herself, as was clearly necessary. She couldn't see any difficulty about this; apart from two remaining weeks of her annual leave, she had additional days coming to her because of the extra turns she had worked over Christmas and the New Year. She could call in at the office first thing in the morning, to hand over her case notes.

When she had made her call and secured her leave, she saw DCI Kelsey, talking to the desk sergeant. She went across and stationed herself near by. As he turned from the desk, she stepped forward to intercept him. She told him about her leave, her appointment with Philip's solicitor, and that she would be calling in at Workwear after seeing the solicitor, to let Shannon know what she understood of the new situation, with regard to the firm. 'Then I'll go along to the hospital,' she went on. 'Have you any idea how long the post-mortems will take?'

'There's no need for you to be at the hospital at all,' the Chief returned at once. 'It could be 8.30, nine, even later, before the post-mortems are finished. I should get off home, if I were you, as soon as you've been to Workwear. We'll let you know the results of the post-mortems tomorrow morning.'

She shook her head with decision. 'I couldn't rest if I went back to the flat. I'd rather wait at the hospital.'

Greg Mottram was in the habit of calling in at a newsagent's for an evening paper, on his way home from work; today he made sure he was supplied with the latest edition. A handful of customers stood about, chewing over the Beechcroft happenings. He didn't stop to hear what they were saying but left as soon as he had made his purchase. He halted a yard or two from the shop, as he always did, to begin his scrutiny of the paper. But this evening it wasn't the job opportunities he sought out but the stop press. By the time he took out his doorkey to let himself into his flat, he had read the paragraphs several times.

His first action, once inside his flat, was to switch on the radio, tuning it into the local station, turning up the volume, in order not to miss a word of any report on the Beechcroft deaths.

He had a quick wash, snatched a bite to eat, drank a cup of tea and settled down in an easy chair with the radio close at hand. Every few minutes he picked up the phone to ring Lorraine but he got no reply. Every nerve in his body cried out for a drink but he was determined to resist; it would be the height of folly to give in now.

He roamed from room to room, he made himself strong coffee, forced down a biscuit, tried to read, to watch TV, in desperation even set about giving the kitchen a good clean.

All to no avail. At seven o'clock he abandoned his efforts at housework and made yet another attempt to ring Lorraine; still no reply.

That was it. He could hold out no longer. He slammed down the receiver, plunged from the flat, not stopping to switch off the radio, turn off the lights, put on a coat. He made with all the speed he could muster for the off-licence.

As soon as he was back inside the flat, he went along to the kitchen, opened the bottle and took his first glorious gulp. The thought of ringing Lorraine dropped away from his mind.

* * *

The house directly across the road from Beechcroft belonged to a middle-aged, childless couple. When the house-to-house team called there on Monday morning they found only the wife at home; her husband had gone to London for the day, on business, and wouldn't be home till 7.30. The wife was anxious to be helpful but could tell them little. They had lived in the house for two years; they had only a sketchy acquaintance with the residents of Beechcroft and had known nothing of recent developments there. The wife had seen and heard nothing of any consequence over the weekend; her husband hadn't mentioned noticing anything out of the ordinary over there. The officers told her they would, nevertheless, make a return call in the evening, to speak to him.

And at 8 p.m. precisely, they were back on the doorstep. The husband's attitude was as co-operative as that of his wife; unlike her, he was able to supply one interesting gobbet of information. On the previous day, Sunday, he had been upstairs in the front bedroom, overlooking Wedderburn Road, at a few minutes after 9 a.m. He was about to go along to the newsagent's for the Sunday papers and looked out of the window, to check the sky, see if it was likely to rain while he was out. He saw the two girls – Vicky Jarrett, whom he knew slightly, and her friend. He didn't know the friend's name; she was a chubby girl, always in and out of Beechcroft. She was like Vicky's shadow; whenever you saw Vicky, you were likely to see this mate. Yesterday morning, the pair had come running up the road, laughing as they ran. When they got to Beechcroft, they stopped running and their manner became what he could only describe as furtive. He saw them go cautiously along the drive and then he turned from the window to go downstairs and along to the newsagent's. He imagined – in so far as he gave the matter any thought – that they were engaged in some youthful prank.

He bought his papers, stood chatting for a minute or two and then set off for home. When he still had twenty or thirty yards to go, he saw the two girls racing out of the Beechcroft gates, laughing loudly as soon as they got out on to the pavement; they seemed in high spirits. They didn't return the way they had come but turned and sped off in the opposite direction, still shouting with laughter.

*   *   *

It was 9.15 when DCI Kelsey came out into the hospital corridor at the end of the double post-mortem and stood chatting to the senior pathologist. As they parted company a few minutes later, the Chief didn't at once move off but remained where he was, reflecting on the initial findings. He had forgotten all about Lorraine Clifford. If any thought of her had crossed his mind he would have taken it for granted that common sense had in the end prevailed and she would by now be at home, doing her best to get a good night's sleep.

He chanced to glance along the corridor and was mildly irritated to catch sight of Lorraine's face peering round the corner at him. He uttered a groan. Foolish young woman, he thought, can she not heed good advice?

She came fully into view and set off towards him; she looked weary but determined. He awaited her with what patience he could muster. He didn't waste his breath uttering any reproaches but gave her a brief outline of the main autopsy findings.

The time of death in both cases had been put at between 10 p.m. on Saturday night and 1 a.m. on Sunday morning. In both cases, death was due to the ingestion of alcohol, together with some sedative or narcotic drugs; the combination would have rendered the pair speedily insensible before death. The full analysis of the stomach contents would require further time.

Lorraine listened intently but made no attempt to detain him further with question or comment. She bade him goodnight and left the hospital.

She chose the quickest route back to Wychford; it didn't take her past Greg's flat. All she wanted now was to get to bed, at the end of what had proved to be an exceedingly long and very draining day. In the brief time she had spent with Philip Harvey's solicitor, he had informed her that she had inherited the bulk of Philip's estate. It would be some time before all matters were finally settled but in effect she was now the owner of Beechcroft and the head of Workwear.

She had gone straight from the solicitor's to Workwear. In spite of the horrifying discoveries at Beechcroft, the visit of the trade delegation had, she was assured, gone ahead successfully, very much as planned. The delegation had been most favourably impressed; a draft contract was to be drawn up and submitted.

It was almost ten o'clock when she reached her flat. As she closed the front door behind her, it suddenly occurred to her that she ought to ring Greg Mottram. She stood for a moment, frowning, then she went to the phone and tapped out his number. She let the ring go on for some little time but got no reply. He must have gone to bed, she concluded.

In fact, he was in his living-room, huddled in his armchair. The overhead light was still on; at his side the radio chatted and played its music but he was far too soundly asleep for any telephone ring, any radio voice or chord to penetrate his brain.

Lorraine replaced the receiver; she didn't try again. A few minutes later she fell into bed and almost at once sank into a slumber as profound as any she had ever known.

At 6.30 next morning Lorraine came instantly and totally awake, fully aware in a single flash of recollection of all the events of yesterday; there were no misty moments in which she sought to disentangle dream from reality.

She sprang out of bed and went at once to the phone, to ring Greg, but got no response. Ten minutes later, she tried again, still without result. In another ten minutes she made a further attempt, this time letting the phone ring on.

The insistent summons finally pierced Greg's consciousness. He was still sprawled in his armchair in the living-room; the lights were still on. The radio had by now begun to greet the new day with its ritual gusto.

He opened his eyes and stared vaguely about. He reached out to switch off the radio. Yes, that was the sound of the phone ringing. He levered himself out of his chair, lurched across the room and lifted the receiver.

12

DCI Kelsey had got back to his flat late on Monday night. His sleep had been fitful and troubled, far from refreshing, his brain stubbornly refusing to switch off, ceaselessly churning over scraps of information.

He was up very early on Tuesday morning, on his way to the police station after a copious draught of strong black coffee, headed for another exceptionally crowded day: as well as the briefing and press conference, there would be local radio and regional TV recordings, appealing for information, to be fitted in at some point.

Among the first members of the team to arrive for duty was a civilian woman employee who sought out DS Lambert, to pass on something told to her, when she got home yesterday evening, by her daughter – a sensible girl, according to her mother, thirteen years old, at the same school and in the same class as Vicky Jarrett and Avril Byrne.

She told her mother that the two girls were far from popular at school and had no other friends. It was chiefly Vicky who was disliked; Avril was looked on as a nonentity, a mere cat's-paw of Vicky's.

What interested Sergeant Lambert was the fact that, according to the daughter, Vicky had long been in the habit of boasting to anyone who would listen that her mother was going to marry Philip Harvey; she appeared to feel that this put her in a position of importance among her classmates, a number of whose parents were employed at Workwear.

Barely ten minutes after the woman had parted company with Lambert, Vicky and Avril came bounding up the station steps and into the reception hall, Avril silent, as usual, Vicky demanding to speak to Detective Chief Inspector Kelsey – she had got his name and rank off pat, from assiduous attention to the local radio broadcasts.

The girls didn't get as far as seeing the Chief, to Vicky's open disappointment, but they were seen by DC Slade, who was interested to hear what was said by a girl (for only one of the pair opened her mouth) who had thought it worth her while to get up early on a cold, dark January morning in the school holidays, when she might have stayed cosily snuggled down in bed, to hurry along to the police station.

What she had to say, in essence, amounted to no more than this: she was very keen to take part in any TV appeal for information. She had seen several such appeals by individuals linked to the victims; she had been greatly impressed by their displays of raw emotion; she was positive such appeals must be irresistible. Above all, she was convinced she would be an outstanding performer.

Slade took the girls back to the exit, to make sure they left the premises. He assured Vicky he would put her offer to the Chief, adding: 'I'm afraid the answer is certain to be no.' Vicky appeared momentarily cast down but said nothing further. He stood for a moment, watching, as the two of them jumped down the steps and went skipping off along the pavement.

An officer had meanwhile called on both Rhoda Jarrett and Mrs Byrne to arrange for the two girls to be interviewed in the presence of their mothers. Mrs Byrne would be working the 10 a.m. to 2 p.m. shift at Ashdene and so an appointment was fixed for 3 p.m., for all four to come along to the police station together.

A good deal to DC Slade's astonishment, the two girls came racing into the station once again, a mere hour or so after their first visit, this time asking for him by name. 'We've decided not to bother with TV,' Vicky announced as soon as Slade arrived within earshot. 'I can just go on local radio, to make an appeal. I know I'll be good on that, I can speak up very clearly.' You can do that all right, Slade said to himself. Aloud, he promised, as before, to put her offer to the Chief, adding, as before, that he couldn't see much chance of her offer being accepted; all the while, as he spoke, he edged the pair towards the exit.

'We're coming back here this afternoon,' Vicky informed him as they reached the door. 'Three o'clock. Detective Chief Inspector Kelsey has asked for us specially.' She gave Slade a glance of open pride. 'We're going to be interviewed, officially. We have to have our mothers with us. I expect that's to make sure we're treated properly.'

Shortly after eleven, a woman came into the station, asking to speak to someone on the investigation team. She was a sales assistant in the knitwear department of a high-class department store in the town. She had had some acquaintance with Mrs Martine Faulkner, as a customer, during the last few years.

Mrs Faulkner had come into the knitwear department last Saturday afternoon, at around 3.30. She had bought an evening top and had also ordered a velvet-trimmed cardigan; she liked the style but wanted a different colour, currently not in stock; she was told it would be to hand within a week.

The woman had been struck by the unusual cheerfulness of Mrs Faulkner's mood.

Both solicitors – the one who had acted for Philip Harvey for many years, and the one who had conducted a short interview with Martine Faulkner on Saturday morning – had willingly agreed to give up part of the Tuesday lunch hour to talk to DCI Kelsey. Philip's solicitor, a man much the same age as Philip, had already talked briefly to the Chief on Monday afternoon, telling him he had last seen Philip on the morning he had left for Europe; Philip had sought his advice about the manner and terms of his severance from Rhoda Jarrett, to ensure there would be no problems when Martine moved into Beechcroft. Philip had also indicated that he intended making a new will shortly after returning from Europe, to take account of his altered circumstances.

The solicitor had described Philip's mood that Monday morning as very much in command of all that was going forward, in no way downcast or perturbed by the sudden turn of events in his personal life; in fact, rather pleased at the way things had been so abruptly set in motion.

His present will had been drawn up some six years ago. There were some minor bequests and there was generous provision for Rhoda Jarrett; the bulk of the estate – house, business, savings and investments – went to Lorraine Clifford. The solicitor had outlined the terms of the will to Lorraine yesterday afternoon, when he saw her for a few minutes – he would be seeing her again at greater length on Wednesday morning.

He knew of no relative of Philip Harvey's other than the elderly crofter cousin Lorraine had made mention of to the Chief. The solicitor had no address for the cousin and didn't even know if he was still alive. Lorraine told him yesterday that she would go through Philip's personal papers, in the hope of finding the crofter's address, as soon as the police and the forensic team had finished at Beechcroft and she would have access to the house.

It was shortly after one o'clock when the two policemen arrived at the solicitor's office for their second interview. He was on the look-out for them today, welcomed them in, sat them down and supplied them with coffee.

The Chief began by asking for a more detailed account of how Rhoda Jarrett stood to benefit under Philip Harvey's will.

He was told that Philip's death in no way affected the generous severance settlement Rhoda had so recently received; every penny of that was hers to keep. Under the will she would receive a sum markedly larger than the one handed over in the settlement; she was also entitled, under the will, to housing provision: a small house or flat of her choice, in the location of her choice, up to a certain specified value, was to be bought and made over to her absolutely. 'Something I feel I ought to say, concerning the legacy to Rhoda,' the solicitor said. 'Philip was an astute businessman, he greatly expanded the scope of Workwear, greatly increased the turnover and profits, in this country and in foreign markets. Lorraine benefits enormously from all that, now that she inherits the firm. And Philip improved Beechcroft a good deal, over the years; he increased its market value considerably. All that, in my considered opinion, more than offsets the double outgoing to Rhoda: the severance payment and the legacy.'

Kelsey asked if Rhoda had known the terms of the present will and was told yes, she had definitely known them; indeed, the housing provision had been made at her express insistence, chiefly, he understood, from concern for her daughter's future.

The Chief went on to ask if there had ever been any real possibility that Philip would marry Rhoda or if he had ever allowed Rhoda to believe it could happen.

The solicitor gave a single, decisive shake of his head. 'Not as far as I was ever aware. When Rhoda came to Beechcroft, she was twenty-seven years old, with a child from some failed relationship, she wasn't an innocent young girl on the look-out for Prince Charming.'

How had Philip got on with Vicky Jarrett?

'Philip didn't have all that much to do with her,' the solicitor replied. 'I never got the impression that he was particularly fond of the girl. I think a benign tolerance would about sum up his attitude. He certainly had no objection to her presence in the household and I don't think he ever found her a nuisance.'

'And Lorraine Clifford?' Kelsey asked. 'What were relations like between her and Philip over the years?'

'Excellent,' the solicitor returned without hesitation. 'Philip was always very generous to her and she fully appreciated that. He was always very kind, very supportive and understanding. I can't ever recall any disharmony.'

'Did Lorraine know the terms of the present will?'

'Not to my knowledge, but I can't be certain. Philip may have spoken to her about the will in recent years, he may have told her what was in it.' He had made two earlier wills, the first at the time of his marriage, when he and Veronica drew up two very straightforward wills, leaving everything to each other.

'Did Philip have anything much to leave at that time?' Kelsey put in.

'He had a fair amount. He'd always earned good money, always saved; he was a shrewd investor. He'd inherited quite a bit from his parents – he was an only child, both his parents were dead by the time of his marriage. Philip was certainly no penniless adventurer. He was devoted to Veronica, very protective. He was devastated when she died.' He had made a new will shortly after Veronica's death, leaving everything – apart from minor bequests – in trust for Lorraine. 'That will stood for six years, when he decided to make a new will – his present will – to take account of what he felt to be his obligation to Rhoda Jarrett.' As to the will Philip spoke of making when he got back from Europe, he had indicated the broad outline: the house and business would go to Martine, with a handsome financial provision for Lorraine, set at a level that he hoped would leave Lorraine feeling satisfied, in no way resentful of Martine. He hoped Lorraine would continue happily along her own career lines, on friendly terms with Martine.

'I always found Philip a highly principled man,' the solicitor added. 'He had a strong sense of justice and fair play. His chief concern, in drawing up a will, was always, as far as he could, to do the right thing by everyone concerned.'

The solicitor Martine had visited on Saturday morning had his offices a mere hundred yards from the offices the two policemen had just left. He was a man of wide experience, somewhat older than Philip's solicitor. He had been greatly shocked to hear of the sudden end of a client he had only just met and still found it difficult to credit that a young woman of her looks and personality, so full of vitality, was at this moment lying in a hospital morgue.

Her appointment with him had been a brief one, to enable her to outline the facts of her situation. She told him on leaving that she would make a longer appointment after Philip Harvey's return, when they had been able to discuss matters thoroughly. The impression she left on the solicitor was that of a determined young woman with all her wits about her and a good deal of character and strength, certainly not someone to be easily deflected or put down. And he found her very far indeed from depressed or despairing; she seemed in excellent spirits, positive and optimistic.

Vicky Jarrett and Avril Byrne, accompanied by their mothers, turned up at the police station with minutes to spare before their three o'clock appointment. Rhoda Jarrett maintained an air of cool composure, Mrs Byrne an air of bemused anxiety; Avril appeared docile and self-effacing; Vicky's look was now coyly demure, sparkled by an occasional glint of something more artful.

The four were shown into a waiting-area and a minute or two later Rhoda and Vicky were taken along to an interview room where DCI Kelsey and DS Lambert joined them. The Chief made it clear that it was Vicky who was being interviewed; Rhoda was present as the parent of a minor; she should not speak, in any way interrupt or seek to influence Vicky's responses. Rhoda gave a nod of acquiescence and understanding, taking her seat – without being so directed – at some little distance from her daughter. Vicky settled herself down as if pleased to find herself in her present situation; she gazed across at the Chief with a look of lively expectancy.

He began by asking if she had been upset to learn, at the end of December, that she and her mother would be leaving Beechcroft and moving away from Cannonbridge. He kept his tone light and even, in no way intimidating.

Vicky replied without hesitation. Yes, she had indeed been upset at the thought of leaving the only home she could remember, leaving her school; above all, leaving Avril, her best friend.

Had she been more than upset? Had she, in fact, been angry at having to leave?

No, she answered calmly, she had not been angry. 'My mother told me she'd find us somewhere nice to live, after we left Cannonbridge, and she'd find a school I'd like. She said Avril could come and stay in the holidays, and we could keep in touch with the phone.' She moved her shoulders. 'I always knew we wouldn't be staying at Beechcroft for ever, my mother always said I should remember we were living there because it was part of her job, it wasn't our real home and never could be.'

'Did your mother explain why you both had to leave Beechcroft in such a hurry?'

That didn't faze her. 'She told me Mrs Faulkner would be moving in at the weekend, and she wouldn't want us there.'

'Did you know Martine Faulkner?'

She made a little face. 'Not very well. I met her a few times when we went to Rivenoak, for the summer fête and the Christmas fair, things like that.'

'Did you like her?'

Again she moved her shoulders. 'She was all right. I didn't know her well enough to have any real opinion.'

'Did you feel angry when you realized there was no chance now of Philip marrying your mother?'

She shook her head with vigour. 'I never expected Philip to marry my mother.'

100

'Didn't you hope, very strongly indeed, that Philip would marry your mother and adopt you?'

Again she shook her head, even more vigorously. 'I never thought that, I never hoped for it. My mother never said anything like that to me.'

'Did you think that if Martine could somehow disappear from the picture, Philip might change his mind and decide after all to marry your mother, you could both go back to live in Beechcroft?'

She shook her head with even greater force, she went on shaking it. 'I never thought any of that. I never ever thought Philip might marry my mother. It never once crossed my mind.'

Kelsey sat back in his chair and regarded her. 'Then how do you explain something we found at Beechcroft?' Stacked beside the dustbins, at the rear of the house, were a number of cardboard boxes, crammed with discarded household and personal items, plainly awaiting the next refuse collection. Three of the boxes had clearly been filled by Vicky. One contained old schoolbooks, paperbacks, gaily coloured posters – and a diary, for the year just ended.

The pages of the diary had been ripped out and torn into small pieces; the pieces had been stuffed into a plastic bag and tucked into a corner of the box. But the endpapers of the diary had not been torn out, and remained within the covers. On the front flyleaf was written in a schoolgirl hand a name and address; the address: the full postal address of Beechcroft; the name: VICTORIA HARVEY, repeated, lower down the page, with variations: VICTORIA TERESA HARVEY, MISS V. HARVEY, MS V.T. HARVEY. Whenever it appeared, the name HARVEY had been carefully ornamented in a variety of ways: with leaves, flowers, scrolls, geometric designs, all neatly coloured in.

Why had she chosen to write her name in this way, in the diary?

She looked coolly back at him. 'I was just amusing myself. I quite like drawing. I picked the name Harvey because I always liked the way it looked, the way it sounded. I used to wish sometimes I could have been called Harvey. I thought it was a much nicer name than Jarrett.' She made a face. 'Jarrett sounds so hard, sort of grating.'

Kelsey switched tack. 'Did you know Philip Harvey had a heavy cold and might return earlier than Sunday evening?'

No, she had had no idea that might be the case.

'You were expecting Martine to be alone at Beechcroft on Saturday night?'

She answered promptly: yes, she was.

'So, as far as you were aware, anything Martine ate or drank at Beechcroft on Saturday evening would be eaten or drunk by her alone? Philip wouldn't share any of it?'

Some hesitation now. She was silent for several moments before answering, plainly assessing the questions from various angles. Finally she came out with a reluctant: 'Yes, I suppose so.'

Again he switched tack. 'Were you upset when you heard of the two deaths at Beechcroft?'

She widened her eyes at him. 'Yes, of course I was upset. Anyone would be upset. Avril and Mrs Byrne and my mother, and everyone else who heard of it was upset. People in the town who didn't know them were upset.' She stared fixedly at him. 'I expect it upset you and all the other policemen, when you heard about it. I expect it upset the people in the radio station and the TV studios and the reporters on the local newspaper.'

'Was it particularly Philip Harvey's death that upset you?'

'Of course it was Philip's death that upset me most,' she threw sharply back at him. 'I'd known him for ten years, I hardly knew Martine.'

Another swift change of tack. 'How did you spend the time between moving out of Beechcroft on Friday and going to bed on Sunday night?'

She answered promptly, in a rapid, mechanical fashion, with not even the briefest pause to think back over her movements. 'Avril and I helped my mother in the bedsit until we went to Ashdene for six o'clock. We worked at Ashdene until we got on the bus at ten past nine.' That bus driver must be found, Kelsey thought. 'We got off at Mrs Byrne's house, we went to bed quite soon after we got in. We were a bit tired, after the move.'

'Did you remain in the house all night?'

She flashed him a look of surprise. 'Yes, of course we did. We got up about eight o'clock on Saturday morning and went along to the bedsit to see if my mother needed any help. We did some jobs for her and we went to the local shops for some things she needed, then we went to Ashdene. We called in at the bedsit again after lunch but my mother didn't need us so we looked round the shops in Cannonbridge. We called in again at the bedsit around five o'clock and then we went to Ashdene for six o'clock. We got the bus back to Mrs Byrne's at ten past nine, we went to bed about ten.' She gave him a cheeky grin. 'We stayed there all night, if you want to know. On Sunday morning we went along to Ashdene for 9.30. My mother had said we needn't call in first at the bedsit, she wouldn't need us, we could go straight to Ashdene.'

'Did you go straight to Ashdene from Mrs Byrne's or did you call in somewhere on the way?'

That brought her up sharp. She made no reply for several moments. She sat straight-backed and rigid, her face set like a mask. She guesses someone saw them, Lambert thought, she's trying to make up her mind if she should come clean and admit it.

She sat back in her chair. 'I remember now,' she said with a half-smiling air. 'We ran round by Beechcroft.' Lambert saw Rhoda jerk up in her seat.

'That's quite a bit out of your way,' Kelsey observed.

She moved a hand with an airy gesture. 'Not all that much. We were running quite fast. It didn't take us long.'

'Why did you go to Beechcroft?'

Another little half-smile. 'Just nosiness, I suppose. We thought we might be able to see Mrs Faulkner, but we didn't see anyone. We only stopped a couple of minutes, then we ran off again, to Ashdene. We went along to the bedsit after lunch and did some more jobs for my mother, then we went to the park for a bit and then we went back to Avril's house, to watch a film on TV, and then it was Ashdene for six o'clock, till we got on the bus at ten past nine.'

Yet another abrupt switch on Kelsey's part. 'Why did you want to go on TV and radio?' Lambert saw Rhoda's features twitch in a sharp grimace.

By way of reply, Vicky said not a word but raised her shoulders and thrust out her lips.

'Did you like the thought that folk would see and hear you?' Kelsey pressed her. 'Did you think your classmates would think you very important?'

That did rouse her into speech. 'That wasn't it at all! I just thought I might be able to help. Everyone would like to help the police in a murder inquiry.'

'What makes you think this is a murder inquiry?' Kelsey came back at her.

She froze in her seat, staring at him, her mouth a little open.

'I ask you again,' Kelsey pursued. 'What makes you think Philip Harvey and Martine Faulkner were murdered?'

Again she made no reply. It was plain from the set of her jaw and the look in her eyes that she intended making no reply, however many times and in however many different ways the Chief might put his question.

Kelsey's next interview – with Avril Byrne, in the presence of her mother – was, by contrast, very brief. He put to her several of the same questions and was struck by the fact that many of her answers were couched in precisely the same words that Vicky had used.

There seemed little point in prolonging the exercise; the Chief let her go, to rejoin the others, but asked Mrs Byrne to remain. Avril left the room with an air of satisfaction and modest pride, as of one who had faithfully discharged her duty. It's conceivable, Lambert thought, as the door closed behind her, that Avril may not at all times have been aware of everything her dearest friend was up to – by day or by night.

Mrs Byrne replied to the Chief's questions in a straightforward fashion. He asked first how Vicky had taken the news that she and her mother would be leaving Beechcroft.

'She was horrified,' Mrs Byrne answered at once. 'She was very defiant at first, she wasn't going to leave Beechcroft, no one could make her, it was her home. She couldn't leave Cannonbridge, couldn't leave her school, couldn't leave Avril, no one had the right to ask her. Martine Faulkner had no right to leave her husband, her little boy, it was very wicked of her. And to want to throw Vicky and her mother out of their home, just so she could move in with Philip Harvey, when she had a perfectly good home of her own, it was really evil of her.' Mrs Byrne rolled her eyes. 'She made a dreadful song and dance about it at first, and then she suddenly went quiet. I must say, I was relieved when that happened.'

Had Vicky been aware of the relationship between Rhoda and Philip Harvey?

'Oh, yes,' Mrs Byrne replied at once. 'She never made any bones about it. She didn't go out of her way to talk about it, but if it came up naturally in the course of conversation, she'd speak of it openly, she just took it as an accepted fact. She was quite certain Philip would marry her mother one day, that struck her as a very good idea. I never expressed any opinion about it, I didn't consider it any of my business, and Rhoda never spoke about it; she's never been a woman to speak of personal matters. I never minded her being reserved, in fact, it made a pleasant change. I've been in caring work all along and you can get pretty tired of folk pouring out their troubles and innermost feelings to you.' She jerked her head. 'A touch of reserve makes a very welcome change.'

How had Vicky taken the news of the two deaths?

Mrs Byrne shook her head slowly and sadly as she expelled a long, mournful breath. 'It was pretty grim, quite terrifying, really. I was the one that had to tell her.' She shook her head again, slowly. 'I never want to hear screaming like that again. I've seen plenty of folk given bad news over the years, but I've never heard screaming like that. She was like someone demented. I thought folk going by in the street would come pounding on the door, thinking someone was being tortured.' She blew out another long breath. 'And then Rhoda turned up. I was that glad to see her. I took Avril away and closed the door on Rhoda and Vicky, I left them to it. I've got to hand it to Rhoda. She got Vicky quietened down in no time at all, then she took her home.' She stared back into that morning. 'Vicky kept shrieking out Philip's name. All the time I was trying to calm her down, she kept shrieking out: "Not Philip! Not Philip!"' She came back into the present, to the interview room and the Chief Inspector. 'And then, do you know, Vicky came round again, that very same afternoon.' She looked at Kelsey with an echo of her old astonishment. 'I'd told Avril not to go round to the bedsit for the rest of the day, give Vicky a chance to get over it. And then Vicky turned up. She seemed as right as rain, quite perky in fact, chatting away about it all, glued to the radio in between, in case there was any more news. The only thing different was her eyes, they were red and swollen all the rest of that day. If it hadn't been for her eyes, I might have wondered if I'd imagined all that uproar.'

13

Rhoda Jarrett wore an air of unruffled composure as she came alone into the interview room, after Mrs Byrne had left it. Sergeant Lambert studied her as she settled herself into her seat. Clearly a woman to be reckoned with, he thought; someone who could steer her boat through tricky waters, with scarcely a hair out of place. Easy enough now on the eye, in her understated way; she would have been a very attractive young woman ten years ago. She must have come into the Beechcroft household like a benignly steadying presence, after all the tumult and grief.

The Chief plunged straight in. 'Before you came here this afternoon, were you aware that Vicky and Avril had paid two visits here this morning?'

Rhoda's jaw tightened, her expression grew flinty. But before she answered she relaxed her features with a visible effort into a more tolerant look. 'No, indeed,' she replied with deliberate mildness. 'I had no idea. But I'm sure they only wanted to help in any way they could.'

'And were you aware that they had looked in at Beechcroft on Sunday morning?'

She had her face and voice well under control by now. 'No, I was not,' she answered easily, 'but it didn't really surprise me.

Girls of that age, they're curious, inquisitive, they wouldn't mean any harm.' She smiled slightly. 'It wouldn't seem like trespassing to either of them. It had been Vicky's home for as long as she can remember and Avril was used to running in and out, over the years.'

A change of tack from the Chief. 'Did you ever really expect to marry Philip Harvey? Did he ever give you reason to believe he had serious thoughts of marriage?'

Another faint smile. 'I'm afraid the housekeeper with the child born out of wedlock only gets to marry her wealthy widower boss in romantic novels. Philip never gave me the slightest reason to suppose that could ever happen and I never imagined it could. In the last year or two I'd more or less known my day was coming to an end, I must be ready for change.' Again a trace of a smile. 'Though when it came it was a trifle more sudden than I'd expected.'

'Did you ever encourage Vicky to believe you and Philip might marry one day?'

An emphatic shake of her head. 'Most certainly not. It would have served no useful purpose for any one of us.'

'Did Vicky ever mention such a possibility to you?'

'No, never.'

'How did she take the news that you would both be leaving Beechcroft, moving away from the area?'

'Better than I had expected. Naturally, she was rather upset at first, but she's resilient, she soon got over it.'

'You signed an agreement, did you not, when you received your severance cheque, promising to leave Cannonbridge?'

'Yes, I did.'

'Why, then, did you not honour that agreement?'

'It was always my intention to honour the agreement,' she replied calmly, 'but I never interpreted it as meaning I must leave Cannonbridge on the very day, at the very hour, that we moved out of Beechcroft. I would have thought that a somewhat excessive demand. I took the bedsit for a month – the shortest time I could take it for. I was sure I would have made up my mind within the month what I was going to do, where we would go. You must remember I had only a few days between signing the agreement and leaving Beechcroft, hardly long enough to make any satisfactory decision about the future, particularly when it meant uprooting Vicky after ten years in Cannonbridge.'

'Philip Harvey's death has, of course, altered your whole situation: there is no longer any need for you to leave the area; you will be a great deal better off when you receive the legacy, so much so, in fact, that it may not be necessary for you to look for another housekeeping post.'

She inclined her head a little. 'All that is so.'

'You were familiar all along with the terms of Philip's will? You knew about the legacy?'

'Yes, I did.'

'Did Vicky know the terms of the will?'

Her eyebrows shot up. 'Good heavens, no!'

'You never discussed the matter with her?'

'Never.' She levelled a steely gaze at him. 'Is there not some danger in all this of forgetting that Vicky is little more than a child?'

The Chief made no response to that but went on to ask: 'Were you aware that Philip intended making a new will after he returned from Europe?'

Her voice remained rock-steady. 'Yes, I was aware. He told me so, the day he left for Europe.'

'You were aware that neither you nor Vicky would in any way figure in the new will?'

'Yes, of course,' she replied with vigour. 'He made that plain. I would, naturally, never have expected to figure in it.'

'Did Vicky know Philip intended making a new will?'

She looked fiercely angry for a moment and then controlled her expression and her tone. 'No, of course she didn't know.'

'How did she take the news of the two deaths at Beechcroft?'

An instant reply: 'She was shocked and horrified, as we all were.'

'Was it Philip's death that particularly shocked and horrified her?'

Again a swift reply: 'Yes, of course it was. She'd known Philip for years. He'd been good to her, she was fond of him. She hardly knew Martine.'

'Was there a hysterical outburst? Screaming?'

This time, a brief pause. 'I wasn't with the girls when Mrs Byrne broke the news. I gather Vicky was very upset at first. She had quietened down by the time I got there.' Another brief pause. 'All things considered, she didn't react too badly. I took her with me, to the bedsit. Later on, she went round to Avril's again, she was quite steady by then.'

A change of direction from the Chief. 'Were you aware, before Philip spoke to you that Monday, that he was involved with Martine Faulkner?'

She shook her head. 'I was not aware of it before that Monday.'

'Did it never occur to you that he might be interested in some other woman?'

'We hadn't been on an intimate footing for some time, I'd always known the relationship would run its course in time. So when he spoke to me that Monday I wasn't altogether surprised.'

Another change of direction. 'Did you know Philip had a heavy cold and might return from Europe earlier than he'd planned?'

She gave a nod. 'Lorraine told me that on the Wednesday morning, after she'd been along to Workwear.'

'Did you pass on that information to Vicky or Avril? Or to Mrs Byrne, perhaps?'

'No, I did not,' she replied robustly. 'I wouldn't have considered it any business of any of them.'

'Did you pass on that information to Tom Guthrie?'

'Certainly not.'

Yet another change of tack. 'How did you spend that Friday evening, after you moved into the bedsit?'

'I went to the cinema,' she replied after a moment's thought. She supplied the name of the cinema, the name of the film, the time she had left the bedsit, the time she returned.

'Did you go to the cinema with anyone?'

She shook her head. 'I went alone.'

'Do you usually go to the cinema alone?'

'Yes, invariably.'

She can't prove she spent the evening at the cinema, Sergeant Lambert thought, and we can't prove she didn't. Easy enough for her to catch the film at some other time, if she felt she might need to give an account of it later.

The interview concluded and Rhoda left the room, free to leave the station now, in company with Mrs Byrne and the two girls.

'I don't know that I can altogether credit that Rhoda had no idea of what was going on between Philip and Martine,' Sergeant Lambert observed to the Chief after the door had closed behind Rhoda. 'I find it hard to believe that Philip never brought Martine to Beechcroft, on one of Rhoda's evenings out. A shrewd woman like Rhoda, worldly-wise, an experienced housekeeper, living for ten years in Beechcroft, she'd know, soon enough, if another woman had been in the house, had been in Philip's bedroom.' He shook his head. 'I can't believe she didn't latch on pretty smartly to what was going on. And when she did latch on, she'd want to find out who the woman was, if it was someone likely to threaten her own position.'

In the early evening the Chief settled down to study the house-to-house reports from teams active in Rivenoak. They had started their operations at the Faulkner stores and business premises, where they had spoken to Harriet Russell and the other Faulkner employees. They had then spread out to take in the rest of the village, moving on further still, to outlying properties and neighbouring hamlets.

Folk in general had professed themselves devastated by the news, shocked, horrified, stunned; this was especially so in the case of Faulkner employees, and others who had some connection with an aspect of the Faulkner activities. No one admitted to having had the slightest inkling of anything amiss in the Faulkner marriage, certainly no knowledge of any serious, recent rift. No one, it would seem, had felt anything but genuine liking for Martine, the highest regard for her as wife, mother, participant in village life; all expressed astonishment at her involvement with another man – and even greater astonishment at the fact that the other man was a local employer, a businessman of standing and repute.

And yet ... And yet ...

All the teams had received the same overall impression: tightly closed ranks. A lack of eye contact with officers on the teams – though, occasionally, by contrast, deliberately sustained eye contact, intended, apparently, to generate an air of guileless truthfulness but actually producing an entirely opposite effect.

The Chief's attention was particularly riveted by accounts of two interviews, taking place within a few minutes of each other, towards the close of operations, in the afternoon, on the farthest outskirts of the village.

Two cottages stood within eyeshot of each other on opposite sides of a secluded lane; no other dwellings near by. Officers had spoken first to the woman living alone in the cottage on the left-hand side of the lane: a Mrs Jephcott, a widow in her late thirties, with the slack remains of youthful attractiveness, a smiling, overtly welcoming manner, with something less appealing peeping out from underneath.

She had the kettle on in a flash, had made the tea in no time at all, scarcely waited for questions but embarked on a series of rapid-fire observations and opinions about the Beechcroft deaths, superficially prompted by sympathy and concern for everyone in any way touched by the dreadful events, but every now and then darting little snide remarks designed to sully the image of Martine and to float suspicion of Owen Faulkner and Harriet Russell, always bracketing them as a pair but never voicing outright accusations.

The officers listened and noted. Mrs Jephcott didn't remain in the house at the end of their visit but followed them down the path to the gate, still in full flow but repeating herself now, her eyes no longer veiled with a show of goodwill but undisguisedly bright with malice. It was only when the officers latched the gate behind them and crossed to the right-hand side of the lane, to the other cottage, that she reluctantly took herself back inside and closed the door.

The woman who received them at the second cottage, also a widow, came across in a very different and much pleasanter fashion. Not far off sixty, with a sensible, competent air, a friendly, forthright manner, she was, it appeared, employed part-time by Owen Faulkner in the Rivenoak stores and had worked there for several years.

The interview didn't take long; she answered their questions readily and concisely but was able to tell them nothing of consequence. When it was finished she stood up from her chair. 'I saw Mrs Jephcott, over the way, chattering to you just now, nineteen to the dozen,' she observed. 'I don't know what she's been telling you but I can make a pretty good guess. I think you should know she's a sworn enemy of Owen Faulkner and Harriet Russell. I don't know the full story – Owen and Harriet are not ones to go spreading tales against anyone – but I do know Mrs Jephcott used to work at the stores. She wasn't there long, she started there a year or two after she was widowed and then she left in a great hurry; she's never had a job since. She can't say anything bad enough about Owen and Harriet but it all wants taking with a very big pinch of salt. She's not a Rivenoak woman.' She named a village some miles away. 'That's where she lived. She came here as housekeeper to an old man, a widower, he lived in the cottage she lives in now. She hadn't been here three months before she married him, he died a matter of weeks later. She got the cottage and his savings – he was worth a bob or two and there were no relatives. There was a lot of gossip in the village at the time but she brazened it out.'

The Chief sat back, digesting the reports. It wouldn't hurt to have another word with Owen Faulkner and Harriet Russell. Faulkner could be rung now, an appointment fixed for him to come in tomorrow morning, immediately after the briefing and press conference. And an officer could go over, unannounced, to call on Harriet Russell for a little chat, at much the same time as Owen Faulkner would be answering questions in Cannonbridge.

14

Owen Faulkner arrived at the police station in good time for his appointment on Wednesday morning. Sergeant Lambert took him along to the interview room where Chief Inspector Kelsey joined them. Owen appeared subdued, with an air of deep fatigue. He answered every question but only after some little delay each time, as if it took an appreciable effort to gather his thoughts after every new query.

Yes, he had known Philip Harvey had a heavy cold and might return early from Europe; Rhoda Jarrett had told him when he called at Beechcroft on New Year's Eve – he had wanted to find out, in so far as Rhoda could tell him, what the situation currently was with regard to Martine and Philip.

No, he had no key to Beechcroft and had never had a key. Yes, there had been occasions in the past when he had briefly had a key in his possession, during a particular job.

Yes, he had walked about, outside and inside the house, that Wednesday afternoon. Rhoda had asked him to cast an eye over the work carried out by the emergency repairers. And yes, he would have had an opportunity to notice any damage not yet dealt with, damage which might have made entry to the premises relatively easy. And yes, again, he had been on his own for some of the time.

No, he did not tell Harriet Russell that Philip had a cold and might return early.

The Chief asked what Martine's attitude had been towards Harriet.

It had always been patronizing, Owen replied. Martine had never been in the slightest degree jealous of Harriet, had never looked on her as a rival, before or after her marriage; she would have been greatly amused at the notion; she regarded Harriet as a dull, dowdy spinster, an old-fashioned countrywoman, much older than herself. She often made fun of Harriet behind her back, though always polite enough to her face. She had certainly never fallen out with Harriet; she made regular use of her for babysitting, knowing she could trust her to look after Jamie with devoted care.

How had Owen spent the evening of Friday, 2nd January? Owen thought back and then replied that he had spent it with Harriet. She had been helping him to look after Jamie ever since Martine had left. Harriet didn't go home from the office that Friday evening but went straight over to his house. She gave Jamie his tea, played with him, in due course bathed him and put him to bed. She prepared supper for herself and Owen,

113

busying herself afterwards with household chores. At around 10 p.m. she said goodnight and went off to her own house.

Before letting Owen go, the Chief asked if he would give permission for the police to have access to such confidential records relating to himself as were held by the inquiry agency he had employed. Owen agreed without hesitation, promising to call in at the agency on his way back to Rivenoak, to see to the matter.

At very much the same time as Owen Faulkner had walked up the steps of the police station to keep his appointment with the Chief, DC Slade was pulling up outside the Faulkner business premises in Rivenoak. Harriet Russell had been at work for some time but was never too occupied to keep a loving eye on Jamie Faulkner, contentedly installed in a playpen in a draught-free corner of her office, engrossed in his toys, gurgling cheerfully to himself.

Harriet appeared in no whit disconcerted when Slade came knocking at her office door. Yes, she would be happy to talk to him immediately. She crossed to a desk opposite and spoke to her young female assistant. A glance at the young woman told Slade it would be a waste of time trying to pump her about Harriet; her attitude to Harriet, the way she looked at her, responded to her, spoke clearly of unshakable allegiance.

Harriet took Slade over to the Faulkner house. She sat him down in the warm kitchen, inviting him to make a start on whatever it was he had come to say, while she made coffee. Her manner was friendly, relaxed and informal. Nothing he asked seemed to give her pause; she answered all his questions readily.

He inquired about her relationship with Owen Faulkner, before and after Owen's marriage. She replied with a frankness that surprised him. There had never been any formal engage- ment; marriage had never in fact been discussed between them but she had always hoped – and believed – until the appearance of Martine on the scene, that she and Owen would marry one day.

But it was only a very short time after Martine came to

Rivenoak that she realized her hopes would now come to nothing; Owen was clearly bowled over by the newcomer. Harriet saw very early on that Martine had set her sights on marrying Owen and she saw with equal clarity that it was only the opposition of Owen's mother that prevented the marriage from taking place pretty speedily. She had steeled herself to accept the inevitable. She had very much wanted to retain Owen's friendship and so had gone out of her way to show kindness to Martine, offer any help she needed. She had, in any case, always liked Martine well enough and could easily understand how greatly Owen had been taken with her.

Owen had been devastated by the break-up of his marriage and she had done all she could in the way of practical help.

How had she spent the evening of Friday, 2nd January?

She didn't have to think back. She had spent that evening as she had spent most other evenings around that time: lending a hand in the Faulkner house.

Slade asked if she was acquainted with a Mrs Jephcott.

She gave a fleeting smile. 'I can guess why you ask. I imagine she's had plenty to say about me – and Owen – none of it very flattering.' She stood up and walked about the kitchen. 'Mrs Jephcott came to the stores a couple of years ago, looking for work. There was a part-time job going and I gave her a trial. Owen wasn't keen – there'd been some gossip about her in the village – but I was sorry for her.'

She halted by the table, took a drink of her coffee and resumed her pacing. 'She hadn't been at the stores very long when it was clear someone's fingers were in the till. Owen decided to set a trap and Mrs Jephcott fell smack into it. We didn't want to bring a court case – though we could have done – so she was simply sacked, there and then, no notice, no wages in lieu, no references; straight out through the door. I saw then by the look on her face that we'd made ourselves a pretty good enemy. She'd protested her innocence loudly enough but she didn't try to take any steps in the matter – she didn't sue for wrongful dismissal, she didn't go to a tribunal. She's done her level best ever since to create mischief for one or other of us, when she can, where she can.'

She dropped back into her seat and finished her coffee. 'She's not the only one in the village ready to give me a sideways look now. Martine had a daily woman, she used to work here for a few hours in the mornings, at other times if she was needed; her husband's one of the tradesmen on Owen's books. She was very competent, she did all the cleaning, the laundry, helped in the kitchen, kept an eye on Jamie, if Martine wanted to go out.' Harriet got to her feet again and resumed her pacing. 'She's stopped coming now, she stopped a week ago, a few days after Martine left. She didn't give in her notice; she sent a doctor's note round, claiming she's got a bad back, she doesn't know how long she'll be off.'

She halted, pulled a little face. 'There have been rumours and gossip about Martine, going round the village in the last few weeks. This woman's always been a great admirer of Martine's, Martine could do no wrong in her eyes. When she discovered Martine had left, I reckon she reached her own conclusions: she decided Martine must have been hard done by, Owen must have behaved like a brute. She's a canny customer; my guess is she's waiting now to see which way the cat jumps, in case, in spite of everything, she decides after all to come back – there aren't that many jobs going in the village and none of them pays better than Owen – and, of course, she's drawing sick pay all the time she stays off without handing in her notice.'

She picked up the beakers and carried them to the sink, where she began to wash them up with vigorous movements. 'Fortunately, there's another woman in the village, willing to come in three or four times a week. I did her a favour or two in the past and she's not forgotten.' She glanced up at the clock. 'If there's nothing else, I ought to be getting back to the office.'

There was one other thing: could she give Slade the address of the daily woman who used to work for Martine and now came no more to the house?

Harriet was silent for a moment, giving him a sharp look, then she relaxed her features into an easy smile. 'Certainly,' she replied and supplied the address, making no comment, asking no question.

After her second, longer talk with Philip Harvey's solicitor – he had fitted her in ahead of normal office hours – Lorraine Clifford made her way to a nearby café where she sat for some time, drinking coffee, mulling over what had been said.

When at length she had reached a decision about the steps to take in the immediate future, she left the café and set off for Workwear, to discuss matters with Shannon and Philip's secretary. She then went along to the police station, asking to speak to Chief Inspector Kelsey.

She explained that she had decided – with the full support of both Shannon and the secretary – to occupy the remainder of her leave by going in every day to Workwear, where she could be reached if the police should wish to contact her.

Did that mean, Kelsey asked, that she had decided to make her future with Workwear?

She shook her head. 'It's far too early for any decision of that kind.' All she had in mind at present was to try to familiarize herself with the workings of the firm, to gain enough understanding of the business to be sure in due course of making the right decision. She could take months, if necessary, to think things over. In the meantime, Workwear would, she was sure, continue to run smoothly under Shannon, along its present lines. She clasped her hands together. 'I'm positive,' she said earnestly, 'it's what Philip would have wanted me to do.'

The Chief asked if Philip had ever discussed the matter with her.

No, never, she told him. She had had no knowledge of the terms of his will, Philip had never once made any mention of them; she had had no idea that she would inherit Workwear.

Who had she thought would inherit the firm on Philip's death?

'I never gave it a moment's thought,' she replied. 'I had my own work, my own life. I wouldn't have considered such matters anything to do with me. I'd expected Philip to live for a good many more years. It would never have occurred to me to spend time wondering what might happen to the business, some day so far off in the future.'

The address Harriet Russell had given DC Slade took him to a semi near the centre of the village. As he set his finger on the bell he could clearly hear a radio in an upstairs room but the seconds ticked by and no one answered his ring. A bad back, Harriet Russell had said. Maybe the woman was lying incapacitated in her bed, unable to totter downstairs.

And then again, maybe not. He pressed the bell once more, long and hard.

A moment or two later, the lower sash of an upstairs window was thrust upwards and the head and shoulders of a woman appeared in the aperture. Her hair was tied up in a floral scarf.

'Yes?' she shouted down at him, little hint of welcome in her voice.

By way of reply he took out his warrant card and held it up to her at full arm-stretch. 'I'd like a word,' he told her.

She looked far from overjoyed. 'Wait there,' she returned grudgingly. She slammed the window shut. The radio suddenly ceased its lively song. He heard her come bounding down the stairs; the door was snatched open.

She stood scowling out at him; a sharp-featured woman, forty or so. Her nylon overall was liberally spattered with paint; her sleeves were rolled up to the elbow. If she's got a bad back, Slade thought, then I'm Jack the Ripper.

'What do you want?' she demanded. 'I can't stand here all day, I'm in the middle of decorating.'

'If I might come inside,' Slade said. 'I won't keep you long.'

She stepped reluctantly back to admit him. 'It'll be about this Beechcroft business?'

'That's right.'

She closed the door and led the way out of the little hall. She was about to show him into the sitting-room but suddenly changed her mind and took him along the passage into the kitchen. 'I could do with a cup of tea,' she flung over her shoulder as she picked up the kettle. 'I'm as dry as a bone. I don't suppose you'll say no.'

'That's very kind of you,' Slade forced himself to reply, though the last thing he wanted at this moment was to send down a cup of tea on top of Harriet Russell's coffee.

He spoke to her about Martine Faulkner as he got his tea down. She volunteered no information, offered no observation, replied guardedly to his questions, pausing each time to consider before answering. Her body language was unfriendly, even hostile. He made a point of referring directly more than once to Harriet Russell. At every mention her face closed up even more tightly. He went on to make an approving remark about the way Harriet was looking after Jamie and at that she couldn't repress a snort, though she made no utterance. He pressed on, saying something about how difficult things must be just now for Owen Faulkner, how shocked and distressed he must be, how burdensome he must find the effort to juggle the demands of everyday life.

She could restrain herself no longer. 'You think so?' Her eyes flashed.

Just as well, Slade continued, that Harriet had been able to find Owen a temporary daily to take over some of the chores.

'It's just a job to that woman that's doing it now,' she burst out. 'She never worked for Mrs Faulkner, she barely knew her. She doesn't care who she works for as long as she gets paid. I worked for Mrs Faulkner right from the time she got married, I always got on well with her. She was a lovely woman, a wonderful mother. And that husband of hers to go and throw her out of the house! Wouldn't even let her take the baby!' All at once she began to cry, noisily, distressingly. 'And Harriet Russell's in the house now,' she got out in between her sobs. 'In Mrs Faulkner's place. Carrying on as if she's got a right to be there –' She broke off abruptly, gulped back her tears, whipped out a handkerchief and dabbed fiercely at her face.

She strode to the back door and flung it open. 'Time you were off. You're getting no more out of me.'

Back in his car, Slade headed for Cannonbridge. Before returning to the police station he must look in, as the Chief had instructed, at the inquiry agency.

But he got little joy from his call there. Both principals, he was told, were currently away on cases. The agent employed on Mr Faulkner's instructions was away in Europe, not expected back before Saturday. Slade's best plan would be to call in or phone on Saturday morning. He would probably then be told the time of the agent's return and could, if he wished, make an appointment to talk to him.

*   *   *

119

Shortly after 3.30 Chief Inspector Kelsey got back from the TV studios where he had again been recording an appeal for information. He found that the analysis of the stomach contents removed during the post-mortems was now to hand; he sat down at his desk to study it with close attention.

The sexton from St John's church had relatives in Berlin, relatives he had never found it easy to get on with. He had been called to Germany on urgent family business, at very short notice, and had left on Saturday morning, to fly to Berlin. When he had dealt with matters as best he could – a process occupying the next few days and proving every bit as exhausting as he had feared, his relatives as volatile and demanding as ever – he thankfully booked his return flight, arriving back in England late on Wednesday afternoon, weary from the emotions and stresses of it all, anxious now only to make his way to the railway station, find a train for the first leg of his journey back to Cannonbridge, to the peace and serenity, the refreshing solitude, of his little cottage.

Mrs Erskine, a Cannonbridge housewife and mother, forty years old, was employed in the general office of a furniture retailer in the town, five afternoons a week. Her widowed mother, living near by, was happy to take charge of her two young grandchildren during the school holidays, while their mother was at work. At 5.45 every afternoon she could expect her daughter's car to pull up by the gate. Today, prompt to the minute, as usual, Mrs Erskine drove up. She jumped out, gathered up her children, kissed her mother, thanked her warmly and sped off again, intent on getting a meal under way before her husband got in from work.

When they reached home, the children darted off to play with their Christmas toys while their mother busied herself in the kitchen. She switched on the TV, to listen to the news as she worked.

Her supper preparations were well advanced by the time the regional news came on and she sat perched on a stool before the set, to give it her full attention. Very soon she found herself watching Chief Inspector Kelsey making an appeal for information. He looked directly out at her from the screen, he asked her, person to person, if there was anything she knew that might be of assistance to them, however slight, in the Beechcroft investigation.

She had a sudden flash of recollection. She sat motionless, staring at the screen, pondering. Could it have any significance? Was it her duty to speak to the police? Would it be worth mentioning? Or would she merely be wasting the time of an investigation team no doubt already stretched to its limits?

After all, what did her recollection amount to? Only that on two occasions in the previous week she had caught sight of someone she had known, years ago. In her first sighting she had caught only a passing glimpse, she could have been mistaken, but she was definitely not mistaken about the second sighting. She had passed quite close to him on that occasion. He hadn't recognized her, he hadn't glanced her way, but she was positive it was Greg Mottram. He was, naturally, quite a lot older and a good deal more careworn, but he was still recognizably the man she had known.

Greg had been employed in the Workwear offices during her own time there – she had taken a job with the firm immediately after leaving secretarial college and had remained there until eight years ago, when she had left, shortly before the birth of her first child.

Greg hadn't been a close friend – he had never made a close friend during his time at Workwear. He was never anything to look at, always diffident and self-effacing. She had been aware, as they all were, that he was some sort of connection of the Cliffords. She was aware also, after Mr Clifford's death, of the strained relations between Greg and Philip Harvey, Greg's increasingly obvious dependence on alcohol, his deteriorating punctuality and work performance, culminating in an explosion on Philip Harvey's part and the instant departure of Greg Mottram. That was twelve and a half years ago now, she calculated, and in all that time she had never once caught sight of Greg in Cannonbridge – until last week.

She had kept in touch with her old mates at Workwear, had

always followed the fortunes of the firm with interest; she had been thunderstruck by the events of the last few days.

Chief Inspector Kelsey reached the end of his appeal with a final exhortation that came to her with direct force, right out of the screen. She switched off the set and sat staring down at the floor, her brow furrowed in thought. Why had Greg come back to Cannonbridge after all this time? Could he possibly have had anything to do with the tragic happenings at Beechcroft? Did the police know of the old friction between Greg and Philip Harvey? Were they even aware of Greg's existence?

When her husband came home a few minutes later, he had scarcely got in through the door before she ran to meet him, to pour out her tale. What did he think? Should she say anything to the police? Or just forget it? She certainly didn't fancy turning up at the police station and making a fool of herself.

Her husband had a compromise idea: she could pop along to a house a few streets away, where a detective constable lived with his wife; Erskine had come across him sometimes; he seemed a quiet, unassuming man who would listen to what she had to say and give a sensible opinion.

She was mightily relieved, she made her mind up on the spot. Right, then that was what she would do. She'd take the car, she wouldn't be away many minutes. She had a very slight acquaintance with the constable's wife from occasional charity coffee mornings; she seemed a pleasant, approachable woman.

But when she rang the bell at the constable's house, his wife told her he wasn't home yet, nor could she say with any certainty at what time he would be home. It could easily be another hour. He was on the team investigating the Beechcroft deaths, they were working flat out.

Yes, she would be sure to give him the message. He would probably call round to see Mrs Erskine as soon as he got in.

DC Slade was hoping to get a word with both Rhoda Jarrett and Tom Guthrie, catch both of them at home, before they might think of going out for the evening. He wanted to ask them about Harriet Russell's access to Beechcroft: when, as far as they knew, she had last entered the house and if at any time she might have had a Beechcroft doorkey in her possession.

But as far as Rhoda Jarrett was concerned he was already too late. There was no one at home in the bedsit and another tenant told him Rhoda had gone out fifteen minutes earlier and wouldn't be back till late.

He had better luck on his next call. He found Guthrie at home, happy to answer questions.

No, he had had no inkling that Philip Harvey might return early from Europe; he hadn't heard that Philip had a heavy cold.

Had either Owen Faulkner or Harriet Russell ever had a doorkey to Beechcroft, even for a very short time?

The question struck Guthrie silent. He looked very thoughtful, pondering its implications. No, he replied at last, he could recall no occasion when either had been given a key, for however short a time.

It was approaching 7.15 when the St John's sexton, standing waiting on the breezy platform, at last saw his train approaching, for the final leg of his journey back to Cannonbridge. He got in and took his seat with a sigh of relief, settling down to relax at last, now that he was almost home.

A few stops later, the passenger in the next seat rose to leave the train. 'You might like to look at this,' he said in a friendly fashion, handing the sexton the newspaper he had been reading. The sexton took it with a word of thanks, giving it no more than a cursory glance: the county evening paper. He couldn't rouse himself sufficiently to read it now; he'd take a look at it when he got home.

15

Sergeant Lambert stole a look at his watch as he followed the Chief into his office. 7.45. Lambert's thoughts were beginning to turn towards getting off to his digs, to the heartening supper his landlady would now be keeping warm, in the hope that he would walk in through the door before it was reduced to a dried-up offering.

But the Chief showed no sign yet of calling it a day. No one awaited his return, no home-cooked supper was keeping warm for him. In spite of the long hours of the last few days he felt comparatively fresh and lively. He had it in mind now to cast an overall look at the jumble of facts painstakingly amassed since Monday morning, to see if some discernible pattern might be beginning to emerge.

He had coffee and sandwiches brought up from the canteen. Sergeant Lambert, still hopeful of sitting down to his hot supper in some sort of reasonable time, wishing to be able to do that supper justice when the time came at last, made do with coffee; at least it would serve to keep him awake.

Kelsey brooded as he ate. Officers visiting Workwear on Tuesday morning had made an appeal for any scrap of information, however small and insignificant-seeming, that might appear to have any bearing on what had happened at Beechcroft; so far there had been no response whatever.

He gave his attention now to the facts as he knew them. There were three drinks bottles in the Beechcroft dining-room: two on the table – a port, one quarter full, and a table wine, a robust red, almost empty; the third – a bottle of whisky, nearly full – was in the sideboard. All three bottles had been laced with the same two sedative drugs, the same two drugs that had been found in the stomach contents of both victims: a narcotic, one of the oldest sleeping drugs still obtainable, once widely used in its liquid form and still occasionally prescribed, chiefly for the elderly; and a barbiturate, also available in liquid form, at one time commonly used but now strictly controlled, after compelling evidence of its habit-forming propensity, its wide abuse and the ease with which it could facilitate suicide.

No adulterant substance had been found in any other article of food or drink in the dining-room, the kitchen, or anywhere else in the house, or in the dustbins outside.

According to Rhoda Jarrett, all three bottles had been in the sideboard since Christmas, the port and whisky bottles opened and the contents partly consumed, the wine bottle unopened – it was one of three bottles of wine bought at that time by Philip. Rhoda maintained – and in this was supported by Lorraine Clifford – that Philip drank little. He never entertained at home and in fact rarely entertained at all; when he deemed it necessary for business reasons he took his guests to a hotel or restaurant. He usually kept a bottle of whisky in the house and would take an occasional glass as a nightcap. Neither he nor Martine could be said to have a palate and the post-mortem had shown that Philip had indeed been suffering from a heavy cold – on its way out at the time of his death – which could certainly have affected his sense of taste and smell.

Owen Faulkner and Bertha Pearce had both stated that Martine was no drinker, though she would take a glass on social occasions.

Kelsey got to his feet and paced about the room. Accident could surely be ruled out. What of a suicide pact? Suicides were certainly more common early in the New Year. And suicide pacts were by no means unknown between lovers, particularly in difficult situations.

But no letter had been left. And no word had been uttered by either to any third party, to suggest a suicidal state of mind. Philip Harvey had arranged important appointments for the week ahead; he was greatly looking forward to the visit of the foreign delegation. Martine had ordered a cardigan; she had bought several personal items, a toy for Jamie, sufficient food for the next few days. None of this suggested suicide.

There was no trace, anywhere in the house, garden or dustbins, of any remainder of the two drugs used, no container that had held either of the drugs; no record of either of the pair ever having been in possession of one or other of the drugs.

What of the theory that it might have been a case of both suicide and murder, one of the pair having decided – without the consent or knowledge of the other – on the death of both?

There seemed nothing whatever to give the slightest credence to such a theory, no reason why either Philip or Martine should have been drawn even to contemplate such a course of action.

Sergeant Lambert looked up at the Chief. 'The fingerprints on the bottles, they seem to me to be the clincher.' The port bottle bore the prints of both Philip and Martine, the wine bottle those of Martine alone; neither bottle bore any other prints whatsoever, not even some indistinct portion of another print. The whisky bottle in the sideboard carried no prints at all – nothing had been found in the contents of either stomach to suggest that any whisky had been drunk during the final hours of the pair. It was plain that all three bottles had been very carefully wiped after being laced with the drugs.

'It's that wiping of the bottles,' Lambert said. 'Why should anyone about to take part in a suicide pact, or about to murder a lover and then commit suicide, go to the trouble of removing all fingerprints from every bottle liable to be drunk from? What conceivable purpose would it serve?' But he could see very good reason for some third person, planning to murder the two people likely to drink from one or more of those bottles, to remove his or her prints from all three bottles, very carefully indeed. 'To my mind,' he declared with conviction, 'that wiping says very positively that it's murder, double murder, we're looking at.'

Kelsey halted in his tracks. The port and whisky bottles, according to Rhoda Jarrett, had been opened some time ago but the wine bottle had been unopened. The bottle opener had not been wiped clean and carried a blurred mix of old prints – and a part of Martine's right thumb-print, undoubtedly more recent. Earlier in the afternoon, Kelsey had sent out for an identical bottle of wine. He had then handed the bottle to a woman constable to see if she could open it and then close it again well enough to rouse no suspicion in someone about to open the bottle, someone who would probably give it no more than a casual glance. The constable went off with the bottle, returning before long to set it down before the Chief. He picked it up, giving it only the casual glance he had spoken of, and opened it, using an opener identical with that found on the dining-room table at Beechcroft. He experienced no difficulty in opening it and if it was indeed Martine who opened the bottle, in her capacity as hostess, and if she was in an exhilarated mood, engaged in a lively, loving interchange with Philip, her mind full of the joy of reunion, with some sideways glancing at the details of dishing up the dinner, anxious that all should be as perfect as she would like it to be, her attention only marginally on what she was doing, then she could well have completed her task without pause, the operation being sufficiently close to normal to occasion no disquiet in someone unpractised and unobservant in such matters, as would seem to have been the case with Martine.

'Do you suppose,' Lambert said, 'that it was only Martine the murderer planned to kill? And that Philip was intended to find her dead when he returned on Sunday evening? Do you think Philip died because he happened to return early?' A mere instant later, Lambert came up with answers to his own questions: 'I suppose it depends on whether the murderer believed Martine was likely to go to the sideboard on Saturday evening and sit drinking by herself.'

It would seem to be only Tom Guthrie, Vicky and Avril who were unaware that Philip might return early – and Vicky would appear to have been the person most genuinely appalled and astounded at Philip's death. 'Ashdene,' Kelsey said aloud on a connected thought – someone must go round there in the morning, to see how carefully medicines and drugs were kept on the premises.

The liquor bottles were most likely to have been doctored between 4 p.m. on Friday, 2nd January – when Guthrie left Beechcroft at the end of his stint – and 8.30 a.m. on Saturday, when Guthrie returned. Friday evening and night were dark and overcast. No one had reported seeing anyone entering or leaving Beechcroft during those hours.

There was certainly no sign of any forced entry but a close inspection had revealed that entry was possible through a window at the rear, opening into a small, stone-floored room equipped with an ancient sink and wooden shelving; it had formerly served as a scullery and flower room but was no longer in use. The window frame and fastenings were old and worn and it was possible with a little perseverance to jiggle the window open. The female constable who had dealt with the wine bottle had got the window open and crawled through it without too much difficulty. She had then crawled back out again, jiggling the window shut behind her.

The driver of the bus which had stopped outside Ashdene at 9.10 p.m. on Friday had now been found and questioned. Yes, the two girls had definitely boarded his bus that evening. He was equally positive that they had got off at their usual stop. He knew the girls as frequent passengers on his bus. And an elderly cousin of his wife's was a resident at Ashdene; he and his wife called there from time to time, to see her. He had had a brief chat with the girls on Friday evening, asking if they had seen the old lady; they had told him yes, they had seen her and she seemed to be going along all right.

'But that's not to say,' Sergeant Lambert observed, 'that the girls went to bed as soon as they got back to Mrs Byrne's house or that they stayed in their beds right through until morning.'

Another thought stopped Kelsey in his pacing. 'Whoever dosed the bottles and left them in the cupboard, surely took a risk that some other person, quite apart from the intended victim or victims, might decide to take a drink from one of the bottles – and die, purely by chance.'

'And that other person,' Lambert responded, 'could easily have been Lorraine Clifford. She might very well have taken it into her head on Friday, after the Jarretts had moved out, to look in at Beechcroft, have a wander round, check that the place had been left secure and in good order. She could have decided to pour herself a glass or two before she left.' He paused to envisage the scene. 'That would surely have brought Martine to a grinding halt on the Saturday morning,' he added with a grimace, 'if she'd gone breezing into Beechcroft to dump her things, full of the joys of spring, and found Lorraine Clifford stretched out cold on the floor.'

It was almost nine when the St John's sexton reached his cottage. It was good to be home again. He let himself in, picked up the few items of mail awaiting him, gave them a glance; nothing of any importance. He dropped them on the table in the living-room, took his bag up to his bedroom, had a quick wash and came downstairs again to put on the kettle, make himself some tea, look out a packet of biscuits.

He paced about as he ate and drank, his head still full of the events of the last few days. At length he shook his head, thrusting these invasive thoughts aside; he crossed the room and switched on the TV.

The news was just coming to an end. It failed to hold his attention and he resumed his pacing, drinking his tea, his thoughts slipping inexorably back to Germany. He picked up another biscuit. As he began to eat it in an abstracted fashion his attention was suddenly caught by the word Cannonbridge springing out from the regional news. He halted, swung round and stared at the set. He found himself looking at a face he recognized, the face of a local senior policeman. A caption at the foot of the screen confirmed the officer's name: Detective Chief Inspector Kelsey.

He dropped into a chair and forced his attention away from Germany. The Chief Inspector was, it seemed, making a fresh appeal for information, however slight, relating to the deaths of two people found dead on Monday morning in a house in a Cannonbridge suburb. As he named the house and the two people – Philip Harvey and Martine Faulkner – the sexton gaped at the screen. He had a sudden vivid flash of recollection: the lean, wispy-haired, bony-featured man he had seen several times, in an attitude of profound grief, before the grave of Veronica Harvey – late wife of Philip Harvey of Beechcroft.

'Don't be afraid to come forward,' the Chief Inspector was urging. 'You may think what you have to say is too trivial to mention. Let us be the judge of that.'

The appeal came to an end; the Chief Inspector vanished from the screen. As the sexton crossed the room to switch off the set, he saw on the table, lying beside his mail, the folded newspaper he had been handed on the train. He snatched it up and opened it out.

There was quite a spread on the case. He dropped into a chair again and read every word. When he had finished, he sat frowning, cogitating. He got to his feet and crossed to the phone. He made to pick up the receiver, to ring the police station, then he drew back, resumed his pacing. What he had to say seemed on second thoughts of no importance whatsoever. He continued to circle the room, halting abruptly as he suddenly remembered with relief a member of the St John congregation, a retired police

129

constable, a good-natured, understanding man who lived only a few minutes' walk away.

He looked up at the clock. Not too late to go calling. He pulled on his coat and plunged out into the sharp night air.

In the dark and silent hours of early morning, Chief Inspector Kelsey woke abruptly with a single word flaring in his brain: murder. Not a scintilla of doubt: calculated, cold-blooded murder, patiently designed and coolly executed by someone with knowledge of the Beechcroft routine, the likely movements of both victims. Someone intending, possibly, the deaths of both, or, conceivably, the death of Martine alone, unaware that Philip might inadvertently fall victim also, or, if aware of that risk, not greatly caring if the casual hand of chance should snatch up Philip, along with his beloved.

16

The public had responded swiftly to the revelations at Beechcroft with phone calls, visits to the police station, letters, both signed and anonymous. The responses had increased in volume with every write-up in the local papers, every radio appeal for information and, most of all, every appearance of the Chief on regional TV.

Personal visits were often from disturbed folk, some well known to the police, turning up regularly, endeavouring to make statements about any well-publicized crime, of whatever nature, not infrequently offering detailed confessions to having committed the crime themselves.

The signed letters were for the most part responsibly written, containing driblets of information genuinely believed by the writers to be important and relevant but scarcely ever of any serious worth. The anonymous letters were usually scurrilous, intent on paying off old scores, and very rarely bore even the slightest relevance to the matter in hand. But all must be noted, all must be considered, however briefly. All consumed valuable time, effort and energy.

Among the earliest folk to put in an appearance on Thursday morning was the sexton from St John's church, supported by the retired constable he had consulted. DC Slade listened with keen interest but the sexton's detailed description of the visitor to the churchyard rang no bells. He got the sexton to promise that if the lean, wispy-haired man were to turn up again at Veronica Harvey's grave, the sexton would at once remove himself unobtrusively from the scene and contact the police.

As soon as the pair had taken themselves off, Slade rang Workwear, asking to speak to Lorraine Clifford. She hadn't yet arrived, he was told, but was expected shortly. He left a message, asking her to call in at the station without delay.

He had barely replaced the receiver when another pair arrived: a detective constable from the murder team, accompanied by an acquaintance, a Mrs Erskine. Again, Slade listened with sharp attention, particularly intrigued by Mrs Erskine's description of Greg Mottram which corresponded closely with the depiction the sexton had just given of the visitor to the churchyard.

Shortly after this second pair had left, Lorraine Clifford came hurrying up the station steps. Slade passed on to her the gist of what the sexton had had to say and asked if she knew who it might be that was so drawn to her mother's grave. Lorraine at once recognized the description: it was undoubtedly a relative – Gregory Mottram.

Slade questioned her at some length about Mottram, asking what she knew of his history, his activities, past and present; she answered fully and without hesitation, speaking of Greg throughout with affection and sympathy.

Was she aware that Greg had been visiting the grave? She shook her head. Had Greg made any mention of the grave? Again she shook her head. 'But I can see nothing odd about his wanting to visit the churchyard,' she declared. He had left Cannonbridge six months before her mother died, he knew nothing of her death at the time, he wasn't at her funeral. 'He was very fond of her,' she added, with a shake in her voice. 'They had known each other as children. It probably gives him comfort now to take flowers to her grave, he may feel it makes up for not being with her at the end. And I can't see anything odd about his saying nothing to me about these visits. He hasn't had an easy life; I don't think it trained him to make any very free expression of deeply felt emotion.'

Slade wanted to know about any visits Greg might have paid to Beechcroft since his return, any encounters he might have had with Philip Harvey. While Lorraine continued to answer readily, her manner made it plain that she was in no wise disposed to share any doubts or suspicions the police might be inclined to harbour about her cousin. Yes, Greg had undoubtedly called at Beechcroft on a couple of occasions since his return to Cannonbridge, but she was positive he hadn't encountered Philip Harvey, either there or at Workwear.

She told Slade where Greg was now living, where he was employed. She knew that today he would be working only until lunch-time.

Slade changed direction. 'As far as you are aware, did Greg ever at any time have a key to Beechcroft? Years ago, maybe?'

'Good heavens, no!' she threw back at him. 'I can't see any reason why he should ever have had a key.'

Had there been any occasion in recent times when she had missed her own key to Beechcroft? Missed it even very briefly, perhaps?

Again she responded with force. She could recall no such occasion. She always kept her key in her shoulder bag.

'Say your bag was lying on a table or slung over a chair,' Slade persisted. 'Couldn't someone remove the key while you were out of the room or attending to something a little distance away? If the key was put back a few minutes later, you'd be none the wiser.'

After a short frowning silence she agreed with marked reluctance that it could be possible.

Slade turned to yet another matter: was it at all likely that she might have taken it into her head to let herself into Beechcroft shortly after Rhoda and Vicky Jarrett had moved out, at some time during that Friday afternoon or evening? To take a look round, perhaps, check that everything had been left in order? Or, maybe, to pick up one or two of her own belongings? And, while thus occupied, might she have decided to go along to the drinks cupboard in the dining-room, pour herself a glass or two?

She shook her head at once, with decision. While it was conceivable that she might have decided to call in at the house – though she very definitely had not done so, being fully occupied at that time with the extra turns she had volunteered for, on top of her normal duties, plus trying to keep an eye on Jessie Dugdale in what little spare time was left – there was no possibility whatever that she would have poured herself a drink. She never under any circumstances touched alcohol. She suffered from migraine and had discovered in her teens that, for her, alcohol was a prime trigger.

Slade asked who might know that she never touched alcohol. 'Anyone who knows me at all well,' she replied promptly.

'Did Greg Mottram know?'

She thought for some moments and then replied slowly: 'As a matter of fact, he did. I can remember mentioning it to him the day we met again, back in November, when we were chatting in the café.'

'Owen Faulkner? Harriet Russell? Did either of them know?'

This time her answer came back almost at once: 'Yes, they did, they both knew. I was at a wedding in Rivenoak, this last summer, Owen and Martine were both there, Harriet Russell was there as well. We were all standing chatting and Owen offered to get me a glass of champagne. I explained then about the migraine and they were all very interested, they all asked me questions.'

Slade let her go on her way to Workwear and shortly afterwards went over there himself, to have a word with Shannon and, separately, with Philip Harvey's secretary, to find out what they remembered of Greg Mottram from his time, years ago, at Workwear and what they knew of any dealings Philip might have had with Greg since his return to Cannonbridge, six or seven weeks ago.

What each had to say about Greg during his time at Workwear was very much as Mrs Erskine remembered. And each told Slade that Philip had mentioned Greg's hopes of getting back on to the firm's payroll, and Lorraine's fruitless attempt to put in a word for Greg. Philip was positive the approach hadn't been initiated by Lorraine but had been engineered by Greg in what Philip considered a devious fashion. He was incensed at what he regarded as Greg's effrontery in attempting such a ploy; he spoke disparagingly of Greg's lack of judgement in believing it remotely conceivable that he could ever again be taken on at Workwear.

When Slade got back to the station he found a constable, newly returned from Ashdene, waiting to see him. The constable had been appalled at the careless way drugs and medications of all kinds, many of them long out of date, were kept on the premises. He firmly believed he would have had no difficulty whatever in pocketing supplies of any he wanted. In his opinion, the relevant authority would be very interested to learn of the state of affairs in the home and would have a good deal to say on the matter to Miss Doris Newman.

At a minute or two before one o'clock Slade halted his car near the entrance to the block of flats where Greg Mottram lived. He didn't have long to wait before he spotted a middle-aged man corresponding closely to the description given by both the sexton and Mrs Erskine, approaching along the pavement; he carried a supermarket shopping bag.

Slade stepped out of his car to intercept him as he was about to turn in through the gates. Greg showed no surprise when Slade revealed his identity and asked Greg to accompany him to the police station for questioning. But he did display a degree of mild irritation – he had been at work all morning, he was hungry, thirsty and he needed a wash. Surely he could be permitted ten minutes in his flat; Slade was welcome to go inside with him.

But Slade wasn't having any. 'You can get all that at the station,' he responded brusquely. 'We won't keep you one moment longer than we need.' Greg made no further remonstrance but got into the car, still clutching his supermarket bag. He didn't ask what all this was about but sat in limp silence during the brief journey. And Slade offered no word of explanation.

At the station he sent Greg off to the canteen in the care of a constable, while he set in motion the business of checking if Greg had ever acquired a criminal record.

A little later, with Greg, marginally refreshed, facing him across the table in an interview room, Slade began a brisk questioning, asking first if Greg had paid a number of visits in recent weeks to the grave of Veronica Clifford in St John's churchyard.

Greg replied at once that he had paid such visits.

Did he have any particular reason for returning to Cannonbridge after an absence of several years?

He shook his head; he had no particular reason.

Why had he sought a job at Workwear when he had left the firm in circumstances that offered little hope of his ever being employed there again?

'It wasn't my idea to try Workwear,' Greg answered promptly. 'It was Lorraine Clifford's idea.' He moved his shoulders. 'I wasn't keen but I thought I'd go along with it. If it came to nothing I'd be no worse off. It was always possible Philip might have changed his attitude in twelve and a half years.' He made a wry face. 'He seemed to have it in for me after John Clifford died, I never really understood why.' A brief pause before he went on: 'I didn't exactly help matters, the way I reacted – drinking too much, turning up late for work, not turning up at all some days, making mistakes in my work. All that gave him a pretty good lever to get rid of me.'

'Were you never hostile to Philip Harvey yourself?'

'No, never,' he replied with force.

'Did you have no objection to his marrying Veronica Clifford? Gaining control of the firm, the house and other assets, on his marriage?'

'No objection whatever,' he shot back with equal force. 'It was none of my business who either of them chose to marry. Veronica was never one to stand on her own two feet, she always needed someone to lean on. She was shattered when her husband died, she found Philip a tower of strength. He was a very able man and I'm sure he did his utmost for Veronica in every way. And I know from Lorraine that he was always very good to her.'

'What was your attitude when you learned that Philip was

135

involved with Martine Faulkner? And that he could be thinking of marrying her?'

He shrugged. 'I had no attitude towards it. It was none of my business. I've found it difficult enough, trying to manage my own life, I've no wish to try to run other folk's lives. If I'd thought about it at all, I suppose I'd have expected him to marry again one day. He certainly waited long enough, it wasn't as if he jumped into it. Veronica's been dead twelve years.'

'When did you learn of the relationship between Philip and Martine?'

He thought back. 'It was Lorraine told me. She'd heard it from Rhoda Jarrett, the morning after the storm – New Year's Eve, that would be.'

The door opened and a constable made a discreet entry. He handed Slade a folded slip of paper and took his noiseless departure. Slade unfolded the slip and glanced down at it; it informed him that Gregory Stephen Mottram had no criminal record of any kind.

Slade looked up again at Greg. 'Did you have any objection to the prospect – if Philip and Martine were to marry – that everything Veronica had left, all that her husband had worked for, might all in the end go to total strangers – children Philip and Martine might have one day, in addition to the son Martine already had, none of them any blood relations whatever of the Cliffords?'

Greg shook his head. 'I never thought of it that way.' He paused. 'I was astounded when I heard they'd both died. I couldn't believe it. To take their own lives like that. It was incredible.' He shook his head again, slowly. 'It seemed such a terrible, pointless thing to do.'

'Is that what you believe? That they took their own lives?'

Greg shot him a look of surprise. 'Well, yes, of course. A suicide pact. That's how it strikes me. I thought that was how it struck everyone. What else is there to think?'

Slade gave him an inquiring glance and Greg enlarged: 'An accident doesn't seem very likely, from anything I've heard and read – which, I grant you, isn't a great deal. I dare say there's a lot that hasn't come out yet but I still can't see it as an accident.'

'You see some motive for a suicide pact?'

Greg spread his hands. 'She'd walked out on the child, she could have been afraid her husband would get custody and she'd lose the child for good. She might think her husband would be vindictive, refuse to give a divorce, make her wait the full five years before she could marry Philip Harvey.' A fresh thought appeared to strike him. 'I suppose,' he said slowly, 'it's possible one of them could have decided on suicide, decided to take the other one along, all unsuspecting – but I can't really see that, somehow, it doesn't seem very likely.'

'Did you have contact of any kind with Philip Harvey after you returned to Cannonbridge?'

He shook his head at once. 'None whatsoever.'

Slade went on to ask what visits Greg had paid to Beechcroft since his return and Greg replied in detail, giving dates and times, the names of those he had met and spoken to, pointing out that he had chosen to call when he was pretty certain Philip would be at work.

Had Greg ever, at any time in his life, for however short a period, had in his possession a key to Beechcroft?

Greg jerked his head back with an air of surprise. 'No, never,' he answered with emphasis.

'When you called at Beechcroft, a couple of days after the storm, did you notice one of the downstairs windows, at the back? It was possible to jiggle the window open, get inside the house that way.'

Greg looked him full in the eye. 'No, I did not notice the window. I was not going round, looking for some way to sneak into the house.'

'Are you able to pick a lock?'

He looked momentarily startled. 'No, it's not one of my skills.'

'On two of your visits to Beechcroft you had ample opportunity to refresh your memory of the house, inside and out?'

'Yes, I did.'

'Ample opportunity to look round the dining-room, take a squint inside the drinks cupboard?'

Greg came back smartly on that: 'I certainly didn't go poking my nose into the drinks cupboard.'

137

Slade changed tack. 'I imagine you've lived through some rough patches over the years? You've probably been prescribed sedatives, you kept by you what you didn't use up at the time.'

Greg made no response at all but sat looking at Slade with a face wiped clean of expression.

After several moments Slade went on to inquire how Greg had spent the late afternoon and evening of Friday, 2nd January.

Now Greg's answer came back at once: 'I was working until five o'clock. I left the store to walk home. I was crossing the road by the entrance to the flats. A car came round the corner, pretty fast, and I had to jump for it. I stumbled and fell down. The car didn't touch me; it went by as close as a whisker but I'd landed awkwardly on my right foot. I came smack down on the edge of the pavement and I fell over. I wrenched my ankle.

'The car pulled up and the driver came running back – he thought for sure he'd hit me. He helped me up. I couldn't put any weight on the foot and it was hurting like hell. He was full of apologies. He was a decent sort, he helped me into my flat, sat me down, did his best to help, any way he could. He made me some tea, asked if I needed a doctor or could he run me to the hospital.

'I told him that wouldn't be necessary, I had a walking stick, I could get about with that if he would go along to the chemist – just along the road – and get me a crêpe bandage. I didn't have to go into work again until the Monday. I'd already done my bit of weekend shopping at the supermarket, I'd brought it home at lunch-time.

'He asked if I was going to report him or make an insurance claim but I told him I didn't want to bother with anything like that. He went off to the chemist's and came back with the bandage, he helped me along to the bathroom. I told him there was no need for him to stay. I'd wrenched my ankle once before, years ago, and I remembered what to do. When he'd gone I soaked the bandage in cold water and put it on tight. Whenever it dried out I soaked it again. I could hobble about well enough with my stick when I had to but I kept my foot up most of the time.'

He half-smiled. 'I can assure you I didn't leave the flat again, on the Friday, the Saturday or the Sunday. By Monday morning, my foot was a lot better, almost normal. I bandaged it up and took my stick, I got along to work without any trouble. I had no difficulty at work. I don't have to keep walking about, I'm sitting down most of the time. My foot's perfectly all right now, no trouble at all. I'm still wearing the bandage but it isn't necessary any more, it's just to remind me to go easy with the foot for the time being.' He stuck out both feet, hitched up his trouser legs. The folds of a crêpe bandage showed above the top of his right sock.

Slade asked for the name and address of the motorist.

'I'm sorry,' Greg replied with an apologetic wave of his hand. 'I never thought to make a note of it.'

'His phone number, then?'

He shook his head. 'No, not that either.'

'The car registration number?'

Another headshake. 'I'm afraid not. Never crossed my mind. I just wanted to get up off the pavement, get inside and sit down.'

'Did anyone here in the flats see what happened?'

'Not as far as I know. There was no one about at the time. No one's mentioned it to me since.'

'Did you have any visitors over the weekend, anyone who can confirm you'd injured your ankle?'

Again he shook his head. 'No, no one called.'

'What about Lorraine Clifford? Did you mention the accident to her? Over the phone, perhaps, or next time she called?'

Yet another headshake. 'No, I never mentioned it. It was perfectly OK next time I had any contact with her.'

'When you went to work again on the Monday morning, did you tell anyone there what had happened?'

A slight smile. 'No, I didn't. I'm not very chatty at work, never have been. I keep my head down, get on with what I have to do. I find it pays.'

'Did you show anyone your ankle? Anybody at all, any-where?'

Once more he shook his head with an air of regret.

'So what it amounts to is this: you have no corroboration of any kind that the accident ever happened or that your ankle was out of commission on that Friday evening.'

'You have my word for it,' Greg pointed out.

To which assurance Slade offered no response.

When Greg let himself into his flat a little later he felt a sense of profound exhaustion. He wasn't in the least hungry now, his thoughts were far too agitated for sleep, he knew it would be useless to try distracting himself with the radio or TV.

What he yearned for, what he needed above all else, what he was desperate for, was a drink. It was all he could do not to throw open the front door and make a beeline for the corner shop. But he knew he must at all costs resist the urge. His brain was flagging up powerful warning signals: he must keep his head clear, his guard up, his wits about him.

He plunged about the flat, in and out of the rooms, for some minutes, throwing himself at last down on his bed, closing his eyes, trying to sink into a merciful slumber.

17

In the middle of the afternoon Slade was lucky enough to find Rhoda Jarrett at home, alone in her bedsit, ready to co-operate in any way she could. Slade asked how recently Harriet Russell had set foot in Beechcroft. Two or three weeks back, Rhoda told him. She had called to ask if everything was satisfactory, after the completion of a repair to the central heating system. She had taken a look round on her own; she hadn't stayed long.

Slade went on to ask about Greg Mottram's visits to Beechcroft and she confirmed Greg's account.

Had she told Philip Harvey Greg had called at the house?

No, she had not.

'You did know Philip had sacked Greg, years ago?' Slade persisted.

She nodded. 'Tom Guthrie told me, after Greg's first visit. But

I take folk as I find them.' She gave Slade a forthright glance. 'For all I knew, Philip could have had reasons of his own, years ago, for wanting Veronica's cousin out of the firm, out of the area, out of the way altogether.'

Slade consulted his watch as he left Rhoda's bedsit: just after 3.30. Thursday was one of Guthrie's Beechcroft days; he could be back there by now, working his usual schedule. He turned his car in the direction of Wedderburn Road.

And he did find Guthrie there, clearing up in the garden, at the end of his stint. He confirmed Greg Mottram's account of his visits to Beechcroft. No, Guthrie had not mentioned his visits to Philip Harvey. He had seen no need to. He had always liked Greg in the old days, he had thought him very harshly treated at the time of his dismissal.

Slade had one more question for Guthrie: when it came to his knowledge that something was going on between Philip Harvey and Martine Faulkner, did he pass that piece of information on to anyone other than Owen Faulkner?

Guthrie came sharply back on that: no, he had very definitely not passed the information on to anyone else. He was not, and never had been, a man for idle tittle-tattle. He had told Owen only after a strong appeal from Owen and an equally strong feeling on his own part of long friendship and old loyalty to Owen. If the positions had been reversed and he had stood in Owen's shoes, he would have hoped to hear the unvarnished truth, however painful, from an old Rivenoak mate.

Twice in the course of her day at Workwear Lorraine had rung Jessie Dugdale to ask how she was. Jessie had tried her best to sound well and cheerful but her voice was hoarse and faltering and the second phone call was interrupted by sharp bouts of coughing. 'I'll look in on you after I finish here today,' Lorraine told her.

As she replaced the receiver she decided to stop at Greg's flat on her way out of Cannonbridge, to ask how he had fared that afternoon – DC Slade would undoubtedly have called on him.

She would leave Workwear half an hour early, that would give her time to hear how Greg had got on, before she drove over to Bowbrook.

At 4.40 she turned her blue Peugeot into the parking space allotted to Greg. He didn't immediately answer her ring; he had fallen into an uneasy doze, lying back in his armchair. Lorraine knew he was in; she could see the light, hear the TV, so she persisted in her ringing till at last she heard him come lurching along the passage.

He looked weary and strained when he opened the door – he had been certain it was DC Slade back again for another bout of relentless questioning. He almost wept with relief when he saw it was Lorraine. He did something he had never done before: he lunged forward and clasped her in his arms.

The double inquest, on Philip Royston Harvey and Martine Emily Faulkner, was set down for 3.30 p.m. on Friday.

Lorraine left Workwear early – for the second day running – in order to attend the proceedings; she was accompanied by Shannon and by Philip's secretary.

Bertha Pearce, in unrelieved black, was already in the court-house, sitting rigidly upright, with a face of stone. When Owen Faulkner and Tom Guthrie entered, Owen glanced across at Bertha. She met his gaze for an instant and then turned her head away. Owen hesitated, as if minded to go over and risk a word or two, but then appeared to decide against it. The two men sat down and looked about them, conversing in low tones.

Rhoda Jarrett came in, on her own. Vicky had begged to be allowed to attend but Rhoda had been adamant; there was no question of her going. There was no exchange of glances between Bertha Pearce and Rhoda but both Owen and Guthrie spoke to Rhoda as she went by. She chose a solitary seat but as she settled into it Lorraine excused herself to her Workwear companions and crossed the room to join Rhoda, halting, on her way, beside Bertha Pearce, to introduce herself and speak a word of sympathy. Bertha appeared surprised – and touched – at the attention. Lorraine halted again to speak to Owen Faulkner and

Guthrie and then went on to sit beside Rhoda, who gave her a little smile of appreciation.

As expected, the inquests were opened and adjourned, the bodies released for burial. When it was all over and the court-room was clearing, Owen Faulkner moved with determination in the direction of Bertha Pearce, making it clear by his manner that he intended to speak to her, whatever her attitude. But she seemed now, however reluctantly, to accept the necessity to speak about the funerals. She followed him outside and they stood in a quiet spot for some minutes, discussing possible arrangements.

Lorraine parted company with Rhoda and waited to one side for a chance to speak to Chief Inspector Kelsey. He saw her waiting and walked across to join her as soon as he could.

She began by telling him she would be too busy over the next few days to devote any time to Workwear; she could be reached, if necessary, at Jessie Dugdale's cottage in Bowbrook – she would be staying there for the present, to keep an eye on Jessie, who was far from well.

She went on to say she had now made contact by telephone with Philip Harvey's elderly crofter cousin. He was greatly saddened to hear of Philip's death, appalled at the manner of it. He wouldn't be attending the funeral but would send a wreath. He would be grateful if Lorraine would handle all the arrange-ments, letting him know, in due course, the date and time, so he could remember Philip in his prayers.

Lorraine added that she had called on Owen Faulkner, to ask what his thoughts might be about the funeral. She had inclined towards a double funeral, the pair being buried side by side, possibly in Martine's native village of Northwick. And she was sure, without asking, that Bertha Pearce would wish the pair who had chosen to be together in life to lie together in their last long sleep. But she had hesitated to suggest this to Owen, having a shrewd notion of what his response would be.

In the event, she never got anywhere near mentioning it to him, as the first thing Owen said to her, in a tone that brooked no argument, was that under no circumstances would he permit a double funeral. He wouldn't even have the pair buried on the same day or in the same place. Martine's funeral would be held on the day after Philip's – whenever that might be. Her funeral would be held at an early hour, to diminish its appeal for the idle and the curious. It would be best, he had decided, to hold the funeral in Northwick, the village of her birth, where she had been raised by a woman who had greatly loved her, to whose home she had chosen to return for what had turned out to be the last week of her life.

Saturday dawned markedly colder, with a sharp frost forecast for Saturday night.

After the first broad sweep of house-to-house inquiries, return visits were, as usual, paid to households where some member had not initially been available. One such call was made to a cottage in an outlying part of Rivenoak. It was occupied by an elderly widow and her middle-aged daughter-in-law, herself a childless widow. The team had spoken only to the daughter-in-law, the old lady being away, due to return on the Friday evening.

She turned out to be a very spry old lady with a mischievous eye; she seemed happy to talk to the officers. Her daughter-in-law planted herself in an easy chair near by, with no apparent intention of leaving the room.

The officers began their questioning but the old lady broke in almost at once, unable to contain her forthright opinions. 'I know someone in Rivenoak who won't be breaking her heart over Martine Faulkner's death,' she declared, 'and that's Harriet Russell.'

'You mustn't say such things,' the younger woman said in despairing protest. She turned an apologetic glance on the officers. 'She enjoys saying things, just to shock folk.'

The old lady ignored the intervention. 'Harriet will be able to get her hands permanently on young Jamie now,' she continued with relish. 'And on Jamie's dad as well, I shouldn't wonder.'

Her daughter-in-law broke in: 'You could get folk into real trouble, talking that way.'

The old lady made a dismissive gesture. 'I'm saying no more than everyone else is thinking.' She directed an uncompromising look at the younger woman. 'I wonder you don't offer these gentlemen some tea, and some of your special biscuits.' The instant the younger woman had taken her reluctant departure, the old lady said in a rapid undertone, laced with significance: 'She feels she's got to keep in with Owen Faulkner – and with Harriet Russell. She does relief work at the stores, she's got her name down for a permanent job there, she's in line for the next vacancy. Those jobs are like gold dust round here.' She needed no further questioning but poured out a stream of utterances.

'I knew Harriet Russell's mother well – I was a neighbour of theirs when my husband was alive.' She jerked her head. 'It was always Owen Faulkner for Harriet, right from schooldays. She was a clever girl, worked hard at school. I know for certain there were three or four very good jobs she could have had, when she finished at the college, but she threw in her lot with Owen Faulkner, helped him every step of the way to build up the business he's got today.'

She fell silent and then went on in another rush: 'They say in the village the pair at Beechcroft were doped – alcohol and some sort of drugs, that's what killed them.' She narrowed her eyes. 'Harriet wouldn't have much difficulty building up a nice little stock of pills and medicines. She helped nurse her parents – and Owen's parents – at the end.'

There was a rattle of china outside in the passage. An officer jumped up to open the door and the younger woman came in, carrying a tray. There was no further questioning while the tea was poured and the cups carried round. A silence charged with unspoken thoughts reigned for a few minutes as the tea was drunk and the biscuits dispatched, then the old lady set down her cup with the air of one getting back to the matter in hand. The younger woman drew a despondent sigh and sat without speaking, hopelessly resigned to whatever might be coming next.

'Martine was a thorn in Harriet's flesh from the moment she set foot in Rivenoak,' the old lady began again with gusto. 'Sixteen years old, a head of hair like you never saw, making eyes at Owen. There wasn't much mystery about what she was after, she set her cap at Owen from day one.' She gave a dry little chuckle. 'Not that he put up much of a fight.' She jerked her head again. 'Well, Martine's out of the picture now. The way's

145

clear for Harriet to marry Owen – and get the baby as a great big bonus, she's always doted on that child. She lost Owen once, she'll make darned sure he doesn't slip through her fingers, this time round – no, sir!' Her eyes sparkled with keen appreciation of the whirligigs of life. 'She'll make him an excellent wife,' she added, on a note of apportioning credit where it was probably due. 'And she'll be a good mother to that boy. She was always the right one for Owen. She'd got him nicely hooked and then along comes that young madam, swinging her hips. If Owen had had the sense to marry Harriet in the first place, none of this would have happened.'

When DC Slade rang the inquiry agency in the course of Saturday morning, he was told the agent who had carried out Owen Faulkner's instructions was expected back in the middle of the afternoon; an appointment was made for Slade to speak to him in the office at five o'clock.

And he found the agent in a side office, waiting for him, when he arrived. A middle-aged man, unobtrusive-looking, slightly built, an unassertive manner, a sharply intelligent eye.

Owen Faulkner, it appeared, had suspected an involvement between his wife and a named man: Philip Harvey. But he had no idea how far matters might have progressed; he had persuaded himself into the belief that it might be no more than flirtatiousness that had begun light-heartedly enough and then got out of hand.

The evidence had been swiftly forthcoming and pointed very strongly indeed to outright infidelity. A report was made and that was the end of the case. A bill was sent and paid immediately, Faulkner expressing satisfaction at the work.

No, Faulkner had never at any time displayed any particular venom. The agent had considered him a very tightly controlled man.

No, Faulkner had at no time made any mention of driving his wife from the marital home. Or of any other course of action he intended taking as a consequence of the report. Nor did the agent ask: it was none of his business.

When Slade left the office he drove to Tom Guthrie's house; he saw lights on as he approached. Guthrie opened the door to him, looking surprised to see him again so soon. But he invited him in, took him along to the kitchen, sat him down, made him tea. No, he hadn't been doing anything special, just reading the evening paper.

Slade asked him about the old attachment between Owen Faulkner and Harriet Russell.

It had certainly been a strong one, Guthrie responded, strong and of long duration. 'They were always together, always a pair. You could say they were childhood sweethearts but it was never in a mushy, sentimental way. I thought it went a lot deeper than that. They were really best friends and I think that's always remained.'

'Even after Owen's marriage?'

'Yes, indeed. The marriage made no difference to that, as far as I ever saw.'

It would seem, Slade continued, that Guthrie was the only person Owen had spoken to at all freely, concerning his thoughts and feelings, after he began to suspect Martine had eyes for someone else. How agitated had he been at that time?

'He was never agitated,' Guthrie came back at once. 'He's not the kind to show agitation, ever. But I could see he was very hard hit, any man would be, that loved his wife. I answered the questions he asked, I believed he had every right to know.'

He levelled an unblinking gaze at Slade. 'I did everything Philip Harvey asked me to do that weekend. I gave Rhoda a hand on the Friday, I gave Martine a hand on the Saturday. That didn't mean I had to approve of what was going on. I do my job wherever I work, I do it to the best of my ability, but I don't get drawn into things that are none of my business. I'm paid to carry out my work, not sit in judgement on folk.'

'But you have your opinions, all the same,' Slade said.

Guthrie jerked his head. 'Of course I do, I wouldn't be human if I didn't. I was never a great fan of Martine's, after the way she set her cap at Owen. She had no conscience about snaffling him from under Harriet Russell's nose.' He stared back into those days. 'Martine was certainly something to look at. You should have seen her at sixteen, she'd have stopped you in your tracks.' He was silent for a moment. 'Then, after she'd married Owen, not to stay faithful to him, to start looking round for better fish to fry, even though there was a young child to think of. Harriet Russell would never have behaved like that, never in a million years, she'd never have broken her marriage vows.'

He fell silent again. 'And Philip Harvey – bringing the wife of another man into the Clifford family home, without a word to Lorraine. Lorraine's a fine young woman, she deserves better than that. And throwing Rhoda and Vicky out at a moment's notice, after ten years. Nobody could defend any of that.'

The owner of the block of flats where Greg Mottram was living had discussed his plans for improvement with his tenants and reached a satisfactory agreement. The tenants understood that the owner would be making the rounds of the flats from 9 a.m. sharp, on the morning of Sunday, 11th January, in company with the building manager of the contractors who would be carrying out the work. The owner had asked all tenants to be present but if any tenant were to be unavoidably absent, the owner reserved the right to enter that flat with the aid of his passkey. He had been assured that all tenants would indeed be present and promptly at nine o'clock on Sunday morning, with the building manager at his side, the owner rang the bell of flat number one.

He got no reply. He rang again, a third and fourth time; still no response. He gave up and turned his attention to flat number two, where they were at once admitted. As they were leaving the flat at the end of their inspection, the owner asked the tenant, an elderly widower, if he knew why Mr Mottram wasn't answering the door. Was he perhaps away? But the tenant couldn't help him. All he could say was that he had encountered Mr Mottram in the hallway last Tuesday evening and had mentioned the matter of the proposed updating. Mr Mottram had appeared pleased at the prospect of improvements, happy to co-operate in every way, and had definitely declared his intention to be in his flat to receive the two men.

The owner returned to flat number one to try another couple of rings. When he still got no reply he went outside and ran his eye over the windows of the flat. All the curtains were closed but an edge of light showed through a tiny gap in the living-room curtains. He went up to that window and put an ear against the glass; he could hear a radio or TV voice.

He was frowning as he went back into the hall. 'I don't like the look of this,' he told the building manager. 'I think Mr Mottram's in there. I think he could be ill. I'm going in.' A few moments later, with the manager beside him, he stepped inside the flat.

He could detect no movement anywhere. He opened the door of the living-room. From the TV a current affairs pundit delivered his opinions. The two men stood frozen on the threshold, taking in the scene.

The overhead light shone down on an easy chair, beside a small table on which stood a whisky bottle and glass. Reclining in the chair, eyes closed, in an attitude of peaceful slumber, Greg Mottram lay fully dressed.

The owner uttered a low-pitched sound. He approached the chair and laid his palm on Greg's forehead, placed two fingers at the side of his neck, reached down and slid a hand over his heart.

No warmth anywhere; not the faintest beat or stir of life.

18

It was almost 10.30 when DC Slade reached Bowbrook. He turned the car down the side road, on the edge of the village, halting before Jessie Dugdale's cottage, which stood alone on that stretch of road. Lorraine Clifford's blue Peugeot was drawn up on a patch of hard-standing to the left of the dwelling.

When Slade rang the doorbell, Lorraine was upstairs in the front bedroom, attending to Jessie Dugdale, who looked and sounded a little better than when Lorraine had moved in on Friday evening. At the sound of the bell Lorraine crossed to the window and glanced down. A car was stationed by the gate. A man stood at the front door, a man in a dark suit. He turned his head and she saw it was DC Slade, from Cannonbridge. Jessie had barely registered the ring; she was drifting off into a doze.

Lorraine went noiselessly from the room, down to the front door.

In the little sitting-room, Slade broke the news as gently as he could. Lorraine drew a sharp breath and put her hands up to her face. 'I'm afraid we must ask you to come over to identify the body,' Slade said after a few moments. 'You would seem to be the nearest relative.' She dropped her hands, sitting with her eyes closed; she gave a nod of stoical acceptance. She opened her eyes, squared her shoulders, got to her feet. He saw that she was beginning to brace herself for the coming ordeal. 'I'll have to have a word with Jessie,' she told him. 'I can't tell her what's happened, she'd be too upset, but I'll have to tell her I'll be away for a while. I'll follow you in my car.'

He shook his head at that. 'I think it would be best if you allow me to drive you over and bring you back.' However prepared she might be for this second trip to the mortuary, he knew how searing the reality could again prove; she might well be in no fit state afterwards to sit safely at the wheel of a car.

She didn't argue but gave another nod of acquiescence. In the doorway she halted to look back at him. 'I saw Greg, just for a few minutes, on Thursday evening. I was on my way over here, I couldn't stop long.' She drew a shuddering breath. 'That was the last time I saw Greg, the last time I spoke to him.' She looked away. 'He was very down, very distressed – you'd been questioning him at the station.' She pressed her hands together. 'He was absolutely exhausted.'

Slade made no response.

She went from the room, up to the bedroom where Jessie opened her eyes a little as she entered. Lorraine explained that she would have to go out for a while but would be back as soon as she could. She saw that Jessie took it for granted she had been called out on some social-work emergency; Lorraine didn't correct her impression.

'She'll sleep most of the time while I'm gone,' she told Slade when she rejoined him. 'I'm not going to tell her about Greg till she's a lot stronger, it would be too distressing for her. She knew Greg years ago, he was a link with the old days.'

*   *   *

At 10.45 Rhoda Jarrett sent a raking glance round her bedsit. Everything in order, clean and tidy. Vicky had left earlier, with Avril, for their stint at Ashdene. She locked the door and let herself out into the chilly morning; she set off at an unhurried pace for Greg Mottram's flat. When she rounded the final bend she came to an abrupt halt at the sight of the police vehicles drawn up in a row, the constable standing guard by the gates – a sight so reminiscent of what had greeted her eyes, outside Beechcroft, less than a week ago.

After a few moments she walked slowly on again till she came up to the constable; he asked her courteously to state her business at the flats.

She explained about the storage of her boxes, her intention now to call in order to remove a few items – Mr Mottram having told her she might call, without phoning, at any time she was likely to find him at home. The constable listened attentively but offered no explanation for his presence, or for the line of cars.

She looked up at him with inquiry. 'Is it all right if I go in?' He regarded her for a moment before replying: 'I think you'd better have a word with the Chief Inspector.' He signalled over to a second constable standing outside the main doorway; the officer left his post and came across. They spoke briefly, in undertones, then the second constable took her inside the building to where a third colleague stood, outside flat number one. She found herself a minute or two later inside the little hallway of the flat where a table and chairs had been set up. She was kept waiting for a very short time before the door of the living-room opened and Chief Inspector Kelsey came out, followed by Sergeant Lambert.

The Chief listened as once again she offered her explanation. He had seen the neatly stacked boxes, marked with the names of the Jarretts. He asked when she had last had contact with Greg Mottram. Last Wednesday evening, she told him; she had called in order to remove some things from the boxes. She had stayed only a few minutes: Greg had seemed much as usual: quiet and helpful. No, he had not struck her as depressed.

At this point, spurred on by Rhoda's increasingly piercing look of inquiry, the Chief gave her the barest outline of what had happened. She took a step back, a hand flew to her mouth. She

151

closed her eyes, dropped her head, remained silent and rigid for some moments. At last she raised her head to look at the Chief. Sergeant Lambert was momentarily astounded to hear her say in a disciplined tone: 'If it turns out that you need some photographs of Greg, Vicky has some very good, very clear ones, she took them quite recently.' All at once she began to weep, silently, with great, racking shudders, as if she would never stop.

Some little time later, when Rhoda had gone on her way, Sergeant Lambert remarked to the Chief in a voice of dispassionate observation: 'Vicky Jarrett seems to have a bent for taking good clear photographs of men who meet an unexpected end shortly afterwards.'

One of the smallest back bedrooms on the second floor at Ashdene was occupied by a very old lady whose days were now largely passed in hazily slipping in and out of a light sleep, for the most part blessedly untroubled, purged of present afflictions and ancient sorrows.

She was scarcely aware of Vicky and Avril moving light-footed about the room, putting it to rights with duster and damp cloth, a spray of polish. On the bedside table, a radio, carefully tuned by Vicky into the local station, sang, played and chatted, but its carefree sounds couldn't get through to the old lady; she was back in some flowery meadow of her childhood, romping with her playmates.

The two girls paused every minute or two in their work to devour another biscuit from the bagful Vicky had purloined from the kitchen and now kept concealed in one of the capacious pockets of the apron she always found it useful to wear during her stints at Ashdene.

The radio suddenly stopped singing and a voice delivered a news-flash, speaking of the discovery of a body in a Cannonbridge flat, the presence of police at the scene, a post-mortem scheduled to start at three o'clock. The two girls froze. They stood in silence, heads cocked, Vicky with a biscuit half-way to her lips, listening intently; they didn't exchange glances.

*   *   *

The Chief had promised to keep Lorraine as short a time as possible, to let her get back to Jessie. When they returned from the mortuary he sent for tea and waited till she had steadied herself before asking if she knew of any other relatives of Greg's.

'I don't know of any actual blood relatives,' she told him, 'but there was a stepmother and a stepbrother.' She didn't know where either of them was now living but she was able to name the town where Greg had lived as a child. 'You might find his old address there among his papers,' she added. Even if, as was highly probable, the step-relatives had both moved away, the address might provide a starting-point for locating mother or son.

That suggestion took the two policemen and Lorraine to Greg's flat, where Sergeant Lambert produced for them an old chocolate box he had come across in a cupboard in the bedroom. Among its contents was a folder of snapshots, much fingered; a few pressed flowers; favours and mottoes from long-ago festive crackers; a small assortment of Christmas and birthday cards, many years old, all from Veronica as a child; Greg's birth certificate, his National Insurance card, a bundle of bank statements – and an address book. Lorraine riffled through it and very soon found an entry showing where Greg had lived as a boy.

From the folder of snapshots the Chief selected half a dozen for Lorraine to look at. All six showed the same trio of children, six or seven years old, maybe. All six snapshots had been taken in the same well-tended garden but on different occasions, at different times of the year. All six showed differing views of the house standing in the garden. On the back of one snapshot, in which the three youngsters were holding balloons, a careful, childish hand had written: 'Gregory Mottram, Veronica Mottram, Constance Whitlock. Veronica's 7th birthday.'

Did Lorraine recognize the house and garden? Did the name Constance Whitlock mean anything to her?

She answered yes immediately to both questions. Her mother had taken her once to see the house and she had often gone by it later. It was her mother's childhood home; it stood in a suburb of Cannonbridge, half a mile from Beechcroft; she was able to give the Chief the address.

153

She couldn't say exactly where Constance Whitlock had lived but she knew it was close to where her mother had lived, as the two had regularly played together as children. She knew the Whitlocks had moved away from Cannonbridge when Veronica was still a child and she also knew that Constance had made occasional contact over the years, when her parents brought her back to the town to visit relatives and friends. Lorraine could remember Constance calling at Beechcroft once or twice, in the years before her mother died. She had never heard of her since, had no idea where she might be living now, what she might be doing, if she had ever married and now, perhaps, bore another name.

Owen Faulkner had been busy for an hour or two in his office, alone in the peace of Sunday morning. He lifted his head from his paperwork and glanced at the clock. Time to think about making his regular cup of coffee. He got to his feet and gave a vigorous stretch, then he stood for a moment, pondering, before leaving the office and moving at a slow pace, still sunk in thought, across to the house and round to the back door, letting himself into the kitchen. He shook his head briskly, dismissing intrusive thoughts, and switched on the radio, tuned into the local station. It gave out a burst of inspiriting music as he set about making the coffee.

He laid out a tray with two beakers and a plate of biscuits. He was making the coffee when the music ceased. Spot on the half-hour, a voice began the regular bulletin, with its news – more detailed by now – of the finding of a man's body in a Cannonbridge flat. As the bulletin progressed, Owen grew rigid. He stood listening intently, staring down at the floor.

The bulletin came to an end but he made no move for another minute or two, then he roused himself to switch off the radio, pick up the tray and carry it along to the glassed-in verandah where Harriet Russell, tenderly smiling, was playing with Jamie.

Tom Guthrie had risen even earlier than usual, determined to catch up on a number of Sunday morning jobs in his house and garden, before permitting himself to look in at the pub for a lunch-time pint. From time to time as he moved between jobs he switched on one of his radios; he had a number of them, strategically positioned, upstairs and down, plus one outside in his shed; the background sound they provided gave him a cheering illusion of company, very welcome these days, now that he lived on his own.

The jobs went very well this morning and he whistled as he returned to the kitchen, just before noon. A wash and shave, change, then off out for an hour – he had put his dinner in the oven earlier, he believed in looking after himself. But before he embarked on any of this he must first wash his hands at the kitchen sink, rid himself of the worst of his grime before going up to the bathroom. He switched on the radio, ran the taps, picked up the soap. The noon bulletin came on and he listened with interest; it was the first news spot he'd caught since breakfast.

A minute, two minutes went by. The radio voice continued, reporting – now at greater length and in more detail – the discovery in the Cannonbridge flat. Guthrie stood transfixed. The taps ran on, the water splashed unheeded.

The bulletin reached its end and a burst of music began. He stirred himself and looked vaguely about. He turned off the taps, dried his hands roughly on the roller towel. He crossed to the radio and switched it off. He pulled back a chair and sat down at the table. He dropped his head into his hands and, with no thought now of any visit to the pub, he stayed there for some time, motionless, furiously thinking, thinking, thinking.

Vicky and Avril had their lunch provided, as usual, at Ashdene, at the end of their stint. They polished off their meal and were gone in a trice, hurtling along towards the bedsit. Avril waited outside while Vicky burst in and out of the room, pausing only long enough to seize a cardboard box from a shelf by her bed, snatch from the box a folder of photographs, with never so much as a glance at Rhoda, who was leaning back in her chair, eyes closed, listening to the radio. Rhoda started up at the irruption

155

but Vicky was gone again before her mother could rouse herself sufficiently to frame a question or a protest.

The two girls raced at top speed, with never a word exchanged between them, for the police station, leaping up the steps, shooting in through the doors, heading straight for the reception desk, where Vicky demanded to see DC Slade.

Slade chanced to be in the building and came swiftly along to the desk, removing the pair immediately to a quiet corner, with Vicky pouring out a non-stop stream of chatter. They had called at Greg's flat on Saturday evening, she informed Slade in a breathless rush, they must have been among the last people to see him alive, maybe even the very last of all. Vicky's eyes shone. This time there could surely be no argument; she must appear on TV – and radio, as well. The moment they reached the quiet corner she thrust her package of photographs into Slade's hands, assuring him he would find no better photographs of Greg anywhere.

Slade delivered them a brief, fierce lecture. They knew better by now than to come running wildly into the police station; anything sensible they had to tell the police must be said in the presence of their mothers, in accordance with due procedure. There could be no question of taking part in any TV and radio appeals for information. 'Your school starts again tomorrow,' he reminded them. 'You should be giving your attention to your studies, not television appearances.'

Vicky pulled a face. 'We never do anything much at school, the first few days. I'm sure they'd let us off to go on TV.' She flashed him a smile. 'They couldn't really stop us if the police wanted us to go. You could ask them, they'd listen to you.'

At 2.45 Chief Inspector Kelsey stood in the doorway of Greg's living-room, running his eye over the scene. All was quiet now, all activity ceased.

Against the opposite wall, an upright chair stood at an angle to a side table. They had found a copy of last Saturday's evening paper on the table, folded into an oblong, showing columns of Situations Vacant, three of the column entries ringed in black ink. A black ball-point pen and a writing-pad lay close by; beside them, three envelopes, stamped and addressed – to the ringed business addresses in the columns – but not yet sealed. Two of the envelopes contained folded sheets of writing-paper: applications for two of the ringed jobs, written with scrupulous care; the top sheet of the writing-pad showed a third such letter half completed; all three letters almost identical in content and layout.

Outside the flat, by the back door, stood a dustbin, nearly full – the bins were emptied once a week, on Mondays. Among the contents of the bin – ordinary household refuse, neatly disposed – were five evening papers, Monday to Friday of last week, all similarly folded, showing columns of job vacancies, similarly ringed.

The dustbin also held five empty liquor bottles: one whisky and four wine; all half-bottles, each one tidily wrapped in sheets of newspaper before being further enclosed in a supermarket carrier bag.

The bathroom cabinet contained everyday items of no significance – and two medicine bottles, almost empty, the labels torn off but leaving fragments still adhering.

The Chief turned from the doorway of the flat and let himself into the main hall. Sergeant Lambert was waiting outside for him, by the car. The Chief glanced up at the other flats. All the tenants had now been questioned about last Saturday evening. No one, it seemed, had spotted any outsider entering or leaving Greg's flat.

Only one tenant, a Mrs Onslow, a widow in her sixties, occupying flat number four on the floor above, had seen anything at all of Greg on Saturday evening. She had been looking out of the window of her flat and had seen Greg approaching, turning into the entrance; he was carrying a newspaper. The time, to the best of her recollection, would be around 5.15, 5.20. She was positive there had been no one with Greg.

As the Chief left the building he spoke a passing word to the uniformed constable standing guard. The officer – PC Venning, born and bred in Cannonbridge, now nearing the end of his service – had known the Chief since the days when the Chief was a raw youngster in the force. Venning had performed the same guard duty at Beechcroft, less than a week earlier.

157

He gave Kelsey a reflective glance. 'I don't know what you make of this one, Chief. A touch early to say, I imagine. For what it's worth, my money's on suicide.'

The Chief gazed back at him with inquiry.

'My guess is: it was Mottram did away with the Beechcroft pair,' Venning enlarged. 'Getting his own back on Philip Harvey for sacking him, years ago. Probably been brooding on it ever since. I reckon he had nothing against Mrs Faulkner, she just happened to be in the wrong place at the wrong time. Afterwards, the whole thing preyed on Mottram's mind – maybe he was upset at Mrs Faulkner dying like that, with a young child left without a mother. He did away with himself in the same way as he'd killed the Beechcroft couple, that could have seemed like justice to him, for what he'd done.' He moved his shoulders. 'Or he could have thought we were on to him. He didn't fancy ending his days inside, so he took the same way out.' He grimaced. 'There was no note, of course, but we all know it isn't every suicide leaves a note.'

19

Greg Mottram's boyhood home was in a town some forty miles from Cannonbridge and DC Slade set off to begin his search there shortly after three o'clock. He had a good clear run and found the house without difficulty: an attractive villa with a sizable garden, in a pleasant residential area.

It belonged now to a retired bank manager and his wife. Yes, they could tell him where to find Mrs Mottram – but she was no longer Mrs Mottram; she had remarried shortly after they had bought the house from her – thirty-two years ago now; her name was now Mrs Squire. She had engaged their interest from their first meeting: a handsome woman with a charming manner, a great many ready smiles, a highly flattering way of listening, with every appearance of keen interest – but behind all that, a suggestion of a sharply active brain, an astute eye for the main chance.

They had read the report of her wedding in the paper and had followed the subsequent fortunes of the former Mrs Mottram and her son with unflagging interest. Her new husband, Mr Squire, was twenty years older than his bride; he was a well-known local businessman, engaged in the manufacture of springs and pressings for the automotive industry; he had a factory on the town's industrial estate. He had long been a widower, with a daughter who had never had a job but had devoted herself to keeping house for her father. A plain, plump woman, the daughter, not the brightest of intellects; mild-mannered and docile, easily pleased; she occupied her spare time with a little charitable work.

Mr Squire had been in indifferent health for some time before the marriage; he had undergone a heart bypass operation a year or two earlier. The business had, in consequence, begun to go downhill. Squire was delighted when his new stepson decided, at his mother's urging, to leave his job in insurance, shortly after the wedding, to join his stepfather as his personal assistant.

Squire survived barely long enough to celebrate his first wedding anniversary; a week or two later, a stroke carried him off. The house went to his widow, who still lived in it. The business, together with all monies and other possessions, went in equal shares to Squire's daughter and his widow. The latter's son, with the approval of Squire's daughter, immediately took over the running of the firm. Three months later, in a quiet ceremony, he married Squire's daughter, who was a good ten years his senior.

The business had prospered since then and was now among the most successful in the region. The son's marriage, it would seem, had also prospered; it had produced two offspring, both now grown up: a son, working under his father, in the family firm, and a daughter, married six months ago to a local solicitor.

The address given to Slade by the retired couple took him to an impressive neo-Georgian dwelling in a select housing development, superbly landscaped, with fine old trees left standing.

He found Mrs Squire at home. He was admitted by a housekeeper and shown into a sitting-room where Mrs Squire reclined at ease on a sofa heaped with cushions, before a coffee-table piled with magazines and newspapers.

She was still a lady to take the eye: slim, straight-backed, elegant, appearing years younger than the age Slade knew she must be. She didn't rise to greet him, didn't extend a hand, didn't squander on him any of the ready smiles he had heard mentioned. He received the strong impression that she would never see fit to expend her charms on a personage of as little consequence as a stray detective constable. She proceeded to deal with him swiftly and efficiently; at no point did she invite him to sit down.

Slade explained the reason for his visit. She expressed herself as saddened at the death of her stepson and made a face of mild distaste at the manner of his passing but Slade saw that it meant nothing whatever to her – except for some slight irritation at the necessity to concern herself with it, however briefly.

She perceived at once that the circumstances of Greg's death would involve continuing police attention, with the possibility, at some stage, of increasing media interest, reaching out, maybe, even so far as to intrude upon the agreeable lives she and her son had constructed for themselves. 'I should be very much obliged,' she informed Slade, 'if you could see that no reference is made to any connection with me or my son – he's a man of some importance in this town, indeed in the whole area. And I do a good deal of work, in my own small way, for charity, in this part of the county. It would never do for either of us to be in any way mixed up in something so unsavoury. I'm sure you appreciate that.'

Slade gave her back a level look. 'I'm afraid we have no control over the media. If they choose to interest themselves in a particular aspect of a case, there is nothing we can do, or would even wish to do, about it.'

She digested that in silence for a moment before going on to inquire with undisguised bluntness if Greg had left enough to pay for his funeral.

Just about, Slade told her, from what he had been able to gather. Enough, at all events, he would think, to pay for the very cheapest funeral.

She didn't offer to pay for a better send-off. He saw that the notion presented itself to her for a fleeting instant and was as swiftly dismissed. Nor had she the slightest desire to oversee any funeral arrangements; she was sure they could be left entirely to Lorraine Clifford. She had been aware, years ago, of Lorraine's existence but had never met her. Lorraine was undoubtedly young but with her social-work background – which Mrs Squire had just this moment learned of, from Slade – she should be capable of dealing with the situation. 'I imagine she would be willing to take it on?' she inquired.

'I'm sure she would,' Slade told her. 'Very willing and more than capable.'

'Good!' Mrs Squire responded with satisfaction. 'That's settled, then; we can leave it entirely to her. I'll write her a letter afterwards, she's sure to appreciate that.' I take leave to doubt it, Slade thought. But he kept his opinions to himself.

Mrs Squire went on to say she wished to be informed, in due course, of the date of the funeral, so she could send a wreath. She'll make sure the card doesn't provide any clue to the identity of the sender, Slade thought; no inquisitive reporter, poking about among the floral tributes, is going to end up, asking questions, on this good lady's doorstep.

No, Mrs Squire would not be attending the funeral. Nor would her son. He and his wife were at present in Italy, enjoying a well-earned break after the rigours of the festive season. 'I know I can speak for him in all this,' she declared with supreme confidence. 'I know his thoughts would be precisely the same as mine.' I don't doubt it, Slade said to himself.

She moved her head. 'You must remember that Greg Mottram was no blood kin of ours. Not in the remotest degree. It's a good many years since either of us have had any kind of contact with him. That was entirely by Greg's own doing. He set out, by his own wish, to make his way in the world, when he was sixteen.' He made his own way, right enough, Slade reflected. His own friendless path that led him, through varying degrees of wretchedness, along endless lonely byways, taking him at last to his solitary death in a rented flat, with TV voices speaking a last goodbye.

'He made it abundantly clear by his actions,' she pronounced

161

with an air of finality, 'and by never communicating with either of us ever again, after leaving the excellent home I had provided for him, that he wanted nothing more to do with us. That was his attitude on the day he left, it very plainly remained his attitude.' She gazed at Slade with unblinking eyes. 'One must be careful to respect his wishes.'

It was turned seven by the time Chief Inspector Kelsey got back to the police station after the post-mortem. It appeared Greg Mottram had died from the ingestion of alcohol together with sedative drugs; the results of the stomach contents analysis would not be available until Tuesday afternoon. Death was thought to have taken place at some time between ten o'clock on Saturday night and four o'clock on Sunday morning. There were indications of a recently healed minor ankle injury to the right foot.

The Chief was greeted with the news that an old lady had now been found, living fifty yards down the road from where Veronica Clifford – Veronica Mottram, as she was then – had lived as a child. The old lady had lived in the house since her marriage, nearly sixty years ago. She well remembered the Mottrams and the Whitlocks; she had known Constance Whitlock well as a child, until the Whitlocks moved to a town some twenty-five miles away, when Constance was fourteen. She had seen and spoken to Constance and other members of her family on several occasions when they returned briefly to Cannonbridge but she had seen and heard nothing of any of them in recent years. From what she recalled, Constance had had a number of different jobs; she didn't seem to settle, always hankered after change. She had never heard that Constance had married.

She was able to tell them, after consulting an old address book, where the Whitlocks had gone, on leaving Cannonbridge, but she had no idea if any of the family were still living there or where they might be now.

After the briefing on Monday morning the Chief arranged to

make appeals for information on local radio and regional TV; he was anxious, in particular, to hear anything of Greg's movements on Saturday, especially from late afternoon onwards. And he directed a special appeal at the motorist – always supposing the gentleman had any existence in reality – Greg had spoken of. Certainly, the post-mortem had given support to Greg's tale of an ankle injury, though that was not to take it as gospel that he had come by the injury in the way he had described.

It had now been confirmed that Greg had left work at five on Saturday and had called at the newsagent's on his way home, to buy his evening paper.

Among the fingerprints in Greg's flat were one or two belonging to Owen Faulkner and Harriet Russell. No immediate explanation for these prints presented itself to the Chief, so, towards the middle of the morning, he dispatched DC Slade, unannounced, to Rivenoak.

Slade went first to Harriet Russell's office but she wasn't there. 'She won't be long,' her assistant told Slade. 'She had Jamie over here but he was getting very sleepy, so she took him back to the house. The new daily woman's over there, she'll be able to keep an eye on him while he's asleep.'

Slade decided not to wait in the office but to go across to the house. He was admitted by the new daily woman; she had a cheerful look and a friendly, bustling manner. 'We've all been having coffee in the kitchen,' she told him. 'You can come along and have a word with Miss Russell there. I can soon fix you some coffee.' He declined the coffee with thanks but followed her along to the kitchen, where Harriet was washing up beakers at the sink; she turned and gave him an assessing glance. Owen Faulkner sat at the table, frowning over some papers. He raised his head and regarded Slade in a silence that could scarcely be called welcoming.

'I'll be getting back upstairs, to finish the bedrooms,' the daily woman told Harriet. Harriet nodded; she gave a sudden little shiver. 'You're cold,' the woman said on a note of concern. 'I can pop up and fetch you down a cardigan, won't take a moment.'

'Yes, please, if you would,' Harriet said. 'You'll find a blue cardigan over the back of a chair.'

No one spoke in the brief interval before the woman returned. Owen went on frowning at his papers, Harriet finished her washing-up.

The woman went off again and Harriet pulled on her cardigan. Owen sat back in his chair and trained a dispassionate eye on Slade. 'You're quite right in what you're thinking,' he observed. 'Harriet has moved in here, it makes it a lot easier for her to run the house and look after Jamie.' His gaze didn't waver. 'And, in case you're wondering, she has her own room upstairs, she doesn't share mine.'

Harriet did not display, either by word or look, any response to what Owen had said. She finished buttoning her cardigan and then glanced across at Slade. 'I don't know if you need me here.' Her tone was crisply businesslike. 'If not, I'll get back to the office.'

Slade felt a strong sense of a close bond between the two of them, unspoken communication, an excellent understanding; they struck him as very much a couple. 'I would like you to stay,' he told Harriet. 'I'll make it as brief as possible.'

She gave a nod of assent and sat down at the table, beside Owen. Slade took a seat opposite them. 'One or two questions I'd like to put to you both,' he began. He made no mention of fingerprints but asked if either of them had ever had occasion to call at Greg Mottram's flat.

'We've both called there,' Owen replied at once. He explained about Lorraine's hope that he might be able to help Greg in his search for work. 'I thought I might be able to do something for him,' he added, 'but I'm afraid it went right out of my head –' he drew a long, ragged breath – 'when all the trouble blew up.'

Slade drove from Rivenoak to Bowbrook, to get a word with Lorraine Clifford. As he came within sight of the turning to Jessie Dugdale's cottage he spotted Lorraine's blue Peugeot approaching from the direction of the village. She smiled a greeting when she saw him. She took the turning to the cottage and he followed her down.

She had driven on to the hard-standing and was taking a box

of groceries from the boot when he got out of his car. 'I've been shopping in the village,' she told him. 'Doing a bit of stocking up.' He carried her purchases indoors for her. She had plainly been hard at work; the kitchen was sparklingly clean. 'I'm afraid Jessie had let it all get into a bit of a state,' she commented as she put her shopping away. 'It had rather got on top of her, poor dear. Hardly surprising, she was struggling to keep going.' She was able to confirm all that Owen Faulkner had just told Slade about the attempt to help Greg.

Slade then went on to tell her about his visit to Mrs Squire, Greg's stepmother. She pulled a face of disbelief and distaste as she listened, remembering all that Greg had told her about his treatment, long ago, at that lady's hands. As Mrs Squire had made it clear that she had no wish to be in any way involved with Greg's funeral, Lorraine willingly promised to see to all the arrangements herself.

Slade told her he was pretty sure the body would be released for burial after the inquest was opened. Did she think Greg had left enough to pay for the funeral? If not, did he have any possessions of value that might be sold?

'He didn't have much,' she replied soberly. 'A few clothes, a radio, a couple of suitcases. His watch, his father's tie pin and signet ring. That's about it.' She shook her head. 'Not a great deal to show for all those miserable years.' Her tone sharpened. 'I'll see he has a decent send-off, I'll pay for it myself, if necessary.' She fell silent for a moment. 'My mother would have wanted him treated with dignity, at the end.'

The Chief's appeals for information had evoked a strong response from the public and a fresh spate of calls of every description began to flood in from Monday afternoon.

Early on Tuesday morning came the call the Chief had greatly hoped for but never really believed he would receive: a visit from the motorist who had caused Greg's fall. He told them he lived some thirty miles away, in the next county. He had seen the Chief's TV appeal on its second showing on Monday evening and had at once determined to present himself at the Cannonbridge police station first thing next morning.

165

He was in his late forties; he came across as intelligent and sensible, anxious to co-operate in every way, to give a full and frank account of the incident, ready to answer any questions.

His detailed recital squared precisely with what Greg had told them, in every particular but one: the instructions Greg had given him when he dispatched him on his shopping errand. Greg had spoken only of requesting a crêpe bandage from the pharmacy but the motorist stated that Greg had also asked him to buy some drink at the corner store.

Greg had given him precise instructions: he was to buy two half-bottles of whisky – any brand, the cheapest available would be fine – and one half-bottle of wine – likewise, any kind, the cheapest available would do. Without being asked, Greg had thrown in an explanation. He wasn't due to go into work again until the Monday morning; it was his rule to restrict himself to wine for his evening drinking when he had to go to work next morning, but when he had the next day off, he was able to indulge his taste for whisky; either way, he never exceeded his nightly limit of one half-bottle.

After the motorist had left, the Chief sat pondering. The motorist's statement would appear to rule Greg out conclusively from any involvement in the Beechcroft deaths.

The discovery of the liquor bottles in Greg's dustbin had already led the police to the corner store the motorist had spoken of. The owner had told them Greg usually called in around seven or 7.30 in the evening. He would class Greg as a habitual, but strictly disciplined drinker, never departing from rules he had plainly laid down for himself. Greg's only other regular purchase had been packets of mints.

Greg hadn't called in at all last Saturday. He had last called in on the previous evening, Friday; his manner had been much as usual: businesslike, quiet and uncommunicative, but civil enough.

In the early afternoon an officer informed Rhoda Jarrett and Mrs Byrne that the Chief proposed to question Vicky and Avril again, immediately after school. The two women should meet the girls and bring them to the police station; both mothers would, of course, be present during the questioning. Neither offered any objection.

Later in the afternoon, the results of the stomach contents analysis, following the post-mortem on Greg Mottram, were delivered to the Chief and he spent some time studying them.

Greg had, it seemed, eaten only a small snack lunch on Saturday and had eaten and drunk nothing further after returning to work. At some time between, say, 6 p.m. and 8 p.m., he had consumed – on an empty stomach – the lethal combination of whisky and drugs: the same two sedative drugs which had figured in the Beechcroft deaths.

The Chief wasn't kept waiting for the arrival of the two mothers and their daughters. The four were taken to an interview room where the Chief and Sergeant Lambert joined them.

Both women wore an air of unease, sitting stiffly upright, their faces tense, but the girls gave no sign of apprehension. Avril seemed calm and untroubled, ready to be co-operative; Vicky appeared blithely cheerful, at ease in her surroundings, stimulated by the occasion, her eyes shining, a little smile on her lips.

The Chief began by addressing the girls: 'You both called at Greg Mottram's flat on Saturday evening?'

'That's right,' Vicky broke swiftly in. Nothing hesitant in what she had to say; she raced through it in a way that seemed well prepared. 'We hadn't arranged to call at the flat, it was just on the spur of the moment. We'd been in town, looking round the shops, in the afternoon; we had to be at Ashdene for half-past six. We called at the flat about twenty to six. We left just before a quarter past six.' She rattled out these times without a moment's pause. 'We stayed at Ashdene our usual time, then we got our usual bus back to Avril's house.'

'What was your reason for calling at the flat?'

Again, Avril made no attempt at a reply; Vicky burst out immediately with her response. 'I wanted to get some things out of my boxes. Greg never minded us calling, he was always pleased to see us. After we'd finished with the boxes, we did a few little jobs for him, round the flat, tidying up a bit, just to say thank-you to him, for being so good about the boxes. He was really pleased about that.'

'Did you say thank-you in any other way?' Kelsey inquired. 'Did you perhaps take him a present? A half-bottle of whisky, perhaps?'

Her eyes widened in a look of astonishment. 'Whisky? No, of course not. Where would we get whisky? You can't buy it in a shop, surely, at our age. It's not legal, is it?'

He let that go, asking another question of his own: 'Did you know that Greg had an alcohol problem?'

Vicky gazed back at him without expression. She gave a slow shake of her head. 'No, we'd never heard that.'

'These photographs you took of Greg – when were they taken?'

Another swiftly winged reply: 'A week ago last Sunday – 4th January, that would be. It was in the afternoon, before we went to the park.'

The Chief took her up on that at once: 'I spoke to you here a week ago about how you spent that Sunday – 4th January. You said nothing at all then of calling on Greg Mottram and taking photographs.'

She shrugged. 'I must have forgotten about it. I can't remember every little detail of every single day. Anyway, we did call in on Greg that Sunday afternoon, we called in to get at the boxes. And we did take the photographs. I'd brought my camera specially, to take Greg's photo. It was a nice, bright afternoon, so I took the photos outside. I intended giving Greg some of the prints but I hadn't got round to it – I didn't have them with me when we called on Saturday. I told Greg then that I'd got the photographs and they were very good; I'd bring them next time we called. He said he looked forward to seeing them, he couldn't remember the last time anyone had taken his photograph. He seemed really pleased.'

Avril had sat throughout like a wooden dummy. Sergeant Lambert studied her mask-like expression. If, indeed, Vicky did have something to do with the Beechcroft deaths, with Greg Mottram's death, then Avril could surely not be hoodwinked for ever; she must by this time be aware, in some degree, at least, of something untoward. Maybe she had the ability to tuck the suspicion – or knowledge – away in some corner of her brain where she needn't acknowledge its existence, needn't allow it to trouble her.

The Chief had no further questions for the girls. He let them go, accompanied by Mrs Byrne, but he asked Rhoda to remain; she made no demur. He had only one question for her: how had she spent last Saturday evening, from, say, five o'clock onwards?

She showed no surprise at the question and her answer came back pat: she had attended the fiftieth-anniversary party of one of the women's groups to which she belonged. The party was held at the headquarters branch, some twenty miles away. The local branch had laid on a coach for its members; she had travelled on the coach both ways, leaving Cannonbridge at 5.15. She had been in the company all evening of two women she was friendly with; it was shortly after ten when she got back to her bedsit. She gave the Chief the names and addresses of both women.

DC Slade called once again on Tom Guthrie early on Tuesday evening. Guthrie took a minute or two to answer the bell; he was upstairs in the bathroom, showering and shaving after his day's work at Beechcroft. He came barefooted down the stairs, clutching a towelling robe around himself, to stick his head round the front door.

'Oh, it's you!' he exclaimed at the sight of Slade. He drew back the door. 'Come in.' He took an old pair of slip-ons from the hall cupboard and thrust his feet into them.

Slade apologised for catching him at an inconvenient time and promised not to keep him many minutes. As soon as they were seated in the living-room he got straight to the point: 'Were you aware that Greg Mottram had an alcohol problem?'

'Yes, of course I was,' Guthrie replied at once. 'I was working at Beechcroft when Greg had his final bust-up with Philip Harvey; I heard all the ins and outs of it from an old Rivenoak mate of mine who was a fitter at Workwear.'

'In recent weeks, after Greg came back to Cannonbridge, did

169

you mention that fact – that Greg had a drink problem – to anyone? Anyone at all?'

Another swift reply. 'I mentioned it to Rhoda Jarrett. She asked me about him, after he called at Beechcroft. I thought if he was goint to keep turning up at the house, she'd better be put in the picture.'

'Did you mention it to Vicky?'

That halted him for a long moment during which he gave Slade a look full of thought. 'Yes, I did,' he replied at last. 'I don't know if her mother had said something to her about it or if she'd picked it up somewhere else but she did ask me about it one day, right out. I didn't go into any details and I didn't pass any judgements, I just told her yes, he did have a problem that I knew of, years ago; as for now, I couldn't say, and I left it at that. She never mentioned it again.'

'What about Owen Faulkner?'

This time there was no pause for thought. 'Yes, I did mention it to him. There was some talk about Owen helping Greg to find a job. Owen spoke to me about him, asked me what I knew about him. It was a straightforward question and I gave him a straightforward answer.'

At the end of the day the Chief sat contemplating the findings so far. The two medicine bottles in Greg's bathroom cabinet and the labels formerly attached to them were, it appeared, several years old; they had been wiped clean and bore no fingerprints whatever. Each held a few remaining drops of a sedative drug – the two drugs found in Greg's stomach, the same two drugs used at Beechcroft.

The whisky bottle on the table by Greg's chair had been similarly wiped and bore only Greg's fingerprints. The glass had not received the same thorough wiping but it too bore only Greg's prints. The dregs showed that the whisky had been laced in the bottle with the two drugs.

This clutch of facts spoke powerfully to the Chief against the theories of accident and suicide. And a man about to commit suicide does not sit down to write letters applying for jobs.

Which left him with murder. And with one basic question:

how did the murderer get Greg to sit down quietly in his armchair and literally drink himself to death?

'Simple enough,' Sergeant Lambert maintained. It looked to him as if Greg had been disturbed while he was writing his third letter at the side table. Disturbed, Lambert guessed, by a ring at the door. He went on to describe the scene as he saw it: the caller, known to Greg, admitted promptly. The caller soon producing from a holdall a half-bottle of whisky, wrapped in fancy gift paper, tied at the neck with a festive bow – in the waste basket in Greg's living-room they had found gift wrapping and decorative ribbon which by their size and the shape they still retained strongly suggested they had been used for this purpose.

The gift-wrapped bottle could have been presented to Greg as a thank-you gift in acknowledgement of some favour received, or given as a friendly seasonal present to enliven Greg's mood; or, maybe, displayed as a prize just won by the caller in some charity draw.

The bottle would then be opened – to drink to the New Year, to success in job-hunting, or some other toast. If it was Greg who did the opening and pouring, he could scrutinize the bottle as closely as he liked; it had in no way been tampered with. Nor did it matter what fingerprints that bottle acquired; it would never be examined by police; it would leave the flat with the murderer.

What happened next, Lambert guessed, was a simple switch. The killer had brought along in the holdall a second, identical half-bottle – bare of festive wrappings – from which a small quantity of whisky had been removed, the rest being laced with the two drugs. This was the bottle which would be left with Greg, the bottle he would sit down and finish as soon as he was alone again.

The actual switch could be carried out easily enough: getting Greg to leave the room for a moment on some errand or directing his attention briefly elsewhere; simpler still, if the caller had not come alone but with a companion who could distract Greg at the crucial moment. The killer must, of course, be careful never to touch the doped bottle with bare fingers; a handkerchief, discreetly held, would take care of that. The innocent bottle would be returned to the holdall, equally unobtrusively, to be dumped on the way home in some skip or bin.

A visit to the bathroom before leaving, to stow away in the cabinet the two old medicine bottles, each with its few drops still remaining. The bottles would heighten, by their presence, the suggestion of suicide – but they could not be left out anywhere in open view, where Greg might see them.

The killer must of course be aware that Greg had a drink problem, that he could be relied on to finish off the contents of the doped bottle.

One last point: if the caller had taken a drink with Greg, the glass used by the caller would also have to be removed; it could not remain behind to display its fingerprints.

'If your thoughts are turning to Vicky Jarrett,' Kelsey observed on a note of scepticism, 'it's not very likely that Vicky would pour out a couple of drinks and stand there drinking toasts with Greg.'

'No,' Lambert returned. 'But she could behave in a playful fashion. Open the bottle, pour him a drink, insist he drink it then and there – certainly not pouring one for herself. All done with merry smiles. He'd take the glass, partly to humour her, go along with the playful spirit; partly because he's pleased Vicky doesn't appear to know he has an alcohol problem – and partly, no doubt, because a glass of whisky would go down very well with him, then or at any other time.'

'And the motive for murdering Greg? Whoever that murderer might be.'

Lambert wasn't to be shaken. 'I'm certain in my own mind that whoever murdered Greg had murdered the Beechcroft pair. I believe Greg had stumbled on some fact about the Beechcroft deaths, without realizing the significance of that fact. The murderer knew that, and also knew that Greg was bound to realize the full significance of that fact before much longer. And in that same moment he would know, beyond doubt, who it was had killed Philip Harvey and Martine Faulkner. I'm sure Greg couldn't have cottoned on to all that yet or there's no way he would have accepted – and drunk – a gift of whisky from the hands of a person – or persons – he was certain had murdered the Beechcroft pair by lacing their liquor.'

*   *   *

The Chief slept heavily on Tuesday night, waking suddenly in the early morning with pictures flashing through his brain: the three children, Gregory, Veronica and Constance, in that long-ago garden. And Greg Mottram, as described by the St John's sexton, standing motionless, sunk in thought, before Veronica's grave.

He threw back the covers, thrust his feet into slippers and began to pace about the room, one thought uppermost now in his mind: was the frail, unquiet ghost of Veronica Harvey rising up now from her grave? Could the solution to the mystery of all three recent deaths lie with Veronica, in years gone by?

A determined attempt must now be made, starting first thing in the morning, to seek out Constance Whitlock. She might have kept in touch with Veronica over the years, she might be able to shed some light on shadowy areas of Veronica's past.

If she was still alive, still in this country.

Reporters from some of the national newspapers made an appearance for the first time at the press conference on Wednesday morning. The questions levelled at the Chief were a good deal sharper in tone. It was now decided that TV appeals for information relative to all three deaths would no longer be restricted to the regional slot but would go out over the national network.

DC Slade was dispatched to make a round of newspaper offices, local and county, evening and weekly, in a search for reports on the inquest, twelve years ago, on Veronica Isobel Harvey.

He found that the inquest had been well covered. Veronica had, it appeared, consumed a random – and lethal – assortment of capsules and tablets, cramming them into her mouth; some undissolved remains were found on her tongue and in her cheeks, when her body was discovered.

Slade made a note of the names of the doctor and nurse from Chelmwood Hospital who gave evidence at the inquest. It was some years now since the hospital had been closed and the site redeveloped but there were regional health authorities, there were doctors' associations, nurses' organizations; it should be

173

possible to locate both doctor and nurse without overmuch delay.

The funeral of Philip Royston Harvey took place at 10.30. In all the circumstances, Lorraine hadn't thought it fitting that he should be interred in the Clifford burial-ground in St John's churchyard, where Veronica lay beside her first husband; Philip, moreover, had never been a member of the St John congregation; he had never, indeed, been a church-goer at all.

There was another, smaller church, not far from Workwear, the church attended by most of the church-going section of the workforce. As head of Workwear, Philip had always supported this church's fund-raising and charitable activities; he had left a generous bequest to the church in his will. The entire workforce had made known their intention of proceeding in a body to the funeral, wherever it took place.

The vicar of this smaller church was aware of all these facts, aware, also, that the burial would attract considerable media attention, as well as a large crowd of onlookers, but he had willingly agreed, when approached jointly by Lorraine and Shannon, that the service should be held at his church and Philip should be buried in his churchyard.

A sizable police presence was evident throughout. Representatives attended from the many business and charitable organizations to which Philip had belonged. There was an impressive array of floral tributes, among them a wreath from the crofter cousin and two eye-catching bouquets, made up by Tom Guthrie, from flowers, foliage and blossoms from the garden and greenhouse at Beechcroft, one of the bouquets bearing a card with his own name and the other – fashioned by Tom at Vicky's fervent request and with the earnest assistance of both girls – carrying a card with the names of both Vicky and Avril.

Vicky had made it plain from the outset that she would be present at the funeral and that Avril would accompany her. They had no difficulty in getting permission from school for their absence and Vicky was prepared, if necessary, to face down her mother over the issue. But Rhoda, who had not the slightest wish to attend herself, made no attempt to prevent Vicky from

174

going, stipulating only that the two girls should go along with Tom Guthrie, who promised to keep an eye on them – and to make sure, as far as humanly possible, that Vicky was kept away from the TV cameras.

Lorraine, as chief mourner, was present from beginning to end, playing her inescapable part with dignity and grace, moving from group to group, speaking a necessary word here and there. Shannon, seeing beneath her unwavering surface composure to the distress and grief beneath, stationed himself close at hand, with Philip's secretary never more than a pace or two away, the two of them striving to spare Lorraine as much nervous strain as possible. When it was all over and the churchyard was emptying, she gave each of them in turn a look full of gratitude.

DC Slade had discovered by early afternoon that the doctor who had given evidence at the inquest on Veronica Harvey had returned to his native Australia when Chelmwood Hospital closed; he was now believed to be working in a psychiatric unit in Brisbane. Nurse Tennant, who had also given evidence, had, it seemed, gone on, after the closure of Chelmwood, to work for various nursing agencies, over a wide area. She was no longer on the books of any of these agencies, having passed retiring age a couple of years back. Slade rang the latest address he was given for her but it turned out to be a rented flat; the present occupant had no idea where the good lady might now be living.

Slade decided he had little option but to forget Nurse Tennant for the present and concentrate instead on trying to track down Veronica's childhood friend, Constance Whitlock. The only address he had for Constance was the one – twenty-five miles away – to which the Whitlock family had moved when they left Cannonbridge thirty-six years ago. It seemed a pretty long shot but he couldn't come up with any better plan. He got back into his car and set off to cover the twenty-five miles.

The inquest on Gregory Stephen Mottram took place at three o'clock; it was attended by a sizable body of reporters, local and national. As expected, the proceedings occupied little time, the inquest being merely opened and adjourned, the body released for burial. Lorraine spoke briefly afterwards to Chief Inspector Kelsey, to let him know she would be asking the firm of under-takers who had dealt with Philip Harvey's funeral to handle arrangements for Greg's burial; it would, of course, be on a far simpler scale. She would be calling at the undertakers right away and would let the Chief know the details as soon as possible.

The Chief didn't keep her talking but let her get off. She looked as if she had by no means fully recovered from the stresses of Philip Harvey's funeral, as if she could do with a good rest, instead of having to brace herself to cope with fresh demands.

Shortly after returning to the police station, the Chief learned that an officer had now spoken to the two women Rhoda Jarrett had named as her companions on Saturday evening. Their state-ments squared precisely with what Rhoda had told them. There could be not the slightest doubt: Rhoda was fully accounted for, from 5.15 onwards, on Saturday evening.

When DC Slade reached the house to which the Whitlock family had moved from Cannonbridge, he was told by the present owners that they had bought the property from the Whitlocks thirty years ago. After a certain amount of searching through bureau drawers and looking through old address books, they were able to tell Slade exactly where the Whitlocks had gone – to an address in a town another forty miles away.

Slade was lucky enough on his first phone call to catch the present resident at that address, who told him the Whitlocks had moved on eighteen years ago. It took three further phone calls to learn that Mrs Whitlock had died a few years back, Mr Whitlock was now living with his married son, some sixty miles further on, and Constance Whitlock – still single – held the post of housemistress in a girls' boarding-school – a somewhat select establishment by the sound of it – a mere fifteen miles away.

Slade's final phone call – to the boarding-school – revealed that term was not officially due to begin until Monday, but the girls would be returning and settling in from Friday morning onwards. Miss Whitlock was expected back tomorrow afternoon. Slade made an appointment to see her at five o'clock.

The passing bell marking the funeral of Martine Emily Faulkner began its sonorous tolling across the Northwick rooftops shortly after 9.15 on Thursday morning. This relatively early hour didn't deter the media contingent, who turned up in force, nor did it put off Bertha Pearce's relatives, friends and in-laws, or the young women Martine had grown up with, but it did succeed, as Owen Faulkner had foreseen, in greatly reducing the numbers of idle gawpers willing to leave their warm beds on this biting January morning, to get themselves over to Northwick.

Vicky Jarrett had made a determined bid to attend the funeral, taking Avril with her, but Rhoda had put her foot down and expressly forbidden any such attempt. Mrs Byrne had strongly sided with Rhoda and Vicky had, in the end, been forced to submit.

Bertha Pearce had assumed the role of chief mourner and Owen Faulkner had shown no wish to displace her. At no time did he do or say anything to draw the slightest attention to himself but stood silent and apart, his head lowered, throughout the service. Harriet Russell did not attend; she had stayed behind in Rivenoak, looking after Jamie.

Bertha had originally taken it for granted that she would bear all the funeral expenses but Owen wouldn't hear of it; Martine was still his wife at the time of her death. Nor could he allow Bertha to saddle herself with a bill she must struggle to pay. Bertha had given way at last, not for either of these reasons but for a totally different, finally compelling reason of her own. She was a fair-minded woman and had lived long enough to believe she could recognize true and faithful love when she came across it. Martine may have chosen Philip Harvey in the closing weeks of her life, but Owen Faulkner had dearly loved her since the day they met. It was Owen who had placed the rings on her finger; he had been unfailingly good to her.

Constance Whitlock turned out to be a tall, thin woman with an air of habitual calm. She received DC Slade in the small flat allotted to her in the school buildings. She was curious to know why a police office should have driven over from Cannonbridge – the town she had left thirty-six years ago – expressly to see her. Slade didn't go into details, merely telling her it might be helpful in an investigation currently going forward to have a little more knowledge of some aspects of the life of Veronica Harvey, whom Constance had known in childhood as Veronica Mottram and, possibly, during the period of Veronica's first marriage, as Veronica Clifford.

Constance digested this in silence for several moments before declaring her readiness to answer any questions to the best of her ability. It soon became abundantly clear to Slade that Constance had no knowledge whatever of the recent happenings at Beechcroft. She had, it seemed, spent the Christmas holidays in Switzerland and had arrived back in England only at lunchtime today.

She did know that Veronica had died by her own hand twelve years ago, while a patient in Chelmwood Hospital; she had discovered this painful fact only two years later when she had attended the funeral of her last surviving Cannonbridge relative – Constance had been working abroad in various countries, teaching English in language schools, for some years by then and had long been out of touch with Veronica.

When was the last time she had seen Veronica?

She had called twice at Beechcroft during Veronica's first marriage: once when Lorraine was four years old, and again, two years later. Veronica had seemed well and happy on both occasions; she had plainly been pleased to see Constance. Lorraine had struck her as a friendly, uncomplicated little girl, cheerful and active. Veronica told Constance on both occasions that she was very interested to hear about her work, her travels; she must be sure to drop in again, whenever she found herself back in Cannonbridge.

But that, as things turned out, was not to be for another four years – Constance had stayed abroad for a longer spell than usual. It was only some months after her return to England that she heard for the first time of John Clifford's death and Veronica's remarriage.

When she did go back to Cannonbridge, some months later still, she was dismayed to hear that Veronica had suffered more than one breakdown since Clifford's death and had, on occasion, been admitted to Chelmwood for treatment. She decided that on her next family visit to Cannonbridge she would make a casual, unannounced call at Beechcroft, hoping to find by that time that Veronica was fully recovered, happy in her second marriage, and that Lorraine was settled and content in the new domestic situation.

Constance's next visit to Cannonbridge chanced to coincide with the half-term school holiday and she found both Veronica and Lorraine at home when she called. Lorraine was then ten years old; she told Constance she could remember her from her last visit, four years earlier, and appeared pleased to see her again. However, Lorraine was no longer a merry little child, busy about a dozen things, but a quiet schoolgirl, with a self-effacing manner and a watchful eye. Veronica looked thin and pale, far from well. Her manner was nervy; she appeared to pay little attention to Lorraine; she seemed, in fact, almost unaware of her daughter's presence. She expressed little surprise or pleasure at seeing Constance again and showed no desire to hear how she had spent the last four years.

Constance felt there was little point in prolonging the visit and rose to leave, a good deal earlier than she had planned. As she got to her feet she heard a car draw up outside. Veronica immediately sat up in her chair; her expression lightened. Lorraine displayed no reaction.

Philip Harvey came straight in and without so much as a glance at Constance went at once to Veronica's side. He reached down and took her hand with an air markedly protective and reassuring. Veronica looked pleased and relieved at his presence, gazing frequently up at him. He didn't leave her side.

Veronica made sketchy introductions and Constance told Philip she had been on the point of leaving when he arrived. Philip was polite but cool; he didn't say he was glad she'd called, didn't try to persuade her to stay a little longer, didn't offer her any refreshment. Neither he nor Veronica asked her to call again. Neither of them saw her out; they remained where they were.

Lorraine, by contrast, had behaved with exemplary good manners, holding the door open for Constance, walking out with her to her car, saying it had been a pleasant surprise to see her again, hoping it wouldn't be another four years before her next visit. But Constance had decided, as she drove away, that this would be her last call at Beechcroft.

And was that, in fact, the last time Constance had seen any of the trio?

She shook her head. 'As I told you just now, it wasn't until ten years ago that I discovered Veronica had taken her own life two years earlier and that Philip Harvey had become the owner of Workwear.

'It was another two years after that – eight years ago now – that I had a surprise visit one day: Lorraine turned up on my doorstep, out of the blue. I'd come back to work in England for good, only a few months before; she must have gone to considerable trouble to locate me. She was sixteen years old by then but I recognized her the instant I opened the door, she was so like Veronica.

'She gave me such an uncertain, searching look, as if she was wondering what sort of reception she'd get, turning up like that, without warning. I made her very welcome; I knew as soon as I laid eyes on her that she'd come to unburden herself about something. She didn't need a lot of encouragement to pour it all out.

'She was still at school, hoping to go on to further education; she talked of going in for social work of some kind. She was still living at Beechcroft, under the care of her stepfather, he hadn't remarried. There was a housekeeper who looked after everything very well, treated her very pleasantly; the housekeeper had a little girl Lorraine liked. Philip took thought for her well-being in every way, she had no complaint to make against him.

'But I did notice a certain deliberation, a wariness, a lack of spontaneity when she spoke of him. I encouraged her to go on talking and after a few stops and starts she did begin to open up. She said she'd never really understood about her mother's illness, how it had arisen, why it had kept recurring, why her mother had been treated in that particular way, why she had never been allowed to visit her mother in Chelmwood, never been allowed to write to her or phone her there, why her mother had never talked to her afterwards about these spells in hospital.

And she'd never really understood why the truth about her mother's death had been kept from her, why she was never told it was suicide, why she hadn't been allowed to know about the inquest, the findings, the reports in the newspapers. She'd only found all this out bit by bit from chance remarks from other folk.

'She'd never felt able to raise the matter with Philip. For one thing, she didn't want to stir up all the old grief and pain, bring it all back to him, and for another, he'd never raised the matter with her himself, she was sure he wouldn't welcome any attempt on her part to speak about it. She thought about it constantly, constructed various scenarios that could explain what had happened. When she was fifteen she made up her mind she was going to do something about it. She went to newspaper offices and looked up the old reports of the inquest; she found out at long last the truth about that. She still couldn't bring herself to speak of it to Philip. Then she remembered me. She wondered what I knew of it all – if, indeed, I knew anything. If I did know, what I had made of it. So she made up her mind to set about finding me.'

When Lorraine had reached the end of her outpouring, Constance had suggested that she should, indeed, attempt to talk it all over thoroughly with her stepfather and then try to put it behind her and get on with her life, concentrate on the present and the future, not the past. Lorraine had listened intently but made no direct response. She had left shortly afterwards, thanking Constance courteously for her time and patience. On the doorstep she had suddenly announced that she intended going over to Chelmwood. She had read in the papers that the hospital was in the process of being run down but she was sure there would still be some members of staff there, medical and nursing, who had been there in her mother's time.

Constance had no idea if Lorraine had indeed gone to Chelmwood or, if she had gone, how she had fared; she had never heard from Lorraine again. 'Of course, I did move on, from time to time,' Constance added. 'Lorraine may have made attempts to contact me again but had no success. I tried to tell myself she had probably gone to Chelmwood and what she was told there had set her mind at rest.'

*   *   *

In the early hours of Friday morning DC Slade woke with dramatic suddenness, shooting upright in his bed, with a face and a name flashing in the forefront of his brain: the face and name of an old Chelmwood nurse, long retired, he had come across a few years back when he was making inquiries for a case he was on, among the staff and residents of a retirement home six or seven miles from Cannonbridge; he had found the lady intelligent and helpful.

He made some rapid mental calculations. She would very likely be in her mid-eighties now – if still alive. It was hardly likely that she had known anything of Veronica; she would have retired long before Veronica ever set foot in Chelmwood. But she could well have been at Chelmwood in Nurse Tennant's time. There was a very slender possibility that she might know where Nurse Tennant could now be found. If at all possible he must make time this morning to drive over to the retirement home.

Lorraine turned her car into the Beechcroft driveway at the time she guessed Tom Guthrie could be taking his morning break. And she duly found him in his shed, drinking his hot Bovril and listening to the radio. He looked pleased to see her. Before she had time to say why she had called, he asked if she had gone to Martine Faulkner's funeral yesterday.

She shook her head, a little surprised at the question.

'I didn't think it right to go myself, taking everything into account,' he told her. 'But I couldn't help thinking of Martine yesterday, when the time came. Such a beautiful young woman, all her life before her. And she was so happy, that Saturday morning at Beechcroft, so friendly and pleasant.' He shook his head. 'And then yesterday, thinking of her going down into the cold ground.' He shook his head again. 'I can well see how Philip Harvey fell for her.' Another pause. 'It seems he left me some money in his will – a very generous sum, to my way of thinking. I certainly never expected it. The solicitor told me he put in his will: "for his long, faithful and devoted service."' He looked on the verge of tears. 'You can't approve of what the two of them did, but you can sort of understand it.'

But it wasn't Martine Faulkner's funeral Lorraine had come to

182

talk about, it was Greg Mottram's. 'It's up to me to make all the arrangements,' she told Guthrie. 'You knew Greg, you knew him years ago, I wanted to ask your opinion about it. I'm arranging the funeral for a week today, Friday 23rd. I very much hope you'll come.'

'I'll be sure to come,' Guthrie replied at once. 'And if there's anything I can do to help, you've only to ask.'

'I really appreciate that,' she responded warmly. 'Would you make me one of your flower and leaf arrangements? I thought the ones you made for Philip's funeral were really beautiful.'

He looked pleased. 'Of course I'll do that. It would be a pleasure.'

'Greg would have liked that,' she said. 'I'm going along to talk to Rhoda now, I'm hoping she'll come to the funeral. And Vicky and Avril, they were always very friendly to Greg, he really liked them, Vicky always cheered him up. I'm sure they'll be able to get off school. And I've spoken to Shannon. He says there are two or three men who worked with Greg way back, in my father's day, he thinks they might like to attend. And I'll talk to the supermarket manager, see if they might send someone from the office.'

'The supermarket might think of sending a wreath,' Guthrie suggested. 'And what about the tenants of the other flats? One of them might like to attend.'

'I'd forgotten them,' she acknowledged.

'I'll see to it if you like,' he offered.

'Oh, would you? I'd be very grateful.'

'I'll see to it today,' he confirmed. 'I'll let you know what they say. They might like to club together for a wreath.' He asked where Greg was to be buried.

'That's another thing I wanted to talk to you about. I've got to decide that pretty well right away. Greg was never a church-goer.'

Guthrie could see little difficulty there. 'He can be buried in the municipal cemetery, surely?'

'Yes, I'm sure he could. But I know where he'd have wished to be buried – and where I'd like him to be buried: in St John's churchyard, in some quiet spot under the trees, not too far from my mother's grave.'

'Then if I were you,' Guthrie advised, 'I'd have a word with the vicar. He'll find Greg some little corner somewhere.' He gave a little smile. 'You could try making a special donation to the church, that never hurts.'

She smiled back at him. 'I'll do that, I'll see about it right away. And I mustn't forget to call in at the police station when everything's arranged, I'll have to give them all the details.'

The afternoon was well advanced before DC Slade managed at last to get away and head for the retirement home.

Yes, he was told, the lady he so clearly recalled was still alive, still a resident in the home, still reasonably active, still interested in life.

She was delighted to see DC Slade again, delighted to be able to tell him she had indeed known Nurse Tennant, had worked with her and liked her, had, indeed, had the highest regard for her.

And yes, she could give him Nurse Tennant's present address. She had received a Christmas card and a letter from her, a few weeks ago, as she did every year. She looked out the letter and gave Slade the address, in a town some forty miles to the north.

He set off at once but found himself caught up in the beginnings of the Friday evening rush. It was close to 6.30 before he located the house, on the outskirts of a market town. He left his car by the gate, hastened up the path and rang the bell, once, twice, three times, with no response. But he was certain there was someone in. There was a light on upstairs and he could hear a radio. He rang again, keeping his finger on the bell, and this time was rewarded by a glimpse of a face at a front-bedroom window.

He stepped back and looked up. A young woman, her head at an angle, squinted briefly down at him. He just had time to raise a hand in a gesture of appeal before the face vanished. He heard a scurry of movement, the door was flung open and he found himself confronting a young woman wrapped in a bath towel, her face flushed and shining.

'Yes?' she barked. 'I haven't time to stop.' She gave a quick, despairing groan. 'What do you want?'

He identified himself swiftly, asked if he could speak to Nurse Tennant on a matter of some urgency.

She was already closing the door. 'She isn't here. She won't be back before eleven.' He held up a hand to halt the door.

'Can you give her a message?'

'I'm off out myself.' She gave another groan. 'I'm on duty in twenty-five minutes, I work at a care home. I won't be back myself till six in the morning.' She began to push the door again. 'You'll have to excuse me, I've a bus to catch.'

'I'll write a note,' he said rapidly. 'I'll have it ready before you leave.'

'She's leaving here at eight in the morning,' she warned. 'She'll be away a fortnight.'

'Then I'll be back here at seven sharp in the morning,' Slade returned. 'I can get a word with her before she goes.'

She gave the matter a flick of thought. 'Yes, that should be OK. She's always up at the crack of dawn. Put it all down in your note.' She banged the door shut and flew back upstairs.

He ran to his car and penned a quick note of explanation, folded it and wrote Nurse Tennant's name on it. He was stationed once more at the front door when it was again snatched open and the missive whipped from his outstretched fingers. 'Put it where she's bound to see it,' he called after her as she vanished upstairs.

A minute later she was down again. 'I've stuck it in her dressing-table mirror. She can't avoid seeing it.' She banged the door shut behind her.

'I'll give you a lift,' he offered. 'Just direct me.'

Her face broke into a broad grin. She leaned forward and planted a smacking kiss on his cheek. 'You're a cracker!' she cried. 'Let's go!'

It had been a slogging, frustrating day for Chief Inspector Kelsey. It was turned nine when he finally let himself into the flat where he lived alone; he had been married once, divorced years ago when his wife found she could no longer stomach the demands of the force; there were no children.

He stood leaning back against the door with his eyes closed, utterly weary and by no means in the best of tempers. He had reached the stage he so often reached in a difficult, protracted investigation when his grip on the discipline he endeavoured to apply to his personal daily routine began inexorably to slacken. Just getting through each taxing day to its conclusion became the only goal of any significance; everything else, little by little, ceased to matter. He worked late, slept badly, lived on scratch meals and snacks. He wrote no personal letters, returned no personal phone calls, remembered no birthdays, forgot there was such a thing as a social life, entertainments, hobbies, relaxation.

When he at last roused himself sufficiently to go along to the kitchen he made himself, careless of the hour, a quantity of powerfully strong coffee. He knew it would interfere disastrously with the sleep he so badly needed but he drank it down all the same, scalding hot, briefly reviving. All at once he felt ravenously hungry. His food supplies had reached the stage – supermarket shopping being currently out of the question – where fresh food was but a memory, his stock of frozen food was reduced to the last couple of packets, and the serried ranks of tins in his larder, those final, indispensable items, were all that remained of the mountains of provisions he always took care to lay in, between cases.

He ran a hand along the larder shelves, selected three tins, whipped them open – still gulping down his coffee – and inside a few minutes had a fearsome panful of stew, from the tipped-in contents, bubbling away on the stove. He found the heel of a stale loaf, wolfed down a bowlful of his stew, topped with his iron-hard crusts, sent down another bowlful after it, followed by a third. And all the time a stifled voice in his brain was striving its pathetic best to issue warnings: You'll suffer for this ... Remember last time ...

Of course he couldn't sleep; how could he expect to? There was tossing and turning, there was clutching the midriff, there was pacing about, there were bitter regrets, self-castigation, rummaging about for every remedy he could lay hands on: aspirin

186

tablets, bicarbonate of soda, patent cure-alls. In the end there was some sort of unrefreshing extinction, scarcely to be dignified with the name of sleep, punctuated by dreams filled with foreboding.

At five minutes to seven next morning DC Slade turned his car round the final corner and saw lights shining out, upstairs and down, from Nurse Tennant's house. This time his ring was answered almost instantly by a lively-looking, briskly-mannered woman, slim and trim with sparkling blue eyes, beautifully arranged snow-white hair, an air of massive competence.

She welcomed him in at once, whisked about to provide him with tea and toast. Yes, she had got his note; she was intrigued to know why he had thought it worthwhile to drive over twice to talk to her. He embarked at once on a rapid explanation of his mission; he was very grateful to her for sparing him her time.

She immediately recalled Veronica's name and the broad outline of her case; the dreadful circumstances of her death ensured that. As they talked, further details returned to her. She had been involved in Veronica's case all along, from the time of Veronica's initial breakdown, after the death of her first husband.

One day, four years after Veronica's death, her daughter – sixteen years old, by then – had turned up at Chelmwood, asking to see her; she had also asked to see the doctor who had given evidence at the inquest on her mother but he was no longer working at Chelmwood.

Lorraine had asked Nurse Tennant a great many questions about her mother's illness and treatment; her attitude, from the start, was clearly slanted in one direction: towards laying all blame for her mother's death at the door of her stepfather. She had obviously been brooding about her mother's illness and death for years without knowing the facts. She maintained that her stepfather had married her mother with only one end in mind: to foster the nervous trouble that had afflicted her after the death of her first husband, to encourage her along the path to suicide and so inherit everything Veronica possessed. Lorraine believed he had also encouraged Veronica to hoard her pills, maybe even supplying her with those she had used to kill herself.

'I remember how vehement she was about her stepfather,' Nurse Tennant said. 'She told me she hated him, had hated him all along, though she had always taken the greatest care never to let him – or her mother – know it.

'I was totally convinced that all these suspicions of her stepfather were outright rubbish. I had seen how devoted he was to his wife, how protective of her. And I knew for certain he'd talked her out of suicidal notions on more than one occasion, as I'd done myself. I'm absolutely positive, beyond any shadow of doubt, that he wasn't responsible in even the slightest degree for his wife's death.

'Lorraine came across to me as highly obsessive, not open to reason in that one area. Her mother's illness and death had come at a formative stage in Lorraine's life. All her theories were based on notions she'd formed as a child. She'd never grown out of those notions the way she should have done. In that respect, she was still operating, at sixteen years old, on the beliefs of a little girl.'

She fell silent for a moment. 'I did wonder if she could have inherited some of her mother's instability.' She fell silent again. 'I wondered if she'd grow out of her obsession in time or if she'd settle into it more deeply as the years went by, if she'd let it rule her life in the end.'

When Slade drove away he pulled in at the first lay-by and sat pondering long and hard. Lorraine had let it be known that she had spent the evening of Friday, 2nd January at Jessie Dugdale's cottage; she'd gone there straight from work and had stayed there until the Sunday evening, looking after Jessie; the only time she had left the cottage during the weekend had been on the Saturday morning, when she had driven into Bowbrook village to do some essential shopping; she had been absent less than three-quarters of an hour.

And she had later let it be known that she had become concerned enough about Jessie's health to move into her cottage on the evening of Friday, 9th January – one week later – intending to remain there until Jessie was better. This meant that she was at the cottage on Saturday, when Greg Mottram drank his

188

laced whisky. Again, she said she had remained in the cottage all day Saturday, except for a brief shopping excursion into the village, during the morning. He recollected the clear and detailed picture she had given them of how devotedly busy she had been over both those weekends, cleaning, cooking, washing, ironing, caring for Jessie. But we never checked one single aspect of those statements, Slade reflected; we swallowed everything she told us, hook, line and sinker.

He pulled himself up sharply; his thoughts were beginning to run away with him. Lorraine could have been speaking the unvarnished truth.

That's easily settled, he told himself a moment later. I can check her statements now. I can call in at Bowbrook on the way back to Cannonbridge, have a word with Jessie Dugdale, see what she remembers of that Friday evening and that Saturday evening, one week later, clear the matter up, one way or the other.

He looked at his watch. By the time he got to Bowbrook it would be a more civilized hour, not too early to go calling on an elderly lady, no longer in the best of health.

Chief Inspector Kelsey was feeling like death warmed up. In spite of a blinding headache he had managed to shave and shower, put on a clean shirt and dress himself. He took neither food nor drink; the thought of either broke him out in a cold sweat. The pain in his middle left him in no doubt about his current condition: his mad folly of yesterday evening had provoked a savage flare-up of his old trouble.

He peered at his face in the glass. Apart from resembling someone dug up after a week underground, he didn't look too bad. He straightened himself, squared his shoulders, took several deep breaths. He would adopt a positive attitude, get along to the station without delay, face the day head-on. Nothing like a spot of application to the task in hand to take your mind off yourself. With luck he should be able to work it off inside a couple of hours.

A downstairs light showed in Jessie Dugdale's cottage and

Lorraine's blue Peugeot was stationed on the hard-standing at the side, as Slade walked up the path to set his finger on the bell. When Lorraine answered the door she didn't appear at all surprised to see him. She didn't look her usual on-the-ball self but wore a weary, dispirited air.

He apologized for disturbing her. 'Would it be possible for me to have a word with Miss Dugdale?' he asked. 'I know she isn't well but I won't keep her many minutes.'

She gazed back at him, her face twisted in distress. She clasped her hands tightly. 'I'm sorry,' she answered in a trembling voice. 'I'm afraid it's not possible.'

'I won't stay long,' he promised. 'I'll do my best not to tire her.'

She lowered her head. 'Jessie isn't here any more.' Tears began to roll down her cheeks. She slipped a handkerchief from a pocket and made unobtrusive little dabs at her eyes. 'I'm afraid she's dead. She's been taken to the funeral parlour.'

20

Slade stood dumbfounded. 'I'm very sorry to hear that,' he managed at last. 'When did she die?'

'Sometime during Tuesday night,' she replied shakily. 'I saw she'd gone, the moment I went into her room on Wednesday morning, I could see she'd been dead some time.'

'I'm so very sorry,' he said again. 'May I come in?'

She held the door back for him. 'It was a terrible shock,' she said in an unsteady tone. 'I was so sure she was getting better.' She squared her shoulders, as if summoning up reserves of strength. 'Come along to the kitchen,' she invited on a deliberately lighter note. 'I'll make some coffee.' She managed to maintain the same easier voice for the remainder of his brief stay. 'I'm going over to Beechcroft tomorrow morning,' she told him as she handed him his coffee. 'I want to make a bouquet for Jessie, like the one Tom Guthrie made for Vicky and Avril, for Philip's funeral. Jessie loved Beechcroft,' she went on. 'I shall use some

Christmas roses, winter jasmine, some sprays from the other flowering shrubs, and evergreen leaves. And I'm going to put in some foliage and winter blossom from her little garden here.' She drew a quivering sigh. 'It helps to keep occupied.'

As they drank their coffee he asked a few casual-seeming questions and learned in this way the names of Jessie's doctor and solicitor – together with the location of the house where Lorraine had made her final call on the afternoon of Friday, 2nd January. He also learned that Jessie's funeral would take place at Bowbrook church, at 10 a.m. on Monday.

When he stood up to leave, he couldn't help observing: 'Jessie died three days ago. In that time you had some contact with the police but you made no mention of Jessie's death.'

Lorraine looked taken aback. 'It never occurred to me to mention it. What had it to do with the police?' He could offer no reply.

He drove only a matter of yards before pulling up near the larger dwelling that stood alone by the turning into the main road. He got out of his car and approached the gate. A name plate informed him that the house was called Willowfield. He walked up the path and rang the bell.

No one answered his ring. There was no sign of life anywhere; the dwelling looked shut up. He got back into his car and drove on, halting at the first lay-by.

Every impulse was urging him to call, and to call without delay, on Jessie's doctor, on her solicitor and at the address where Lorraine had made her final visit that Friday afternoon. He very much wanted to know exactly when Lorraine had finished that call, exactly when she had arrived at Jessie's cottage and if she had, in fact, left the cottage at all during the evening and night of that Friday.

He had no obvious justification for making any of these calls, not the slightest shred of anything that could be called evidence, only an ill-defined sense of suspicion. But from that cloudy unease two facts stood sharply out: Lorraine hadn't seen fit to make any mention to the police of Jessie's death; and shortly after ten o'clock on Monday morning Jessie's remains would be consigned to the earth of Bowbrook churchyard.

Leaving aside the doctor and solicitor, who might prove tricky to deal with, he could at least call at the house where Lorraine had made her final call that Friday; there could surely be no harm in that.

But caution reared its head, caution and common sense. Better get back to Cannonbridge; stick to the normal procedures; speak to the Chief, tell him what he had learned, what he now suspected, what he had in mind; leave it all up to the Chief. After a brief battle, common sense and caution won the day. He switched on his engine and pulled out of the lay-by, heading for Cannonbridge.

At that precise moment, over in the Cannonbridge police station, Chief Inspector Kelsey was collapsing limply into the chair at his desk. He hadn't been able to work it off; in fact, he hadn't really managed to do any work at all, not anything any serious-minded person could dignify with the name of work. He remained for some little time leaning forward, elbows on his desk, his head propped on his hands, his eyes closed. Nothing for it, he thought, I'm doing no good whatever here, I'll have to give in.

He would have a word with the doctor. Not your everyday civilian GP but the police doctor, a man he had known for years, a man who understood life in the force, its stresses and strains, unceasing demands. He'd get the doctor to give him something to get him through the rest of the day, then he'd get off for an early night, with another something from the doctor to guarantee a long, sound sleep. He'd be in considerably better shape by tomorrow morning, able to approach the day's work in something like a normal state of health.

With his decision taken, he began to feel very slightly more cheerful, marginally less like a dying duck in a thunderstorm. He raised his head, sat up, straightened himself, stretched out a hand and picked up the phone.

So it wasn't, in the end, the Chief that DC Slade got to see, but DS Lambert, who informed him that the Chief had just now been ordered home for a rest by the doctor and wouldn't be back till Monday morning.

Slade took himself off at once to the canteen where he sat alone, pondering as he ate. He had three options: speak to DS Lambert and take his instructions; dismiss the entire matter from his mind; or he could act on his own initiative.

By the time he rose from the table his mind was made up. He went swiftly out to his car, bound for Bowbrook and Wychford. He would make his calls, all three of them. His first call would be on Mr Ingram, the old man Lorraine said she had called on at ten minutes to five that Friday afternoon. She said she had left Mr Ingram at 5.15, had driven straight to her flat, picked up the bag she had previously packed and at once driven out to Bowbrook, arriving at Jessie's cottage at around 5.50.

Ingram's address took him to a mid-terrace house in a Wychford suburb. He spoke to the woman who answered his ring. It seemed she lived in the house next door; her name was Mrs Unsworth.

Mr Ingram, it appeared, was an Alzheimer sufferer, in a stage now where it was inadvisable to leave him on his own, day or night, but not yet arrived at a time when there would be no alternative to putting him into full-time residential care.

His family maintained a roster whereby every son, daughter, relative by marriage, old friend, former workmate and neighbour willing to assist, co-operated in keeping him safe and contented in his own home; they had some additional help from local volunteer groups from church and charitable organizations; Mrs Unsworth came in three mornings a week.

Slade asked her if she knew if anyone had called at the house in the late afternoon of Friday, 2nd January but she shook her head at once. She never came in during an afternoon and never at any time on a Friday.

Did she know who would have been in the house, keeping an eye on Mr Ingram, at around five o'clock that Friday? But again she shook her head; she had no idea.

Could he have a word with Mr Ingram? See if the old gentleman had any recollection of that afternoon?

She pulled down the corners of her mouth. 'You're welcome to try, but I'm afraid you'll be wasting your time. He won't pay you any attention. He was pretty noisy, quite aggressive sometimes, before they put him on the medication he has now – he's as quiet as a lamb these days.' She shook her head sadly. 'He was as nice a chap as you could wish to meet, before he got like this. Still, it's much better all round, the way he is now. He hardly ever says a word and when he does it doesn't make much sense, but he seems content enough. Anyway, come along and see for yourself. He's in the front room, watching TV, he likes that.'

She led the way along the passage, into the room where Mr Ingram, a sprucely turned out old man, not far off eighty, sat with his eyes fixed on the TV screen, the fingers of his right hand ceaselessly tapping out a staccato rhythm on the wooden armrest of his easy chair. He didn't look round as they entered, never gave them a glance.

Mrs Unsworth introduced Slade and tried to give Ingram some brief and simple indication of what it was Slade wished to inquire about. Ingram paid her no attention whatever but continued staring and tapping. After some minutes of this and three or four more attempts, on the part of Slade as well as of Mrs Unsworth, Slade gave up.

Outside in his car again, he sat leaning back, his eyes closed. What next? Admit defeat? Clear off, back to Cannonbridge, with his tail between his legs?

Or see if he could get a word with Jessie's doctor? Or Jessie's solicitor?

He set his jaw, opened his eyes and sat up. He was far from ready to admit defeat.

So, the doctor's it was.

An hour and a half later saw Slade back in his car again, returning at last to Cannonbridge. He had managed to get a moment with both doctor and solicitor, two extremely busy men, the doctor rushed off his feet, coping with the flu outbreak, the solicitor with a list of appointments ahead of him. Both exhibited the same instant response to Slade's opening query about the death of Jessie Dugdale: a surprised jerk of the head, a sharp upward glance. Why were the police showing interest?

Slade had had his answer ready, the vague, all-embracing response he regularly made use of: the mention of routine inquiries that might just conceivably have some marginal bearing on a case – not specified – currently under investigation.

As he drove, Slade chewed over what he had learned in the course of his two brief visits: the doctor had not been at all surprised to be informed by Lorraine Clifford, early on Wednesday morning, that Jessie had died in the night, nor had he had the slightest hesitation in issuing the death certificate.

According to her solicitor, Jessie had made a will two years ago; short and uncomplicated. She had little to leave; Lorraine was named as sole executrix. There were a few modest bequests to charities and to the Bowbrook church; small items of furniture, ornaments, pictures – of no great value – to go to named individuals. The rest of her savings and all other possessions to go to her dear friend, Lorraine Clifford, who was also her residuary legatee.

DC Slade could have taken the whole of Sunday as a rest day but a little after one o'clock he found himself getting into his car and driving to Bowbrook, arriving at the turning for Jessie's cottage at what he hoped might be a suitable time to find the occupant of Willowfield at home.

But he was again out of luck. His ring brought no one to the door; the house still wore its empty look.

He got back into his car. Nothing for it but to go back to Cannonbridge. But his wheels had something else in mind, taking him off, a minute or two later, in the opposite direction, bearing him inexorably into the village, halting him in the carpark – almost empty – of one of the two pubs in the village. Small and old-fashioned, this one, little different now from what it had been fifty years ago, unlike its larger, much more up-to-date, livelier and a good deal more prosperous rival, situated bang in the centre of the village.

The publican, a pleasant-looking widow in her fifties, was polishing glasses behind the bar; she gave Slade a warmly welcoming smile. A few old men sat over their pints at corner tables, reading their newspapers, exchanging occasional comments; they paid Slade no attention beyond a passing glance.

He ordered an alcohol-free lager and a sandwich. He sat at the bar, talking to the publican, who seemed happy to have someone to chat to. 'You're not from round here?' she hazarded. He shook his head. 'I'm trying to contact whoever it is that lives in a house called Willowfield.' He indicated the location. 'I've called a couple of times but I can't seem to find anyone at home.'

'It's Miss Agnew lives there,' the publican returned at once. 'Everyone in the village knows Miss Agnew, she does no end of good work round here. She lives there by herself now, since her father died. She's away at present, staying with friends, she went off on Thursday afternoon. She'll be back late this evening. She definitely intends going to Jessie Dugdale's funeral, she told me so herself. Very well liked in the village, Jessie was, there'll be a good turn-out tomorrow.'

Slade asked if Jessie had been a customer of hers.

She smiled as she shook her head. 'Not only never a customer, she never set foot in this place. She always made out she was a teetotaller, like her parents.' She smiled again. 'But I do know she took a drop on the quiet.' She gave a confidential wink, able to speak with the freedom of one talking to a total stranger, never likely to be encountered again. 'I have a sister-in-law used to work on the drinks counter of a Wychford supermarket, years ago. She told me Jessie used to stop by regularly for a bottle – Jessie was working in Wychford in those days.'

When Slade left the pub he sat in his car, penning a note for Miss Agnew. On his way back to Cannonbridge he halted by Willowfield and slipped the note in through the letterbox.

It was almost midnight when Miss Agnew returned to Bowbrook and let herself into Willowfield. A vigorous woman in her sixties, a face of character and decision; somewhat weary now, after her journey, her spirits a little lowered at the prospect of the funeral in the morning.

She set down her travel bag and scooped up the post from behind the door. She didn't permit herself so much as a glance at it, in case she came across something that might give rise to thoughts that could prevent her falling into the deep sleep she felt more than ready for. She laid the mail down on the hall table;

196

tomorrow would be time enough to give attention to whatever it might contain.

She slept as soundly as she had hoped. She woke early, refreshed and invigorated, feeling more cheerful than she had expected, ready to face the sorrows of the morning. She put on her dressing-gown and slippers, to go down to the kitchen to make herself a pot of tea. The morning was almost silent: fitful country sounds, the intermittent passage of early traffic. She switched on the radio; a cheerful voice greeted her, played her some lively music, told her the latest news. As she took milk from the fridge she remembered her mail and went along to the hall. She picked it up from the table and returned to the kitchen, glancing through it as she went. Nothing very exciting: a couple of bills, a receipt, the usual junk mail.

And DC Slade's note: no envelope, just a sheet of paper, folded in four, bearing her name, in a hand she didn't recognize.

She unfolded it, skimmed through it. She switched off the radio, poured herself a cup of tea. She sat down and began to drink her tea, reading through the note again, slowly, this time, considering its contents, the possible implications. She sat thinking, frowning, drinking her tea. Ring me at any time, DC Slade had urged; day or night. He had given her two phone numbers: at work, and at home, in his flat.

She looked up at the clock, still pondering, then she suddenly drained her cup, stood up and went rapidly along to the sitting-room. She sat down by the phone, lifted the receiver and tapped out the number for DC Slade's flat.

When the phone beside Slade's bed shrilled him out of his slumbers at 5.30, he came instantly awake. Twenty-five minutes later he was easing his car out into the dark morning, bound for Bowbrook. He had no need to ring the Willowfield doorbell; Miss Agnew, by now fully dressed and groomed, was watching out for him. Five minutes later, over a fresh pot of tea and hot buttered toast, they were sitting at the table in the warm kitchen. He gave her the absolute minimum of explanation for what he was about; he went on to ask what acquaintance she had had with Jessie Dugdale and Lorraine Clifford.

197

A pleasant, neighbourly, landlady-and-tenant relationship with Jessie, she told him; they had never been close friends. Lorraine Clifford she knew both as a social worker dealing with folk in the village and as a family connection of Jessie's. She added that when she heard, in recent times, that Jessie wasn't too well, and that Lorraine was keeping an eye on her, she had called twice at the cottage, to inquire after Jessie.

Did she, by any chance, know anything of Lorraine's movements on the evening of Friday, 2nd January?

She gave him a long, thoughtful look, replying at last: 'I'll tell you what I do know, I'm afraid it isn't much.' On the two occasions she had called at the cottage to ask after Jessie, Lorraine had treated her somewhat brusquely, telling her Jessie was on the mend, she would be sure to pass on her messages of concern and good wishes, but not allowing her to go up to see Jessie – saying, on the first visit, that Jessie was asleep, and on the second, that she was resting and had said she didn't wish to be disturbed.

'But I do have a key to the cottage,' Miss Agnew told Slade with a glint in her eye. 'We've always kept a key here, at Willowfield, though it's rarely been used. I don't know if Lorraine knows about the key and I certainly didn't go out of my way to inform her.' So one evening when she chanced to look out of her bedroom window at around 6.15 and saw Lorraine in her blue Peugeot turning into the main road, driving off in the direction of Cannonbridge, she decided on the spot to pop along at once to the cottage to wish Jessie a happy New Year – this was on the Friday, 2nd January.

She hurried off, let herself in and called up to Jessie who responded at once with pleasure, calling down to her to go up. 'She was delighted to see me. Lorraine hadn't mentioned that I'd been inquiring about her. She said we could have a good old chinwag – Lorraine hadn't told her where she was going but she'd said she'd be gone about an hour, an hour and a half. I stayed for half an hour. Before I left, she said it might be best if she didn't tell Lorraine I'd called.' She smiled grimly at Slade. 'She said Lorraine had referred to me more than once as an interfering busybody who liked nothing more than running other folk's lives. Jessie thought that was quite amusing but it was clear to me she'd never dream of disagreeing openly with Lorraine, she'd just let that sort of remark slide past her – the last thing she'd ever want to do would be to fall out with Lorraine.' Miss Agnew was silent for a moment before going on to say she'd been very surprised when she heard in the village that Jessie was dead.

Slade asked if she knew anything of Lorraine's movements eight days after her chat with Jessie – the evening of Saturday, 10th January.

Again she thought back. 'That would be a week ago, last Saturday. Yes, I do recall something about that evening. I don't know if it's of any use.'

She explained that she belonged to the League of Friends of Wychford Hospital and often used her car to run village folk with no transport of their own, to and from the hospital, for appointments or to visit patients. On that Saturday, 10th January, she had arranged to run a pensioner to the hospital to visit her husband; the woman would be making her own way home by bus. Miss Agnew had left Willowfield at 5.10, to pick the woman up. 'I can show you the entry in my desk diary,' she told Slade. 'I always make a note of any arrangement.' As she drove past Jessie's cottage she saw Lorraine's car on the hard-standing and lights on in the cottage. It was half an hour later when she again drove by the cottage, on her return to Willowfield. She saw that Lorraine's car had gone and there was only one light on, upstairs, in Jessie's bedroom.

When she got in, she busied herself attending to her correspondence. At five minutes to seven she put on her coat to walk to the postbox – she had been keeping an eye on the time as there was a TV programme at 7.30 she always liked to watch. Her route took her past Jessie's cottage, along to the next turning, then a further hundred yards to the postbox. As she passed the cottage she saw Lorraine's car had not yet returned and there was still only the one light on.

When she reached the postbox she met an acquaintance on a similar errand and they stood chatting for a few minutes. On her way home again, passing the cottage, she saw Lorraine's car was now back on the hard-standing and there were lights on, upstairs and down. It would then be about 7.25. She was pretty sure of that as by the time she got in, took off her coat and switched on the TV, her programme was just beginning.

One further question: could she say if Jessie liked a drink? Would she be likely to keep liquor in the house for her own consumption?

Miss Agnew gave a little reminiscent smile. 'Jessie always made out she was a strict teetotaller but this I do know: she was helping out at the harvest supper in the village hall a couple of years back and I came on her unexpectedly in the kitchen quarters. She had a tray of glasses, she was pouring out wine for the tables; she had her back to me. I happened to go in quietly and she didn't hear me. I saw her very quickly draining a glass, filling it up again, putting it back on the tray. I went out again very quietly and went back in with a lot more noise. She spoke a word, carried out the tray, as innocent as the babe unborn. I don't know how much more she had that evening but whenever I saw her, she seemed to be enjoying herself; she was quite jolly by the end of it.'

Slade couldn't be sure that the Chief would be back at work this morning. He gave the matter a flick of thought and asked Miss Agnew if he might use the phone.

In fact the Chief was feeling considerably restored after his enforced rest. He had woken early and was determined to get along to the station without delay, catch up on what had been happening in his absence. He was shaved, showered and dressed, he had just finished a breakfast composed strictly in accordance with the doctor's orders – one of the canteen ladies had very kindly been along yesterday afternoon to do a little supermarket shopping for him – when the phone rang and DC Slade came on the line. The Chief listened with keen attention to what Slade had to say.

Five minutes later, the Chief was on his way to the police station and over in Bowbrook DC Slade, with Miss Agnew beside him in the passenger seat, was turning his car into the main road, headed for Cannonbridge and their rendezvous at the station with the Chief.

DS Lambert's watch showed ten minutes to ten as he opened the door on the passenger side of a marked police car, for the Chief to take his seat. With a police van following, Lambert took the road to Bowbrook. The traffic was fairly heavy and they had to endure more than one hold-up before they came in sight of the mourners' cars drawn up by the church.

They swept in through the gateway and up the sloping path. The funeral procession was already making its reverent way across to the graveside. The police vehicles came to a halt, doors were flung wide; the officers jumped out, breaking into a run.

Startled faces turned to stare. The procession slowed to a stop. The police slackened pace. Lorraine stood motionless, looking across at them with an air of calm inquiry.

21

Shortly before noon Chief Inspector Kelsey and DS Lambert took their seats opposite Lorraine Clifford in an interview room in the Cannonbridge police station. Lorraine still wore the mourning clothes she had put on for Jessie's funeral: a dark-grey, high-buttoned jacket and straight skirt. She had shown not the slightest reluctance to accompany them back to Cannonbridge and had made it plain that she was anxious to assist in any way she could. She was present on an entirely voluntary basis, to answer questions.

The Chief and Lambert were due to leave for the hospital at one o'clock, in readiness for the start of the post-mortem on Jessie Dugdale. In the absence of any relative, the body had been formally identified by Miss Agnew, who had now been driven back to Willowfield.

An officer had spoken to Jessie's doctor who had merely expanded slightly what he had said to DC Slade on Saturday morning: he had visited Jessie three or four times in recent weeks, he had believed her to be making some progress. There was no question of sending her to hospital; every bed there was occupied because of the flu outbreak, with some patients forced to wait on trolleys in corridors before being admitted to a ward.

He had every confidence in Lorraine's nursing; he knew Lorraine in her social work and had a high regard for her. He had not gone round to view the body when Lorraine called to tell him she had found Jessie dead in her bed; he had not considered it necessary; nor had he had a moment's hesitation in issuing the death certificate.

Forensic teams had now carried out an inspection of Lorraine's flat and car, as well as of Jessie's cottage, and had come up with nothing of any significance. It was evident that the cottage had been cleaned with great thoroughness in the last day or two; Lorraine's flat and car, while both very clean and tidy, had not recently received the same meticulous attention.

In the interview room, Kelsey was just about to open his mouth to ask his first question when Lorraine said suddenly in a little rush, with an air of frankness, a suggestion of throwing herself on his mercy: 'I'm not sorry it's all going to come out, I'm glad to be able to get it off my chest, I was never very happy about getting rid of evidence.'

Kelsey digested this in silence for several moments before asking: 'Evidence of what?'

She shot back at once: 'Evidence of what I took to be suicide.'

'You believed Jessie Dugdale took her own life?'

'I can't be one hundred per cent certain and I can't really prove it, but it did look very much like suicide to me.'

'You'd better start at the beginning,' Kelsey said. 'What precisely do you know of what took place that Tuesday night?'

'As I said, I went into Jessie's bedroom in the morning, it would be about seven o'clock. I switched on the light and spoke to her but I got no reply. I looked across and saw at once that she was dead. It struck me within the first few moments that she had taken her own life: there were two old medicine bottles, almost empty, on the bedside table – I'd never seen those bottles before. There was a beaker beside them and a half-bottle of port, about a third full.'

'Were there any labels on the medicine bottles?'

'Yes, old labels. They'd both been made out for Jessie's mother, years ago. They didn't show the actual name of what was in the bottles, they never did at one time, it was always "the mixture" or whatever. I had a sniff at the beaker and it was clear she'd poured the contents of the medicine bottles into the beaker, along with the port, and drunk it down.'

'How come you never saw the medicine bottles when you cleaned and tidied the cottage?'

'She could have kept them in a cupboard or drawer in her bedroom – I never went poking or prying in there. I had to go through her things after her death, of course, decide how to dispose of them. I want to be out of there as soon as possible, get back to my flat. I intend handing over the keys to Miss Agnew on Friday.'

'Did you know there was a half-bottle of port in the house?'

'No, I didn't.'

'How would Jessie have got hold of the port?'

'There'd be no difficulty there. She'd have had it by her, in her room.' She gave a little smile. 'I discovered a long time ago that she liked a drink but she could never admit to it. She was well enough to do her shopping until this last illness, she used to go on the bus into Wychford once or twice a week, for things she couldn't get in the village. And she wouldn't need to worry herself about the empties, she could drop them in the bottle bank in the village. She could have had the port hidden away in her room for some time.'

'Were you surprised when the idea of suicide crossed your mind on Wednesday morning?'

She gave a swift shake of her head. 'No, I wasn't. Jessie often said she'd never want to live to be very old, dependent on other folk. I know why she felt like that, she spoke to me about it more than once. When she was a child they had her grandmother living with them after she was widowed. After a year or two she had a stroke and then a second stroke. They were all sure she'd die from the second stroke but she lingered on for another couple of years till a third stroke finished her off. It coloured Jessie's attitude for the rest of her life about growing old. She said she'd never want to inflict that sort of burden on anyone herself. Her eightieth birthday was coming up – it would have been this coming Thursday. I believe now she saw that as the beginning of real old age. And I also think she was more affected by poor Greg's death than she'd let me see – I'd had to tell her about it, she'd have found out from the radio and newspapers. She believed he'd taken his own life.' She fell silent for a moment and then added with force: 'I made up my mind on the spot there wasn't going to be any inquest, any post-mortem – no police investigation, no press hullabaloo, she would have hated all that.'

What had she done with the medicine bottles, the port bottle, the beaker?

She waved a hand. 'It was very simple. I put the lot in a plastic bag, put it in the boot of my car. Later the same morning, on my way over to Cannonbridge for Philip's funeral, I dumped the bag in a rubbish skip.' She smiled wryly. 'I thought I'd dealt with everything. And then DC Slade turned up at the cottage, asking to speak to Jessie. I had the strong feeling he suspected something.' She gave another trace of a smile. 'I can't say I was completely taken by surprise this morning when you stopped the funeral. In a way, it was a relief.' Another ghost of a smile. 'Though it did strike me as a touch over-dramatic, the police charging up the path like storm-troopers.' She was briefly silent again before asking: 'How serious an offence is it – covering up a suicide? Does it rate a prison sentence?' When the Chief let that pass without a reply, she added: 'Whatever the punishment is, I'm ready to face it.' She shook her head sadly. 'There'll be a post-mortem after all, they'll cut her up.' Tears shone in her eyes. She took out a handkerchief and dabbed them fiercely away.

Kelsey changed tack. 'If I could take you back to the evening of Friday, 2nd January, when you went to Jessie's cottage for the weekend. You told us you didn't leave the cottage that Friday evening.'

'That's right,' she confirmed.

'We have information,' Kelsey continued in the same even tone, 'that you did in fact leave the cottage, you drove away at about 6.15, you were away more than long enough to drive over to Cannonbridge and back.'

Lorraine's eyes gleamed, but not now with tears. 'I can make a very good guess about the source of your information,' she came back sharply. 'Miss Agnew from Willowfield.'

Kelsey made no reply.

'You need to understand Miss Agnew,' Lorraine continued. 'She certainly does a great deal of good work round here but she looks on Bowbrook as her own particular territory. She seems to have a special down on social workers, she sees them as outsiders interfering in her domain. Whenever I come across her in the course of my work, she's never the slightest help. Polite, yes, but never any actual help. If she can obstruct me in any way, she does so, always skilfully, neatly, nothing you could ever make an official complaint about.' She levelled a forthright glance at the Chief. 'If she can persuade herself now to recall events in some fashion likely to be troublesome to me, then that's how she'll persuade herself to recall them.'

The Chief let all that go. 'If you would cast your mind back to another evening, eight days later, the evening of Saturday, 10th January. You told us you didn't leave Jessie's cottage at all that evening.'

'That's right,' she acknowledged with a wry smile. 'And now you're going to tell me it just so happens that you have information that I did leave the cottage that evening.'

'We do have such information,' he responded calmly.

She closed her eyes and blew out a little breath. 'And I'll tell you where you got this piece of information: from the same helpful lady, Miss Agnew of Willowfield.'

Shortly after three DC Slade applied himself to studying in greater detail the forensic reports and other data relating to Beechcroft and to Greg Mottram's flat. His attention returned more than once to a matter that would appear so far to have aroused little interest, if any at all: among the contents of the waste basket in Greg's bedroom were some tiny, seemingly related items: a sales tag of thin white card, bearing the logo of a hospice charity shop in the town, and two halves of a white plastic tie of a type commonly used to attach price tags to garments in charity shops – one half of the tie was still attached to the tag, which showed a price, a chest measurement and a ledger identification number. On a shelf in Greg's kitchen lay a folded plastic carrier bag, bearing the same hospice-shop logo.

Might be worth while, Slade mused, paying a visit to the charity shop. Such establishments usually closed at five. He looked at his watch; he couldn't go along to the shop yet; one or two jobs he must attend to first.

The garden Tom Guthrie tended on Monday afternoons

belonged to a widow in her seventies. Today she was out at her class in Italian cookery, at the local College of Further Education, where the new term had just begun.

When Guthrie took his break at 3.30, he settled himself down in the garden shed and switched on his radio, tuning in for the first time today to the local station. Within a minute or two he found himself listening with increasing stupefaction to a report of a funeral at a church in Bowbrook being stopped shortly after ten o'clock this morning by the Cannonbridge police. The funeral was of a Miss Jessie Dugdale, an elderly spinster. The chief mourner, a twenty-four-year-old social worker, had been taken in for questioning. A post-mortem on the remains of Miss Dugdale was now taking place. It was understood that the police officers involved were part of the team currently investigating three recent deaths in Cannonbridge.

Guthrie dropped his head into his hands and remained sunk in thought for some considerable time, then he left the shed and paced about the garden. He had a sudden flash of memory: Jessie Dugdale, here in the garden in the old days, on one of her visits, stopping to talk to him, always so pleasant and friendly, so interested in the garden, so kind and unassuming; asking about his family, genuinely interested, always remembering their names, what they were doing.

All at once his mind resolved itself. He would get off home, a quick wash and change, then take himself along to the police station.

Half an hour later he managed to get a word with DC Slade, but it was only a word, Slade could spare him only a minute as he was still anxious to finish his clearing up, to allow him to get along to the charity shop in good time. If Guthrie cared to sit in reception and wait for him – it could be as much as half an hour – he could ride along with him in the car, tell him what was on his mind as Slade drove to the charity shop. Guthrie made no objection; he found a seat and a newspaper, sat himself down and prepared to wait for as long as it took.

PC Venning was driving back to the police station after a couple of routine calls. A clock over a jeweller's showed ten minutes past four as he slowed his car on the approach to a pedestrian crossing by a supermarket.

A knot of folk, laden with shopping, stood on both pavements, waiting for the signal to cross. As Venning halted, his gaze lighted on the foremost pedestrian on his left, poised no more than a foot or two from the bonnet of his car, ready to make his forward dart. Their eyes met. Venning knew the man, Jack Phelan by name, he had known Phelan for years. Phelan was retired now; until a year or two ago he had manned the petrol pumps and the forecourt kiosk at a garage where Venning often filled up; they had always exchanged a word. Venning raised a hand in greeting, he gave Phelan a friendly smile. But Phelan offered no smile or nod in reply. A look of marked discomfiture flashed across his face; he dropped his gaze, averted his head.

The crossing signal sprang to life and the pedestrians surged forward. When Venning moved on again he didn't continue on his way back to the station but took a turning that brought him to a patch of waste ground where he could pull up and give a moment's concentrated thought to what might be troubling Phelan.

Very few seconds elapsed before his brain sent up a hint of explanation. Venning had been one of the uniformed officers in the teams making inquiries of fellow tenants and neighbours, after the discovery of Greg Mottram's body. It was the statement of Mrs Onslow, in flat number four, on the floor above Mottram, that surfaced now in Venning's memory. Mrs Onslow occupied the flat, together with her aged mother; it was Mrs Onslow who had seen Greg returning from work that Saturday evening. When asked if she had seen or heard anything from Greg's flat in the course of that evening, Mrs Onslow told them she had spent the evening at bingo with a woman friend, as she did every Saturday evening. Her brother had come along, as usual, to keep an eye on their mother in Mrs Onslow's absence; the police could ask him if he had seen or heard anything. The police had later spoken to the brother; he told them he had seen and heard nothing from Mottram's flat that Saturday evening.

The name of that brother was Jack Phelan.

It seemed to Venning now, sitting pondering in his car, that Phelan's unwillingness to meet his eye could have been prompted by one of two things: in his statement Phelan could have told them something he knew to be untrue; or, for reasons of his own, he had chosen to omit from his statement something he knew full well he ought to tell them. Either way, a word with him now wouldn't go amiss. He switched on his engine and drove off.

Phelan, a long-time widower, without children, lived on his own. He had got in with his shopping only a minute or two before Venning rang his bell; he was in his kitchen unpacking his purchases. He showed no surprise when he opened the front door; indeed his expression said clearly enough that he had fully expected Venning to appear on his doorstep.

He put up little resistance to Venning's challenge but went back to the kitchen with Venning following, uninvited. Phelan continued to stow away his shopping in a dogged fashion, not looking at Venning, uttering not one syllable in reply to anything Venning had to say. It was only when Venning announced his intention of returning to the flats and questioning Mrs Onslow again that Phelan suddenly ceased what he was doing and gazed at Venning in alarm.

'Don't do that!' The words jerked out of him. 'I'll tell you what you want to know, as long as you give me your word you'll say nothing of it to my sister.'

Venning pulled down the corners of his mouth. 'I can't give you any absolute guarantee. If any of this gets as far as the courts, what must come out will come out. All I can say is that I certainly won't go out of my way to repeat to your sister anything you tell me now.' And with that Phelan had to be satisfied.

He dropped into a chair and waved Venning down into a seat opposite him. Phelan launched into what he had to say with rapidity, as if he'd gone over it time and again in his mind since he had last spoken to the police.

His mother, it appeared, had been slipping downhill for some time, drifting into episodes of forgetfulness and confusion, but his sister was determined to keep her at home for as long as possible. When Phelan retired, his sister told him that from now on she expected a considerable degree of practical assistance from him in the day-to-day care of their mother. He agreed to present himself at regular times, on regular days, to look after the old lady, freeing his sister to go out.

It was the evening stints that particularly irked Phelan. He had long been accustomed to while away his evenings in his local pub and he found it tedious beyond bearing to spend endless hours with his mother, trying to make conversation, playing childish games, watching the very simplest TV programmes. It wasn't long before he hit on a solution. As soon as his sister had gone off for the evening he gave his mother a cup of one of her usual beverages, laced with a sleeping pill, and settled her into a comfortable armchair. He never had long to wait before her eyes closed. He made sure all was safe and then took himself off to his pub, returning in good time before his sister got back. Nothing untoward had ever occurred; he had never been caught out.

Venning had given an assurance that he would, as far as possible, say nothing to Mrs Onslow but he had no intention of allowing Phelan to continue this treatment of his mother, as he now made abundantly clear. Phelan gave a dismal nod by way of response, foreseeing only too plainly the return of those interminable hours of nursery amusements.

And now came the question to which Venning was determined to get a truthful answer: what was it Phelan had seen or heard that Saturday evening that he hadn't troubled to tell the police?

Now that the jig was up, Phelan replied without hesitation. As he had approached the flats that Saturday evening at about 6.15, he had passed a nearby cul-de-sac and had glanced down it, as he always did. He saw, parked a little way down, the blue Peugeot car he had seen on three or four occasions parked in the space allotted to Greg Mottram. Phelan knew the car belonged to the young woman – a relative of Mottram's, he'd been given to understand – who often called at his flat. It crossed his mind to wonder briefly why she had chosen to park her car there this evening and not in the usual spot.

When he went in through the entrance gates he saw that Mottram's parking space was unoccupied. He certainly wasn't mistaken about the blue Peugeot; he knew its number and was able to give the number now to Venning; he had been associated with cars all his working life, it came as second nature to him to register the number of any car that for some reason caught his attention. The blue Peugeot always took his eye by virtue of the fact that it was never less than immaculately clean and shining.

Phelan had gone into the building and up to his sister's flat, letting himself in with his key; his sister had a word with him and left a minute or two later. When Phelan let himself out of the flat again, bound for his pub, it would be 6.45, near enough. He had just stepped out of the flat when he heard Greg Mottram's front door open, the sound of voices. He at once drew back, out of sight, not wishing Mottram to see him leaving, in case by some chance conversation between his sister and Mottram it should come out that he had left the old lady on her own.

Mottram had emerged, chatting amiably to his companion: the young woman who drove the blue Peugeot. Mottram saw her out and then went back into his flat and closed the door. Phelan gave a clear description of the young woman, adding that she wore a shoulder bag and also carried a shopping bag – not a plastic supermarket carrier but a stouter, more durable type of holdall.

22

As soon as DC Slade collected Tom Guthrie from the reception area, to drive with him to the charity shop, he pressed Guthrie to make a start on telling him whatever it was he had come to the station to say. Guthrie needed little urging and by the time he had got his seat belt fastened he was well under way.

He told Slade in some detail something that had taken place at Beechcroft on the Friday morning of the Jarretts' move, something known to both himself and Rhoda Jarrett.

'It's been bothering me,' Guthrie owned, 'it's bothered me a lot. I kept thinking about it when I woke up in the night but I kept pushing it away, I kept telling myself it was only a tiny trifle, there was bound to be some good explanation.'

By the time Slade pulled up in the shopping area he had grasped the significance of what he was hearing but he was forced to leave it aside for the moment, to give his attention to his business with the charity shop. As soon as he had dealt with that he would call at Rhoda Jarrett's bedsit, see if she was in, if she could confirm what Guthrie had just told him.

Guthrie remained, as directed, in the car while Slade went into the charity shop. At this hour on a Monday afternoon, so near closing-time, the shop was almost empty and Slade was able to get a word immediately with the manageress.

Yes, he was told, the label did come from one of their garments. The number on the label took her to a ledger entry which revealed that the garment in question was a man's cable-knit sweater, dark-green, winter-weight, in good condition; it had been sold on Saturday, 10th January.

The manageress spoke to an assistant who had worked in the shop that day; she had no difficulty in recalling the sale. She had just come on duty; the time would be 1.30, 1.40. A man had entered the shop, plainly in a hurry. He had gone straight to the rack of men's sweaters, selected the green one and approached the counter, where a young mother with two small children in tow had just begun to unload the armful of small garments she had chosen.

The man had asked the young woman very politely if she would allow him to go before her, explaining that he was in his lunch hour and had to get back to work. She agreed at once. He thanked her, made his purchase and left the shop, taking his sweater in one of their carrier bags. By the assistant's description, the man was clearly Greg Mottram. At the time of his death, Greg had been wearing a dark-green, heavyweight, cable-knit sweater.

When they arrived at Rhoda Jarrett's bedsit, Slade again asked Guthrie to remain in the car while he went inside. He was lucky enough to find Rhoda at home; there was no sign of Vicky.

He asked Rhoda to cast her mind back to the Friday morning of her departure from Beechcroft and before long he had her recalling the incident Guthrie had spoken of. She had been so busy that Friday morning, so preoccupied, with a hundred and one things to attend to, that the incident had very soon slipped her mind, but she was able now to recollect it in sharp detail, confirming in every respect what Guthrie had just told Slade.

Shortly after 5.30 Chief Inspector Kelsey and Sergeant Lambert left the hospital at the end of the post-mortem on Jessica Anne

Dugdale. They spoke little on the drive back to the police station; it had been a long, weary day, by no means over yet.

On the station forecourt Lambert halted the car; they got out in silence and approached the steps. As they came in through the doors, the little group who had been waiting in the reception area, watching out for their return, rose to their feet. DC Slade and PC Venning went across together to intercept the Chief; Tom Guthrie and Jack Phelan stayed where they were, ready to go forward at the beckoning of a hand.

It was turned 6.15 when Lorraine Clifford was again conducted to an interview room. She was no longer in the police station on a voluntary footing but had now been placed under arrest, a process she had taken in her stride. She appeared far from apprehensive. In the few hours that had passed since her first interrogation, she had eaten, rested, had even been able to drift into a light sleep. She looked refreshed and energetic as she took her seat under the lights; upright, shoulders squared, eyes glinting; still in her dark mourning clothes.

Again the Chief asked if she would like a solicitor. 'In my opinion,' he told her with strong emphasis, 'you would be well advised to have one.' But again she declined, this time adding with a touch of impatience: 'I've told you exactly what happened, exactly what I did. I'm not seeking to deny any of it. I'm ready to take the consequences. Why should I need a solicitor? To protect me from some trumped-up allegations on the part of the police?'

Unperturbed, the Chief went on to say that if she were to change her mind at any stage, she should at once speak up and a solicitor would be sent for. She received this with a barely perceptible, acknowledging movement of her head.

The Chief then turned to the matter of the post-mortem findings, pointing out that the full analysis of the stomach contents would not be to hand for a couple of days, although they had been given a preliminary report.

The cause of death was clear. Jessie had not died from influenza, bronchitis, any congestion, infection or affection of the lungs, heart or other organ. Death had plainly resulted from the ingestion of a quantity of alcohol, together with sedative drugs. This combination had very probably been swallowed in three or four roughly equal doses, over a period of some thirty to forty minutes, the first dose being taken on an empty stomach.

'Philip Harvey died in much the same way,' Kelsey continued. 'He died after drinking alcohol at the same time as sedative drugs. Martine Faulkner died in the same way. So did Greg Mottram.' Lorraine made no response. 'Is it not something of a coincidence,' Kelsey pursued, 'that Jessie Dugdale should also die in the same way?'

She moved her shoulders. 'I can't comment on that. I have no idea of the relevant statistics, no idea how usual or unusual it is to die from such a mixture.'

'Jessie would appear to have drunk the mixture in spaced-out doses. How do you account for that?'

She returned an unwavering gaze. 'I can't see that I can in any way be called upon to account for it. I didn't provide the alcohol. I know nothing of the drugs she took. I certainly didn't supply them, nor did I administer them.'

He executed a swift change of direction. 'Eight years ago, you went to see Nurse Tennant, who gave evidence at the inquest on your mother. You indicated clearly to her that you believed Philip Harvey was responsible for your mother's death. Your attitude, when you spoke of him, was very hostile.'

She brushed that aside with a wave of her hand. 'That was a long time ago. I was a very young, very naïve schoolgirl. My mother's death had come as a shattering blow, while I was still a child. I was told nothing about her illness, given no proper information about her death. I understood nothing about it, I jumped to some very foolish, ignorant, childish conclusions. I hope I've grown up since then. I discovered, among other things, over the years, that Philip was a good, kind, caring man, utterly devoted to my mother. He always treated me with the utmost kindness and generosity. I grew to appreciate all that, to respect him, to realize that he had greatly loved my mother and had always done his very best for her.'

Another change of direction from the Chief: 'When precisely was the last time you set foot in Greg Mottram's flat?'

She gave a small sigh. 'As I told you the last time you asked me that question, and the time before that, I didn't set foot in Greg's flat after Thursday evening, 8th January.'

'Cast your mind back. Take your time. Think about it. What was Greg wearing that Thursday evening?'

She closed her eyes, she fell silent for some moments before replying: 'He was wearing grey slacks and a dark-green sweater.'

'Can you describe the sweater?'

She fell silent again before answering: 'It was quite a good-looking sweater, thick and warm, with a cable pattern.'

'Are you positive, beyond any shadow of doubt, that Greg was wearing the sweater you describe on that Thursday evening, 8th January?'

She responded on a note of rising impatience: 'Yes, I am absolutely positive.'

At a nod from the Chief, Sergeant Lambert picked up from the seat of the chair beside him, the green sweater – now bagged and tagged – that Greg had been wearing when his body was found. The Chief took the bag from him and held it out before her. 'Is this the sweater Greg was wearing when you called at his flat that Thursday evening, 8th January?'

She stared down at it for several moments. 'Yes, it is,' she confirmed at last.

'Do you positively identify this sweater as the one Greg wore that evening?' he persisted.

Irritation sounded clearly in her tone as she snapped out her reply: 'Yes, I do positively identify it as the sweater Greg wore that evening.'

The Chief regarded her for a long moment. 'We have witnesses to state that Greg bought that sweater, the sweater he was wearing when his body was found, at a charity shop in the town, during his lunch hour on Saturday, 10th January, the last day of his life. He didn't own that sweater on the Thursday evening, 8th January. If, as you state, you saw him wearing it, then you must have called at the flat on the Saturday evening, 10th January. That was the only evening Greg could possibly have worn that sweater.'

Lorraine had listened to this with an air of half-smiling scepti-cism. Now she settled herself back in her chair. 'I imagine your witnesses are ladies from the charity shop. They're either plain mistaken or looking for a little excitement, a little colour in their

214

lives. I deal with members of the general public every day of my working life. I know, when you're doing your best to establish the reality of any situation, just how difficult it is to persuade folk to stick to the facts, the actual, unadorned facts, rather than what they think you want them to say.' Her tone grew a little sharper. 'Saturday must be a busy day at the charity shop, there must be a great many purchases made. It's really rather conveni-ent that your witnesses happen to remember so clearly that particular purchase.' She leaned forward. 'I repeat: Greg was definitely wearing that sweater on the Thursday evening, there-fore he must have bought it, at the latest, sometime on Thurs-day.' She stabbed a finger at the air. 'Furthermore, I did not leave Jessie's cottage at all that Saturday evening, 10th January, so I could not have been calling at Greg's flat.'

The Chief's manner remained imperturbable. 'We have a wit-ness to say you did, in fact, leave the cottage that Saturday evening, 10th January. You were away more than long enough to drive into Cannonbridge and back.'

She exhaled a long, noisy breath. 'Not again! Not Miss Agnew again! Just happening to be on the spot to record my comings and goings! But who else would it be? We needn't go into all that again. You know my opinion of that lady and any statement she's only too ready to make about me.'

The Chief continued in the same even tone: 'We have another witness to say he saw your car in the cul-de-sac by the flats, as he went by at 6.15 that Saturday evening. Half an hour later, at 6.45, that same witness saw you come out of Greg's flat. Greg was beside you, walking with you to the main door, going back into his flat after you'd left. That witness has no conceivable animus against you, he knows you only by sight – he had seen you visiting Greg on previous occasions, he had seen your car at other times, parked in the space allotted to Greg.'

She came back roundly at that: 'Then your witness – whoever he is – is quite simply mistaken. I have never left my car in that cul-de-sac, I have never had any reason to. I have always left it in Greg's parking space. It was some other car he saw – my car is not the only blue Peugeot in existence.' She moved her shoul-ders. 'Then again, your witness may have his own agenda, something you know nothing about, some reason I can't guess

215

at, for saying what he did. And if he can make a misstatement about the car, for whatever reason, he could be equally ready to make a misstatement about the time, about seeing me leave the flat, even about what day it was. Are you so positive this witness of yours is someone who always speaks the unvarnished truth?' She appeared to grow a little warm; she unbuttoned her jacket and let it hang open.

Kelsey eyed her in silence for several moments. She bore his scrutiny with no show of irritation. 'Will you now take your mind back a little further?' he asked at last. 'When precisely was the last time you set foot in Beechcroft, before the two bodies were discovered on Monday, 5th January?'

'And my reply now is precisely the same as the last time I answered that question,' she replied in a voice that began to tremble on the edge of anger. 'I never set foot in Beechcroft for so much as one single moment after the morning of New Year's Eve, Wednesday, 31st December, until the Wednesday one week later, after the forensic team had left, and I was given access to the property again.'

'Are you absolutely certain of that?' he pressed her. 'Is it possible you entered the house at some time during that week, just for a few minutes, maybe, to pick up one or two of your belongings, perhaps?'

She shook her head vigorously. 'No, I did not set foot in the house again during that week, not for one single moment, not for any reason whatsoever.'

He leaned forward. He stabbed a finger in the direction of a locket she was wearing, clearly visible now in the opening of her jacket: a silver locket and chain. 'Then how come,' he asked, 'Tom Guthrie saw you wearing that locket at around three o'clock on the afternoon of Monday 5th January, as he stood talking to you, here in this police station, asking you what he was to do about his duties at Beechcroft? At the time he merely registered the locket for a moment in passing, thinking: "Oh, she found it, then." His mind was too full of what was happening that day to dwell on the full implications of that thought. Tom Guthrie has no agenda of his own. He has excellent eyesight, an excellent memory. He had the highest regard for your parents, he has been fond of you, all your life. It was only some time after his encounter with you in the corridor here that Monday after-noon that he began to realize the significance of what he had seen: the fact that you were wearing the locket. He has had a considerable struggle with himself before he could bring himself to come forward and speak to us about it. But there had been four deaths, deaths of four people he had known; in the end he could no longer keep silent out of some mistaken feeling of loyalty to the Clifford family; he was compelled to speak out.'

She stared back at him, frozen into immobility, her mouth a little open.

'On the Friday Rhoda Jarrett was leaving Beechcroft,' the Chief continued in the same relentless tone, 'she went down to the summerhouse, to see if Vicky had left any of her belongings in the summerhouse cupboards. Rhoda found Tom Guthrie near by. He moved the deckchairs to one side for her, so she could get at the cupboards. That locket and chain, the locket you are wearing now, fell out of the canvas folds of one of the deckchairs. Tom Guthrie and Rhoda both saw it fall, both recognized it at once.' A Victorian locket, belonging originally to Veronica's great-grandmother, descending from mother to daughter, through the generations, passing to Lorraine on the death of her mother. Lorraine had always treasured it, frequently wore it. She had missed it a few months ago, couldn't find it in spite of much searching. She had spoken of her loss at Beechcroft, asking everyone to keep an eye open for it, in case she had lost it there. 'She must have lost it when they were putting away the deck-chairs,' Rhoda had said to Guthrie when the locket fell out of the canvas folds. She remembered Lorraine spending a Sunday afternoon at Beechcroft during the last warm spell of the declin-ing year. Philip and Lorraine had sat out in the garden that afternoon, chatting, taking their tea on the lawn.

'Rhoda Jarrett took the locket from Tom Guthrie that Friday morning,' Kelsey continued now. 'She told Guthrie she would put the locket on the dressing-table in your bedroom, with a note to say how it had been found.' But Rhoda had been very busy that morning, she had never got round to writing the note. She had simply darted into Lorraine's bedroom and left the locket on the dressing-table, intending to dash off a note before she left the house. When asked by DC Slade an hour or so ago, to cast her

217

mind back to that Friday morning, Rhoda had clearly recalled the incident, confirming in every detail what Guthrie had just told Slade.

Kelsey now had a straightforward question for Lorraine: 'Can you explain how you came to be wearing the locket on the afternoon of Monday, 5th January, the locket that had been placed on the dressing-table in your bedroom at Beechcroft during the morning of Friday, 2nd January, if, as you maintain, you never set foot in Beechcroft for a full week after December 31st?' Lorraine gazed back at him without speaking. 'You could not have slipped into Beechcroft that Monday, 5th January, after the bodies were found,' Kelsey went on. 'The house was guarded by police, forensic teams were at work. The teams have just now assured us there was very definitely no silver locket and chain on the dressing-table in your bedroom when they went over the house, that Monday and Tuesday.'

Still Lorraine said nothing.

'You picked up the locket on the Friday evening, 2nd January,' Kelsey continued, 'after Rhoda and Vicky had moved out, and after Tom Guthrie had locked up and gone home. Miss Agnew saw you leaving Bowbrook at around 6.15 that same Friday evening, you were driving in the direction of Cannonbridge. Miss Agnew took the opportunity of your absence to go along and let herself into Jessie's cottage, she stayed chatting to Jessie for half an hour. Jessie told her you'd said you'd be back in an hour, an hour and a half; that gave you plenty of time to do what you'd planned to do at Beechcroft.

'You let yourself into Beechcroft, you dosed the drinks bottles. Upstairs in your bedroom you saw your locket on the dressing-table. That was when you picked it up, the only time you could have picked it up.'

Lorraine continued to regard him for another long moment before suddenly erupting into passionate speech. She leaned forward, clenching her fists, her cheeks flushed, her eyes brilliant.

'I have no regrets.' Her voice was high and brittle, pouring out the pent-up bitterness of the years. 'Not the smallest regret. Philip was responsible one way or another for my mother's death. So I killed him. A life for a life. That's fair, surely? That's justice.'

Kelsey raised a hand to arrest the flow, administer the caution, advise her yet again to see a solicitor. She interrupted him to demand: 'What good can a solicitor do? He can't alter any of what's happened.'

When Kelsey had quite finished she burst out again, as if intent on having her viewpoint, her actions, understood at last. 'Philip harried poor Greg Mottram till he drove him out of Cannonbridge, so my mother would have no one to help her, no one to turn to, no one to see what he was up to, no one to save her.' She clasped her hands tightly. 'I was the only one to make sure Philip paid for killing my mother, there was no one else to do it, it had to be me. She was my mother. I couldn't let him get away with it. I owed her justice.'

Again the Chief broke in with a caution, again he urged her to see a solicitor; again she thrust his words aside.

'Martine Faulkner?' the Chief said. 'What did you have against Martine Faulkner?'

She made another sweeping gesture of dismissal. 'Martine was nothing to me. She was no innocent virgin, no green schoolgirl. She was a married woman with a young child. She knew what she was doing, she had no business to do what she did. She put herself into the situation of her own free will, for her own purposes. She'd chosen to throw in her lot with Philip. She was simply caught up in what had to happen.'

'How did you come by the drugs?' Kelsey asked.

She smiled a little. 'No difficulty there. I'm always dealing with old folk. Some of them have stocks of medicines going back for years. When one of them dies and you clear out a cabinet, you can find enough old stuff in there to finish off a regiment.' She fell briefly silent. 'It was only by the purest chance, back early in December, I discovered Philip was involved with Martine – they didn't realize I'd found out. I thought: Right, that's it, I'll have to act now. I couldn't stand by and let them marry, have children, let the children take everything one day, my whole inheritance, everything my father had worked for all his life, everything that belonged to me by rights. Those children would be total strangers, not one solitary drop of Clifford blood in their veins. How could it be right that one day it would all come to them?

'I was holding my breath for the right moment, then Rhoda told me she'd been dismissed, Martine was moving in, Philip was out of the country.' Her face broke into a smile. 'I knew the moment had come. I didn't much mind if I put paid to Philip on his own or if Martine went along at the same time – that could be all to the good, could make it look like a suicide pact, but it wasn't essential; I wasn't much bothered about Martine, either way.' She grimaced. 'She took her chances and she lost.'

Cold-blooded, deliberate, carefully planned double murder, Lambert thought, with a prickle along his spine.

'You realize,' Kelsey said, 'that if you stand trial, if you're found guilty, none of your inheritance will go to you? The business, the house, the money, not one penny of it.'

She stared at him in frozen silence. She looked for a moment savagely stricken, then her features relaxed into a smile of sorts. 'I guess you're right,' she replied at last. 'I suppose it will all go to Philip's ancient cousin, up in his island.' She laughed outright. 'The cousin will sell up, he'll sell the lot, lock, stock and barrel. I hope he has a riotous old age on the proceeds.' She added with conviction: 'Shannon will get the firm. He'll mount a buy-out, he'll raise the money all right. He'll make a roaring success of it.' She jerked her head. 'At least Philip and Martine's children will never be born now, they'll never get their hands on any of it, that's some consolation. Anything's better than that.'

'And Greg Mottram?' the Chief said. 'What had you got against Greg? Why did you kill him?'

Her expression changed abruptly. 'I had to do it.' No angry outburst now; a defensive tone, almost apologetic, but tinged with contempt. 'I had no choice. He forced me into a corner. He'd got his mind set on going over to see Jessie, he wouldn't be put off.' She shook her head slightly. 'I knew then he'd have to go. Greg was a lonely man, he'd have latched on to Jessie, he'd have kept going over to see her and she'd have been glad of his company, she always liked him. They'd have got talking. I'd never have had a moment's peace, I couldn't take the risk of him finding out I did leave the cottage that Friday evening, I'd never have felt safe. Greg was no fool. Once he knew that, it wouldn't have taken him long to realize who it was killed that precious pair of lovebirds. He'd have done one of two things: he'd have gone to the police or he'd have blackmailed me, wanting a very substantial slice of my inheritance, probably with a sinecure at Workwear thrown in.' She flung out a hand. 'I couldn't have that wretched drunkard round my neck for years. I'd been sorry for him up till then. I'd done what I could to help him but that changed everything. It was either him or me.' She sat back in her chair. 'So I did what I had to do. I didn't enjoy it, but he brought it entirely on himself. I told him when I left him on the Thursday evening that I'd speak to Jessie and see what I could arrange about him going over. I called in on the Saturday evening to tell him Jessie would be very happy to see him.' She gave a trace of a smile. 'We fixed it up for tomorrow – he wouldn't be working tomorrow afternoon. I said I'd drive over to pick him up and I'd run him back afterwards. He was delighted, it really cheered him up.

'I had no difficulty at all about the drink. I wrapped the bottle up in fancy paper and ribbon. I told him I'd just been given the whisky as a thank-you present by the son of an old lady I'd been able to help over community care. Greg knew I can't touch alcohol. I never let on that I knew he was drinking again – I'd have had to be pretty dim not to catch on, every time I called he was sucking a mint, and he was forever buying some fancy new air freshener device to take away the smell.

'I opened the bottle and poured him a drink, to wish him good luck in his job-hunting. He drank it straight down. I'd got the second bottle, the doped bottle, in my holdall. It was easy enough, switching them.'

She didn't have to go to any trouble, fiddling with the neck seal of the second bottle, Lambert thought; Greg had watched her open the first bottle.

'I left him the doped bottle,' Lorraine went on. 'He was in an upbeat mood when I left, pleased with my visit, pleased I was leaving him the whisky, pleased he would be seeing Jessie. He walked me to the outside door. He said: ' "I'll see you Tuesday, then. I'll get a nice bunch of seedless grapes to take over to Jessie." ' She fell silent again. 'I knew he'd set about finishing the whisky the instant he got back inside.' She stared back at that moment. 'He was a shiftless drunk, a pretty useless human being.' Her voice shook with old anger, old bitterness. 'My mother was always fond of him, always kind to him, and what did he do for her? Nothing, nothing whatever. He never lifted a finger to help her when she needed it, he never tried to protect her against Philip. He let Philip manoeuvre him out of Workwear, out of Cannonbridge, he thought only of himself. He did nothing to save her, he ran away and left her at Philip's mercy, when he should have stayed and fought for her.' She flung out a hand. 'He'd had a wretched life, he lost nothing by dying. And I'd no intention of having him round my neck, sponging on me, for years.'

Into the silence that followed, Kelsey asked: 'And Jessie Dugdale? Did she deserve to die?'

Lorraine closed her eyes, drooped her head. The silence lengthened. Sounds drifted in from the corridors: footsteps, voices, approaching, passing, departing. Lorraine raised her head at last. 'I had to do it. I never planned it from the beginning. It was just that one thing led to another. I had no choice.'

Jessie's the one that will come back to haunt her, Lambert thought, the one that will jerk her awake in the dark and silent hours.

She plunged on, her voice tense. 'I was absolutely forced into it. I never knew Greg had the box with the old cards and photographs, he never showed them to me. The moment the police started asking me about the photographs, I knew then it was only a matter of time, they'd catch up in the end with Constance Whitlock and Nurse Tennant, they'd hear what those two had to say and then the finger would start pointing at me. I couldn't have Jessie questioned about where I was that Friday evening.' She jerked her head. 'And I was right – DC Slade did come over to the cottage, asking to speak to Jessie.' A moment's silence. 'But he came too late.'

'A piece of ruthless, cold-blooded planning,' Kelsey came back at her. 'You moved in with Jessie to be ready to deal with her if it became necessary to remove her.'

'She was an old woman,' Lorraine said flatly. 'She didn't have many years left, in any case. She died in full possession of all her

222

faculties. You don't do everyone a favour by letting them live out their full lifespan, outliving their physical and mental capacities – I see enough of that in my work. Jessie had had the best of it, it would have been downhill all the way for her, into real old age.'

'But she had no particular dread of being eighty?' Kelsey demanded. 'You invented that to make the notion of suicide plausible.'

She shrugged. 'Maybe so. But she was happy when she went. I told her the doctor had said a drop of port would act as a tonic. I gave her little drinks, ten or fifteen minutes apart, she really enjoyed them. She fell asleep after the last one. It was all very peaceful. She didn't suffer, not the tiniest little bit. None of them suffered – I don't know if you realize that. All four of them died happy.' I can see how social work suited her, Lambert thought; it gave her a position of control over disadvantaged lives, from a stance of supposed compassion.

Lorraine fell silent again. At last she looked across at the Chief, faintly smiling. 'I think perhaps I'd better have a solicitor after all, I'm beginning to see the wisdom of it.' She mentioned the firm her parents had employed. 'I'll have someone from there. If there's anyone there who remembers my mother, that's the one I'll have. If not, any one of them will do.' Another faint smile. 'Whichever one's most experienced in this kind of case.'

When she was taken from the interview room a little later, she didn't appear distressed or nervous; she looked tired but entirely composed. She wore an air of calm satisfaction as if at the end at last of a long and difficult task it had, for many a long day, been her clear duty to carry out.

By the time a solicitor from the firm had been located, been apprised of the situation and come hotfoot to the police station, Lorraine had already been charged with the murders of Philip Harvey, Martine Faulkner and Gregory Mottram. No charge was made against her in the case of Jessica Dugdale; there was not one shred of direct evidence to show that Jessie's death was, in fact, murder; Lorraine's outpourings on that score would not stand as proof in a court of law.

The solicitor had known neither of Lorraine's parents. He was a well-seasoned practitioner in late middle age, with a reassuring, fatherly manner. He remained closeted with Lorraine for some time, promising, on leaving, to attend to all practical matters concerning her flat, her car, the vacating of Jessie's cottage; he would also inform her department at work of what had happened.

He had asked her, early on, if there was any relative Lorraine wished him to contact but she had shaken her head. 'I haven't a single relative now, that I know of,' she had told him, adding with a wry hint of a smile: 'Greg Mottram was the last one left.'

'Some close friend, perhaps?' the solicitor had suggested.

Again, she had shaken her head. 'I'm afraid not. I've never gone in for close friends.'

In sudden recollection she had gone on to say: 'It's Greg's funeral this coming Friday. Everything's arranged. I'm sure Tom Guthrie and Rhoda Jarrett will see it through, if you'd have a word with them.'

Last of all, on the verge of departure, he asked if there was, perhaps, some personal item she might wish him to bring her from the flat or the cottage – subject, of course, to official regulations.

Just the one item, she told him: the silver-framed studio photograph from the bedroom in her flat, showing her mother, at very much the same age as Lorraine was now, newly engaged to be married, radiant and smiling, looking to the future with joy and hope, in the long-ago shining days, before it all began.

SOUTH LAN

HOUSE

138

009